HOTWIFE

A Husband Watches His Cuckold Fantasy Become Reality

Scarlett Duffy

CONTENTS

THE ACHE OF
ROUTINE

The office felt particularly sterile that morning—fluorescent lights casting a harsh glow across the beige walls, the faint hum of computers blending with the occasional tap of fingers on keyboards. My desk was cluttered with the remnants of a long week: half-drunk cups of coffee, scattered papers, and a blinking inbox that seemed to multiply by the hour. Outside the large glass windows, the city stretched far into the distance, a patchwork of gray skies and bustling streets below. The office's artificial air was slightly too cold, the kind that makes you wish for the warmth of home. Yet, here I was, surrounded by the relentless drone of corporate life.

The dull ache of routine was momentarily broken by the shrill ring of my phone, vibrating slightly on the desk beside me. I glanced at the clock—right on time. It was Lucy, as predictable as ever, calling after her lunch break. I smiled to myself, my hand already reaching for the phone before the second ring. I leaned back in my leather chair, trying to ease the tension in my shoulders. Even in the most mundane moments, hearing her voice always stirred something in me—a reminder that life outside these walls still existed.

"Hello, dear. How was your morning?" Her voice was as light as ever, sweet and familiar, the same greeting she offered each day.

"Oh, not too bad. Same old, same old," I replied, staring absently at the stack of papers in front of me. "How was your lunch break? Did you happen to try that new restaurant you were talking about last night?"

There was a slight pause on the line before Lucy's voice returned, softer, almost playful. "Well, I didn't go to lunch with the girls today."

That caught my attention. She usually met the same group of women from her department, a predictable ritual in her daily routine. I leaned forward slightly, the chair creaking beneath me.

"You remember that guy I told you about? The new one, Lewis, in my department?" There was a teasing lilt in her voice, something that immediately sent a familiar, hollow sensation to the pit of my stomach.

Lewis. Yes, I remembered. We had a little game, Lucy and I—a subtle way to tease my deepest fantasy. Whenever she found a man attractive, she'd mention him casually, never missing the opportunity to see the effect it had on me. But this time, it wasn't during one of our usual intimate conversations. This was different.

I shifted uncomfortably in my seat, the sensation of dread creeping up my spine. "Yeah, I remember. Why do you ask?"

The question hung in the air, and though my voice remained calm, I could feel my pulse quickening. Something about the way she said it, the casual mention of Lewis outside of our usual playful moments, set off alarm bells in my mind.

There was a long pause on the line, and when she spoke again, I could hear the barely-contained excitement in her voice. "Well... I finally asked him out," she said with a giggle that sounded almost mischievous. "And you'll never guess how my lunch went."

A flush of heat shot through me as her words sank in. I shifted in my chair, my hand gripping the armrest, trying to maintain some semblance of composure. My mind raced, battling between anticipation and the strange thrill that had started to pulse low in my body. Beneath my desk, I could already feel my erection stirring, thickening against the fabric of my trousers, the fantasy I had tried to bury so many times now dancing on the edge of becoming real.

"Oh, really?" I managed to say, my voice steady but tinged with eagerness. "Did you go to lunch with him?"

There it was—the moment I had secretly craved, though I'd never expected it to happen like this. The words came out more breathless than I intended, as though the idea itself was oxygen. Could this be the beginning of something we'd only ever teased about, a step toward finally fulfilling the desire that had gnawed at me for so long?

This obsession of mine had started in the most unintentional of ways—blurting it out in the heat of passion during one of our more intense sessions. I hadn't meant to say it, not then. For months, I had debated broaching the subject, but fear held me back. Fear that Lucy might find it strange, even repulsive.

But in that moment, mid-orgasm, the words slipped out before I could stop them. "Tell me how big Steve's dick is."

The shock on her face had been immediate, but what followed shocked me more than I could have ever predicted. Lucy's body stilled, her breath catching in her throat. And then, she moaned, long and low, as her eyes fluttered shut.

Steve was someone Lucy had been telling me about recently —a waiter at the little restaurant where she and her friends often lunched. She described him as tall, with broad shoulders, muscular, and possessing a pair of blue eyes that she called 'gorgeous.' She'd said it casually, mentioning him offhand as part of our game, never offering more than her surface attraction to the men she noticed. But this time, something was different.

I could almost hear the smile in Lucy's voice as she continued, her words rolling out as if they were some playful confession. "Oh, it's so much bigger than yours," she moaned, her voice laced with a new kind of teasing. "At least two or three inches longer."

The words hung in the air, and for a split second, I froze. My mind spiraled. The casual way she said it hit me like a punch to the gut. Bigger. Three inches longer. My body reacted before my mind could, a twinge of insecurity flaring up as her words echoed. I knew she was only playing our usual game—feeding into the fantasy that had become part of our sex life. But still, hearing her compare me to another man, telling me how much bigger Steve was, stirred something complicated inside me.

A sharp pang of jealousy mixed with an unexpected rush of arousal. How could I feel both things at once? The idea of her fantasizing about Steve—tall, muscular Steve with his perfect blue eyes and supposedly larger cock—left me feeling exposed, vulnerable. Like I wasn't enough. And yet, even as that insecurity crept up, it was tangled with something darker, something more primal that drove my arousal higher.

What was it about this? The thought of her comparing me to another man, knowing she found someone else's body more alluring, more… satisfying. It stung, sure, but it also made me harder than I'd been in days. My pulse quickened, and I could feel the heat radiating off my skin as my erection pressed painfully against my pants.

I shifted in my seat, the sensation of desire and conflict building within me, pushing me closer to the edge. Could Lucy tell? Was she playing into it, feeding that gnawing hunger inside me that I didn't quite understand?

My thoughts swirled, and as I listened to her soft, breathy moans on the other end of the line, I couldn't help but wonder—was she thinking about him? Right now? About Steve's larger cock? The image of her, lost in pleasure, imagining him as she moaned and writhed beneath me... it was almost too much to bear. The jealousy cut deep, but the thrill of it, the way it electrified my senses, was undeniable.

As I neared the brink, my breaths coming faster, more erratic, the question clawed its way to the forefront of my mind. Is she thinking of him right now? Is she imagining Steve filling her, stretching her more than I ever could?

The thought sent me over the edge. My body tensed, pleasure crashing through me in waves, but my mind was somewhere else, lost in the vivid image of Lucy with another man. Even as I came, I couldn't shake the feeling—the mixture of dread and desire twisting inside me.

After we finished, we lay there together, limbs intertwined, the warmth of our bodies still radiating from the shared moment. The room was quiet, save for the soft sound of our breathing and the faint hum of the ceiling fan overhead. The sheets were tangled around us, a comforting mess that anchored me in the afterglow of what had just happened. Lucy's head rested on my chest, her hair tickling my skin, her fingers tracing lazy patterns across my stomach. For a moment, everything felt perfect, suspended in that peaceful haze that only comes after sex.

"You really surprised me with that one," she murmured, breaking the silence with a small laugh. Her voice had that lightness to it, the kind that comes from being completely relaxed. "I decided to just go with it, and it kind of helped me cum." There was a playful edge to her words, as though she was letting me in on a secret, something private that she had just discovered about herself.

I tilted my head down to look at her, my brow furrowing slightly. "What do you mean, helped you cum?" I asked, the question slipping out before I could stop it. A flicker of insecurity passed through me. Hadn't I been doing enough? Was there something

5

lacking in what I'd done to make her feel like she needed more?

Lucy rolled over onto me, her lips finding mine in a soft kiss that quickly melted away my doubt. "Oh, stop it," she said with a teasing smile, brushing her fingers across my cheek. "You know what I mean. It was just... kind of hot, that's all."

Her words hung in the air between us, and though I smiled back, my mind was already working overtime. The idea that something I had said, something that had brought her to the edge of this fantasy, had made her cum harder—it stirred something deep inside me. Maybe I was reading too much into it, but I couldn't help the thrill of excitement rising in me, a slow burn that was becoming harder to ignore.

I shifted slightly beneath her, trying to keep my voice casual, though I could feel my pulse quicken. "Are you saying you're considering... fucking around, and telling me about it?" My heart was racing now, my excitement intensifying at the possibility. The idea of her stepping further into this fantasy, of actually doing it and then sharing every detail with me—it was intoxicating. My breath hitched slightly as I waited for her reply.

Lucy let out a soft giggle, her lips curling into that mischievous smile I knew so well. "Well, I don't know about all that," she said, rolling onto her side and reaching for her vape from the bedside table. She took a slow pull, the tip glowing faintly as she inhaled, and exhaled a soft cloud of sweet-scented vapor. The smell of vanilla and something floral filled the room, blending with the lingering musk of our lovemaking. "I'm just saying, I kind of found that a little hot," she continued, her eyes finding mine again, a glint of something playful, something a little dangerous, in her gaze.

The way she said it—so casual, so offhanded—sent a wave of heat through me. Was she teasing me, or was there something more behind her words? I couldn't quite tell, but I knew one thing: this was getting to me, and fast.

She took another pull from the vape, the vapor swirling around her as she rolled back into her previous position beside me. Her skin was warm against mine, her leg draped lazily over my thigh. "You surprised me," she said softly, her voice barely above a whisper. "And I guess I surprised myself."

She paused for a moment, then let out a soft laugh. "I instantly came when I thought about how big his dick would be. Just picturing it got me so hot, so quickly."

Her words sent a jolt through me, a mix of emotions hitting all at once—jealousy, insecurity, and the undeniable arousal that this entire conversation stirred within me. It was all tangled together, a confusing blend of feelings that left me both unsettled and completely captivated. The image of her imagining another man, of her getting off on the idea of his size, should have stung, should have made me feel inadequate. And yet, there I was, growing harder again just thinking about it.

I turned my head to look at her, my mouth suddenly dry. "You were really thinking about him, weren't you?" I asked, my voice low, almost hoarse. There was no judgment in my words—just a burning curiosity, a need to know more. Lucy met my gaze and smiled, a secretive smile, as if she knew exactly what effect she was having on me.

"Yeah, I was imagining that nice big cock of his."

After Lucy confessed that she had been imagining Steve, a silence lingered between us, thick with tension, yet laced with something different—an unspoken understanding that had never been there before. The jealousy still simmered under the surface, but it was overshadowed by the heat that was building again. My mind should've been racing, angry even, but instead, my body betrayed me.

Before I even had a chance to process it, Lucy's hand slid down between us. She felt me twitching beneath the sheets, her fingers curling around my hardening cock. Her smile was slow and knowing, like she'd discovered something she hadn't expected but had always suspected.

"Well, would you look at that," she murmured with a soft laugh. Her thumb stroked along my length, and I couldn't hold back the sharp inhale that followed. "Seems like I've unlocked something in you." Her eyes sparkled with amusement, her earlier confession suddenly taking on a whole new level of playfulness.

Without breaking eye contact, she placed her vape down on the nightstand and shifted beneath the covers. I swallowed hard, watching her head disappear as she moved between my legs. It had barely been a few minutes since I'd cum, and yet here I was, hard again, something that had never happened so soon after. I could feel my heart pounding as her lips brushed against me.

"You're thinking about Steve now, aren't you?" she teased, her voice muffled as she took me into her mouth, her tongue swirling expertly. "About how big he is… how much bigger than you."

Her words, her playful tone, sent a bolt of pleasure through me, mixing with the remnants of insecurity. I should've been embarrassed, or angry, but all I could focus on was the way her mouth felt on me, and how the images she was painting were only making me harder. I was helpless against the pleasure, every word she spoke drawing me deeper into the fantasy I had unknowingly craved.

"Do you think he'd fuck me better?" she mused between strokes of her tongue, glancing up at me with those mischievous eyes. "I bet he could fill me up in ways you can't." She moaned softly, the vibration of her voice against my skin sending shivers through me. My breath hitched, my body responding faster than I wanted it to.

I didn't have a chance to reply—didn't even trust my voice to work—before my body began to betray me again. The sensation was too much, too overwhelming. She hadn't even been sucking me for long, but already, I could feel myself teetering on the edge. The embarrassment was creeping in, but I was too far gone to stop it.

"Lucy, I'm—" I managed to gasp, my hips involuntarily bucking toward her, but she knew. She always knew.

Just as I felt myself about to tip over the edge, Lucy pulled her mouth away, leaving me aching, my cock pulsing in the cool air. She flashed me a wicked grin, her hand wrapping around me as she began to stroke, slow and deliberate. "You know I don't do cum in my mouth," she said lightly, but there was a teasing edge to her voice.

Her hand moved faster, her grip just right, and within seconds, I was done. My orgasm ripped through me, much stronger than I anticipated, and I groaned as she stroked me through the finish, my cum spilling onto her hand and the sheets.

When it was over, I lay there panting, utterly spent and slightly humiliated by how quickly it had happened. Lucy just laughed softly, wiping her hand on the sheets before settling back beside me.

"Well, hopefully Steve could last a little longer," she teased, her voice light and playful, but with that same undercurrent that made my heart race.

I chuckled, still catching my breath, the embarrassment fading into amusement. "Maybe," I replied, shaking my head. "But you're so damn good... I'm not sure anyone could last long."

Lucy just smirked, rolling over to curl up against me. "You're cute," she murmured sleepily, her head resting on my chest. The room seemed to calm again, the tension dissipating, leaving only the quiet comfort of her body pressed against mine.

And as we drifted off to sleep, I couldn't help but wonder what this new dynamic between us would bring. But for now, everything felt strangely right.

THE FIRST STEP

T hat was how it all started. For a while, it never went beyond the fantasy—talking about who she would choose, what they might do. It made for some intensely erotic times, but never the full fantasy I had craved. We played around with the idea in bed, teasing each other, spinning scenarios, but it always remained just that: talk. I was beginning to wonder if it would ever go further. Then today—out of nowhere—she told me she actually went to lunch with a man we had talked about while fucking, and that she asked him out?

My mind was racing, half with excitement, half with disbelief. I sat up a little straighter in my chair, gripping the phone tighter, trying to stay calm. "So... what did he say? Or, better yet... how did you ask him, and what did you ask exactly?" I blurted out, my voice barely containing the eagerness that had been bubbling up since she mentioned him.

She giggled, that same shy giggle she always used when she knew she had me hooked. "Well, we've been flirting for a few weeks like I told you," she began, her voice teasingly casual, like this wasn't a bombshell she was dropping. "And today, in the break room, while I was getting my morning coffee, he told me I looked pretty."

I raised an eyebrow, impatience creeping in. "And that led you to ask him out?" I asked, unable to hide the skepticism. It seemed so simple. A guy compliments her, and suddenly we're inching closer to a reality I'd only dreamed about. That was all it took? Just some interest?

"Not exactly," she said, a smirk audible in her voice. "I thanked him, and then he asked if I had any plans for lunch. I told him nothing I couldn't break, and asked what he had in mind."

I leaned forward, my excitement getting the better of me. "So... you went to lunch? Where did you wind up going? What did you talk about?" The questions spilled out one after the other, a million thoughts swirling in my head. I needed every detail. Had this been just a friendly lunch, or was there something more? What had they talked about? Had there been flirting? I could hardly keep my mind from racing ahead, filling in the gaps with every dirty scenario I'd ever imagined.

Lucy laughed softly, clearly amused by my eagerness. "Wow. Someone's excited," she teased, her voice light but knowing.

"Well, hell yeah I'm excited," I replied, my heart pounding in my chest. "My wife just went out to lunch with someone she thinks is incredibly sexy, and you know I get off on this stuff. What's not to be excited about?" My pulse was quickening, the thrill of the conversation hitting me in waves. "Even if he's not the one you choose... or if this never goes any further, it gives me plenty for the spank bank. Just imagining what you could've done."

There was a pause on the other end of the line, and I could practically hear Lucy smiling through the phone, her coy silence driving me wild. She knew exactly how this was affecting me, how much her little tease was pushing all the right buttons. And I couldn't help but wonder—had she imagined it too? Had she thought about what might happen if this did go further?

The line crackled slightly as she exhaled, her voice soft when she finally spoke. "Maybe I'm just warming you up for something more," she said, the words dripping with possibility.

"Uh... you don't mean..." I hesitated, my mind racing with

possibilities. I could feel my pulse thudding in my ears, wondering just how far this conversation had gone.

Lucy laughed, a light, playful sound that immediately made my tension spike. "No, nothing happened. We just talked," she said, amused by my eagerness, clearly enjoying how ready I was to jump to conclusions.

Relief washed over me, but it was mixed with the simmering excitement that never seemed to fade when she teased me like this. My thoughts swirled, questions piling up as I tried to keep my voice steady. "Did you tell him about us... or that you find him attractive?" The words came out more quickly than I'd meant them to, betraying the curiosity that had been gnawing at me since she mentioned him.

There was a brief pause on the line, and when Lucy finally spoke again, her voice had dropped into a seductive tone, dripping with suggestion. "Um, yes, I did," she purred. "I told him you get off on me talking about fucking other men... but that I've never actually done it."

Her words hit me like a shockwave. My breath caught in my throat. She actually told him. The confession made the fantasy we'd only played with feel dangerously real, as though we were one step closer to crossing that invisible line we had danced around for so long.

"What did he say?" I asked, not expecting an answer, but needing to know. The curiosity burned in my chest, mingled with a strange sense of vulnerability. How had he reacted to hearing that his co-worker's husband fantasized about her with other men? How had Lucy presented it?

"He thought it was interesting," she replied, her voice lilting with amusement. "He'd never heard of anything like that before."

I could hear the smile in her voice, the mischievousness curling at the edges. "And he blushed, rather adorably," she added, letting out a soft titter. "When I told him I thought he was unbelievably hot."

That sent another jolt through me. The thought of her, sitting across from him, watching his face flush as she openly admitted her attraction, had me clenching my fist tighter around the phone. My mind raced with images I hadn't allowed myself to fully entertain until now—Lucy, effortlessly charming him, playing with him the way she played with me.

"And then?" I pressed, leaning in. "What happened next?"

"Oh, we just talked a little more about odds and ends," she said, as if it were nothing. "You know, casual stuff. Then we headed back to the office."

"That's it?" I asked, trying to hide the disappointment in my voice. "When did you ask him out?"

Lucy exhaled loudly, drawing it out deliberately, like she knew exactly what she was doing to me. I could tell she was toying with me now—she always did this when she had something more to tell, but wanted to watch me squirm first. "Well," she began, drawing out the word slowly, "we had taken his car, and on the ride back to the office, he brought up our... relationship again." There was a slight pause, just long enough for my heart to race before she continued. "I just asked him if he wanted to get drinks this weekend."

The rush of excitement hit me like a tidal wave. My chest tightened, my breath quickened—this was really happening. She was actually going to go out with another man. "So, this weekend, then? Just drinks?" I tried to keep my voice steady, but I couldn't contain the thrill creeping into my words.

Lucy's tone turned playful, almost condescending as she teased, "Well, to start, I guess. I'm not going to ask someone I work with every day to just come over and fuck me in front of my husband," she snickered, the sound low and sultry.

"Yeah, I guess you're right," I laughed, shaking my head at the absurdity of the thought. "Wouldn't have been great if he said no."

But as we ended the conversation, I could already feel the excitement building. I barely slept that night, my mind buzzing with images and possibilities. The two days that remained until the weekend were pure hell. Hours at the office dragged, every meeting a blur as I obsessed over what might happen. I couldn't concentrate on anything else. The anticipation weighed on me heavily, and by the time Friday finally rolled around, it felt like my thoughts had been consumed by nothing else.

This was it. Tonight was the night. Lucy was going out with another man—something we had talked about endlessly but never acted on. The reality of it hit me all at once as I drove home. My heart raced, and my hands gripped the steering wheel tighter as I tried to control the excitement that had been building all week.

When I pulled into the driveway, my stomach flipped. I knew she'd be getting ready, but nothing could've prepared me for what I saw when I opened the door.

Lucy was sitting on the couch, dressed to kill. She wore a short red dress that hugged her curves, showing off her legs in a way that made my breath catch. My eyes trailed over her body, taking in every inch—her tall, thick frame, her curves accentuated perfectly. She was 5'9", with a round ass and full 34C breasts that strained against the fabric of her dress. Her blond hair was sleek and straight, falling to the middle of her back, with those bangs that just barely swept into her eyes, making her look even more seductive.

But it was when my gaze dropped lower that my excitement spiked even more. I had always had a severe foot fetish, and Lucy knew exactly how to play into it. She wore high-heeled, open-toed black shoes with delicate straps wrapping around her ankles, highlighting her long legs. But it was her toes that really grabbed my attention—her nails painted in that hot pink polish I loved so much. It was by far my favorite shade in her vast collection, and she wore it just for me, knowing how much it would drive me wild.

"Wow," I muttered, my voice barely a whisper as I stood in the doorway, taking her in. The sight of her like this, all dressed up to go out with another man, left me speechless. My heart raced in my chest, and the feeling of excitement, jealousy, and arousal swirled together in a heady mix.

Lucy smiled at me, her lips curving into a knowing smirk. "You like?" she asked, standing up slowly, her heels clicking against the floor as she moved toward me. Her dress clung to her in all the right places, showing off just enough to leave me craving more.

"You look... amazing," I managed, my eyes still glued to her legs, and then, instinctively, down to her feet. The hot pink polish gleamed under the soft light of the living room, and my body reacted instantly.

She noticed where my eyes were drawn and let out a soft laugh, lifting her foot just slightly so I could get a better view. "I thought you'd like this," she said, her voice teasing. She took a step closer, her presence filling the space between us. "I picked this dress... these shoes... just for you. To drive you crazy before I leave."

And it was working. God, it was working.

"Planning a late night, are we?" I asked, trying to sound casual, though my heart was already racing.

Lucy smiled, that same teasing, knowing smile she always gave when she had me wrapped around her finger. "Maybe. I'm not sure yet. We'll see how it goes." She walked across the room, grabbing her coat from the closet with a kind of nonchalance that only heightened my anticipation. "I wanted to wait for you to get home, to see me before I left," she continued, slipping her arms into the sleeves, her eyes flicking to mine with that spark of playful mischief. "I told him to meet me at Brasserie Lyon at five."

I could only nod, my throat suddenly dry as she moved closer. When she leaned in to kiss me, I could feel the electricity in the air between us. "I guess I'm off," she said brightly, her lips brushing mine, sending a jolt of excitement straight through me. "I love you... and I wouldn't wait up, just in case," she added with a wink, her tone light but layered with possibility.

The words hit me hard, stirring something deep in my chest. Just in case. The reality of it was setting in, but instead of fear or doubt, all I felt was that same rush of excitement I had been chasing.

"Oh, you know I will. I'll want all the details," I replied, trying to keep my voice steady.

"I know," she said with a soft laugh, before turning toward the door.

I followed her, watching as she stepped outside and walked to the car. The sight of her—dressed in that red dress, those heels, her hair perfectly styled—was almost too much. She looked incredible, sexy in a way that made it hard to believe she was mine. But she wasn't going out for me tonight.

I waved as she backed out of the driveway, my heart pounding harder with each second that passed. The excitement swirled in my chest, but as her taillights disappeared down the street, the waiting set in. It was going to be hours before she came home, and the thought of what might happen between now and then gnawed at me in a way I hadn't anticipated.

For a moment, I considered jerking off right then—just imagining what she might be doing was enough to drive me to the edge. But no, I wanted to save it. I wanted to hold on to this energy, to let it build until she came back, until I could hear it all from her lips.

The hours stretched out unbearably, each minute crawling slower than the last. Eventually, exhaustion took over, and I wound up drifting off on the couch, my mind still buzzing with images of what might be happening.

Then, my phone buzzed, startling me awake. I blinked against the dim light of the room, groggy but instantly alert as I saw Lucy's name flash across the screen. My heart leaped into my throat, a surge of excitement flooding through me. Hands trembling, I clicked on the message.

"Can I fuck?"

That was all it said.

The rush that washed over me was overwhelming, a mixture of excitement, fear, and disbelief. Did I really want my wife to fuck another man? This had been my fantasy for so long, but now, faced with the reality of it, the weight of the decision settled on me heavily. My pulse quickened, my mind racing as I stared at the screen. One word. That's all she had sent.

I could feel my chest tighten as I hovered over the keyboard, debating. I knew she wouldn't go through with it if I texted back with a no. Lucy had always been careful, always made sure I was comfortable with the boundaries we had set. She had been the only woman I had ever trusted enough to share this with, the only one I had even considered bringing this up with.

But now... now it wasn't just talk. It was real.

My fingers hovered over the screen before I typed back, trying to keep my message short, even though a thousand thoughts were racing through my head.

"Are U at the restaurant?" I sent.

A moment later, my phone buzzed again.

"No."

The simplicity of her reply hit me harder than I expected. She wasn't at the restaurant anymore. My mind whirled with the implications, the thrill of it spiking as I imagined where she might be. Was she with him already? In his car? A hotel? The questions bombarded my mind, each one adding to the excitement that surged through me, knowing I was on the edge of something that could change everything.

It was eight o'clock now. Three hours had passed since she left, and my mind was running wild with possibilities. Maybe they were still at the restaurant, just talking and flirting, but I couldn't shake the feeling that something more was happening. The silence was maddening, and with every passing minute, the anticipation grew. I picked up my phone, unable to wait any longer.

"Are you drunk? Where are you?"

I hit send and stared at the screen, willing a reply to come. A few minutes passed—though it felt like an eternity—before my phone buzzed again.

"At his house."

The words sent a jolt through me. My heart pounded in my chest, and my stomach tightened. She was already at his house. A thousand thoughts flooded my mind. What were they doing? Had anything happened yet? I hated how short her messages were, how they left so much room for my imagination to fill in the gaps. And then, another text.

"Well... can I?"

My breath caught in my throat. She was asking for my permission. My fingers trembled as I typed back, trying to keep calm, though my mind was racing.

"Can I call you, without interrupting anything?"

The seconds dragged on, each one stretching longer than the last, until finally, my phone buzzed again.

"I guess you can."

I didn't waste a second. As soon as I read the message, I clicked her picture on speed dial, my heart racing as the phone rang in my ear. It felt like ages before she finally picked up, her voice soft and breathy.

"Hello." Her voice was barely a whisper, and I could immediately tell something was different. There was a tension in the way she spoke, a softness that hinted at what was happening on the other end.

"Hey," I said, trying to keep my voice steady, though I was already on edge.

"Yes," she whispered again, waiting.

I hesitated for a moment, unsure of how to start. "What are you doing?" The question came out awkwardly, but I needed to know. I needed to hear it from her.

Lucy let out a soft chuckle, the sound sending a shiver down my spine. "Do you want the short version, or do you want to know the details?" she asked, her tone playful yet dripping with impatience. "If you say I can fuck him, I'll give you all the details when I get home."

My breath quickened, the weight of her words pressing down on me. My mind raced with a million questions, but I forced myself to focus. I wanted to know, and yet… I wanted this to happen. The thrill of it was undeniable. "How about a few details… and yes, you can fuck him," I said, my voice trembling slightly.

There was a brief pause on the line, and then Lucy spoke, her voice low and sultry. "Well, we're laying here naked," she began slowly, her words deliberate, teasing. "His fingers are in my pussy, and I'm stroking his cock, waiting to continue sucking him off… and for our phone conversation to end with the good news that I can take this massive dick inside me tonight."

Her words sent a shockwave through me. My pulse quickened,

and I felt my body react immediately. The image of her lying there, naked with him, her hand wrapped around his cock as he touched her—God, it was everything I had fantasized about, and yet now that it was real, it hit me harder than I ever could have imagined.

I swallowed hard, trying to steady my voice. "Um... yes," I managed to say, the words almost catching in my throat. "You can fuck him."

There was a soft, satisfied sound on the other end of the line, a noise that sent another rush of arousal through me. But before I could lose myself in the moment, one last question slipped out.

"But first," I asked, still slightly bewildered by her earlier choice of words, "how big is 'massive'?"

Lucy guffawed on the other end of the line, her voice tinged with amusement. "Well... how big are you, Jordan?" I heard her ask, her tone playful but with an edge of something more—something eager. A man's voice responded in the background, muffled but unmistakable. I couldn't make out the words, but then Lucy answered for him, her voice filled with a readiness that made my pulse quicken.

"About nine inches... and it's pretty thick," she said, her words dripping with excitement. "I've never had one that big before."

I swallowed hard. That part was true. Lucy had been with several men before we met, but I'd always been the biggest—until now. I'm about seven inches, which I knew was above average, but damn. Nine inches? Seriously?

My mind was racing, trying to process the weight of what was happening, but I pushed through the flood of thoughts, wanting to keep things moving. "Okay, you have fun, baby," I said, my voice strained as I prepared to hang up and let her night continue without me.

"Oh, I will," she purred, her words sending a final jolt of

excitement through me before the line clicked dead.

I stared at my phone, heart pounding. Whoa. She was really going to have sex with him. This wasn't just talk anymore —it was happening. The excitement hit me like a wave, but underneath it all was the sharp sting of jealousy. That jealousy was what fueled me, though, wasn't it? The thought of her with another man, the image of her moaning under someone else, that was the whole point. And yet, now that it was real, the complexity of my feelings left me both aroused and slightly unsettled.

I glanced at the clock—it was only 8:15. Damn. She'd probably be gone for hours. The thought of her spending all that time with him, doing things I could only imagine, left me restless. I couldn't just sit there, waiting and torturing myself with thoughts of what might be happening. I needed to distract myself.

I flipped through the channels, trying to settle my mind, but every show, every commercial, everything seemed meaningless compared to what Lucy was doing. Eventually, I drifted off on the couch, exhaustion winning over my racing thoughts.

It wasn't until the sound of keys jingling in the door woke me that I realized how long I'd been out. I glanced at the clock—4:00 a.m. Damn! She's been gone all night.

Lucy quietly shut the door behind her, and I immediately sat up, my heart racing again. As she stepped closer, the first thing I noticed was how disheveled she looked—her hair was a mess, strands sticking to her damp skin. There was a musty scent to her, the unmistakable smell of sweat and sex lingering in the air. Her red dress, the one that had clung to her so perfectly earlier, was now tousled and wrinkled, clinging to her in all the wrong ways. She looked worn out, completely spent.

As she tossed her purse onto the couch, I noticed something else—her panties, wadded up and hanging out of the bag. My stomach flipped as my eyes traveled back up to meet hers, and I couldn't help but smile wide, my excitement getting the better of me. "Well... how was your night?" I asked, my grin ear-to-ear, already knowing the answer but needing to hear it.

"Oh... my... god... it was fucking amazing," she replied with a gleeful sigh as she plopped down next to me. She slapped her hand on her leg, laughing softly, still glowing from whatever had happened. "I came at least seven times," she said, shaking her head in disbelief. "Amazing, absolutely amazing."

I felt a rush of arousal just from hearing her say it. Seven times? My mind buzzed with the images of what she'd done, what he'd done to her, how her body must have responded. My excitement spiked again, and without thinking, I leaned over and began to nuzzle her neck, desperate to feel her, to have her again.

But Lucy cocked her head in my direction and kissed me gently on the cheek—just a light, fleeting kiss, almost a brush-off. It wasn't what I expected. My heart sank slightly.

"What?" I asked, the disappointment creeping into my voice. "Is something wrong?"

She shook her head, looking at me with tired eyes. "I'm just really tired... and worn out," she said, letting out a sigh. "I honestly don't think I can have any more sex tonight. I spent all night doing that, and now my pussy is sore." Her words hit me hard. I knew she was being honest, and I understood—she had to be exhausted—but still, my heart sank. I had wanted this so badly, wanted her so badly, especially now that she was back. But I could see it in her eyes—she was spent.

I nodded slowly, swallowing the disappointment. "I understand," I muttered, though it stung.

Lucy leaned back into the couch, looking at me with a small pout. "I'll talk to you while you jerk off," she offered, her expression apologetic yet still teasing, knowing exactly what I was feeling.

I tried to smile, but the mix of emotions in my chest—jealousy, arousal, disappointment—made it hard. Still, the thought of her talking me through it, giving me the details of her night, made my pulse quicken again. It wasn't what I had hoped for, but it was enough to keep the fantasy alive.

"Okay," I said, feeling slightly better as I started to pull my pants down. I was already rock hard and knew I wouldn't last long, but I wanted to take my time, at least get the whole story before I exploded.

Lucy leaned in closer, her eyes locked on me as I began to stroke myself. "Where do you want me to start?" she asked, her voice soft but full of suggestion.

"At the beginning," I replied eagerly, my breath catching. I was desperate to hear every detail of her 'fucking amazing' night.

She smiled, leaning back into the couch, licking her lips as if savoring the memory. "Well, let's see..." she began, her eyes drifting to the ceiling as she collected her thoughts. "When I got to the restaurant, he was already there, waiting in a corner booth."

I nodded, hanging on her every word.

"He stood up, kissed my cheek as I sat down," she continued, her voice slow, almost teasing. "We talked for a while—awkward at first, you know? But the sexual tension was there. You could feel it."

I could see the memory playing out in her mind, the way her eyes grew heavy, her lips curling in that satisfied smile. It only made me stroke myself harder.

"And?" I prompted, feeling the heat rise in my chest.

She let out a small, breathy laugh, leaning her head back on the couch. "Well, fast-forwarding through the small talk and mundane parts," she said, licking her lips again. "We had about an entire bottle of wine. I was getting a good buzz going, and we started flirting more, playing a little footsy under the table."

Her words, combined with the image of her playing footsy with another man, sent a thrill through me. My hand moved faster, but I forced myself to slow down. I wanted more.

"Then what?" I asked, almost breathless.

"Two hours must've passed before he finally brought up leaving... going somewhere more comfortable." She shot me a sideways glance, biting her lower lip. "I agreed, and we decided to take his car."

I could hear the subtle satisfaction in her voice, like she was reliving the moment.

"Whose idea was it to go to his house?" I asked, my voice shaky as I stroked my cock steadily, trying to maintain control.

"Oh, that was mine, believe it or not," Lucy said with a huge smile on her face, her eyes gleaming with excitement.

Hearing that made my heart race even faster. She had wanted this. She had made the move. My stroking quickened, my hand moving faster than I realized, too close to the edge. I forced myself to slow down, my mind too captivated by what she was saying. I needed more.

"When we got to his car," she continued, her voice dipping lower, teasing me with every word, "he asked where we should go. And I asked if we could go to his place."

I groaned softly, feeling a surge of excitement as I imagined her asking him that. My wife, after thirteen years of marriage, wanting another man that badly.

"He said sure, and that's where we headed," she said with a soft laugh. "He didn't live far from the restaurant, so there wasn't much time to 'make a move,' but god, I wanted to. I wanted to just lick all over him."

I slowed my hand further, trying to stay in control, but every word she said pushed me closer.

Lucy's eyes darkened as she leaned in closer to me, her hand sliding over my inner thigh. "So, I started touching his thigh while he drove," she whispered, her breath hot against my ear. "He snickered a little and looked at me. Oh god, his face... the way he looked at me... I could feel my panties getting damp just from that look."

Her hand moved slowly, teasing me, and I couldn't help but moan softly in response. The way she was telling this, the way she was leaning into every detail, was driving me wild.

"I then began to fondle his bulge," she whispered, her voice dropping even lower, "and it was huge... especially for not even being hard."

That sent another jolt of excitement through me. My hand started moving faster, the tension building again. This was it. My wife was touching another man—something I had fantasized about for years, but now it was real.

"I slowly undid the button on his jeans," she continued, her eyes locking with mine, "just so I could stick my hand in there and feel what that bulge was hiding."

I could barely focus on my breathing, my heart pounding as she spoke.

"And as I pulled him out," she said, her lips curling into a wicked smile, "he started to get stiff. Oh my god... he was fucking huge. The biggest cock I've ever felt."

That sent me over the edge. My body tensed, and I had to stop my hand entirely just to hold back from cumming too soon. The thought of her touching him, of her wrapping her hand around another man's cock—one bigger than mine—was too much.

Lucy noticed, her smile deepening. She knew what effect this was having on me, and she loved it.

"I know you have a thing for men who are bigger," she said,

teasing me, "and trust me, baby, this one was bigger."

I could barely manage to nod, my mind a blur of arousal and jealousy, the two emotions tangling together as I tried to keep my cool.

"Once he was hard," she went on, "I bent over and put him in my mouth. I could barely get him in, though—I couldn't even come close to deep-throating it."

My breathing grew ragged, my hand instinctively moving faster again. The image of her struggling to take him in was overwhelming.

"I only managed to go down on him three or four times," she said, her voice hushed, "before we got to his place."

I groaned softly as I pictured it, her lips wrapped around him, the heat in my chest intensifying.

Lucy's eyes twinkled as she leaned back, her hand still teasing my thigh. "I quickly lifted my head as he shut off the car," she continued, "and then he leaned over and kissed me. His lips were so soft, and his tongue intertwined with mine..."

She let out a soft, satisfied sigh. "He was such a good kisser."

I was growing more excited, knowing exactly what was coming next. They were at his house, and I could only imagine what was about to unfold. The sex—this was it. But then another thought hit me. Lucy had left at five, they'd spent two hours at the restaurant, which put them at around seven, and she didn't come home until four in the morning. Did she fuck him for nine hours?

That idea alone made my dick even harder, if that was possible. My hand moved faster, and I had to force myself to slow down. I needed to last until the best part of the story.

Lucy leaned in closer, her eyes glinting with excitement. "When we got into his house, he immediately started kissing me and grabbing my ass," she said, her lips curling into a wicked smile.

"He had my dress hiked up to my waist, spreading my cheeks so wide that my thong started to slide in."

I groaned softly, the image hitting me like a wave. Her in that red dress, now bunched up around her hips as he pulled her close, touching her in ways only I had before. My heart raced as I stroked myself harder.

"He muttered something about loving my ass," she continued, biting her lip seductively as she watched my reaction, "then quickly removed my dress completely."

Hearing that, I felt a jolt of arousal. My hand moved faster for a moment, picturing her standing there naked before another man. But what came next caught me off guard.

"He started sucking my tits," she said, her voice lowering with a hint of pleasure. "And biting my nipples."

Her eyes flashed at me as she bit her lower lip. I could see how much she loved reliving it, the way she smiled at me, knowing how it was affecting me.

"He picked me up," she added, her tone turning breathless.

I froze for a second, shocked. Picked her up? Lucy wasn't a lightweight—she was 155 pounds, with a big, sexy ass. And this guy just lifted her like she weighed nothing? My mind struggled to process it, the image of him holding her up, his hands on her, her legs wrapped around his waist. I could only imagine how it looked.

"I wrapped my legs around him," she continued, her smile growing as she saw the shock on my face. "The kissing got even hotter, and I could feel his cock pressing against my pussy—my panties were still on, but I could feel him rubbing against me."

My hand picked up speed again, my pulse racing as I listened. The image of her, legs around another man, his cock rubbing against her, her panties soaked—it was almost too much.

"He carried me to the couch," she said, her voice growing

breathier, "still kissing me the whole way."

I groaned softly, picturing it all—her body wrapped around him, the way he must have laid her down.

"And then," she said, her eyes flashing as she watched me, "he slid down between my legs."

I blinked, caught off guard. I hadn't expected that. It had always been Lucy giving the oral, not receiving it. It was something I had never given much thought, but now... now the idea of another man going down on my wife hit me like a gut punch. A surge of jealousy rushed through me, catching me off guard.

"He pushed my panties to the side," she whispered, her voice dripping with satisfaction, "and started licking my pussy."

What? I could barely process it, my mind racing. He was going down on her, licking her? My wife? The shock of it made my hand falter for a moment, but then I felt a strange surge of arousal mixed with the jealousy.

"I was dripping wet," she moaned softly, "and he knew exactly what he was doing. He licked my clit, then slid two fingers deep inside me."

My breath caught in my throat. Hearing her describe it in such vivid detail, knowing how much she had enjoyed it—it was making me crazy. My jealousy burned hotter, but so did my arousal.

"He made me cum so fast," she said with a breathy laugh. "He'd ram his tongue into me every now and then, as deep as he could, while his fingers worked me."

I groaned again, unable to help myself. The image of him between her legs, his face buried in her, was almost too much to bear. I stroked myself harder, barely able to hold back.

Lucy slid her hand from my thigh to my balls, gently kneading them as she leaned in closer. "That was just the first orgasm," she grinned, her voice full of mischief. "There were many more after that." Her hand moved from my balls to take over where mine had left off, stroking me slowly but deliberately.

I could barely focus, my body already betraying me, edging closer to release. "You should skip ahead," I pleaded, my voice strained. "I'm not going to last."

She chuckled softly, slowing her strokes as she leaned in by my ear, her breath hot against my skin. "Well," she whispered, "long story short... before I called you, he continued to eat me out. I sucked his big cock until he came in my mouth, and then we just sat naked on the sofa and talked, kissed... until I realized I just had to fuck him."

My body tensed. He came in her mouth? The words echoed in my mind, sending a sharp jolt through me. My breath caught, and for a moment, I was at a loss for words.

"He came in your mouth?" I blurted out, my voice thick with disbelief.

Lucy paused, glancing at me with a playful smirk, her eyes narrowing as if to gauge my reaction. "Yes," she said slowly, clearly enjoying the effect this revelation was having on me. "Why? Does that bother you?"

I struggled to form a coherent response, the shock still hitting me hard. Of course I knew she had amazing sex with him, and yes, I had expected her to give him head—it was all part of what we'd talked about. But her swallowing? That was something else entirely. She hated the taste of cum. She'd always avoided it. I couldn't even remember the last time she swallowed for me.

Lucy raised an eyebrow, sensing my hesitation. "I mean," she continued, a slight note of awe in her voice, "you know I love giving head. And you're worried about me giving him a blowjob?"

I shook my head, still trying to process. "No, it's not that," I managed, my voice uneven. "I figured you'd suck him off. I just didn't think you'd let him cum in your mouth."

Her lips curled into a small, knowing smile. "Oh?" she asked, her tone light but laced with curiosity. "And why not?"

I swallowed hard, forcing myself to meet her gaze. "You... you don't like the taste of cum. You never have," I said, the words slipping out more quietly than I'd intended. "I mean... I can't even remember the last time you swallowed for me."

The truth of that statement hit me harder than I expected. It had been so long since she'd done that for me—always dodging, pulling away at the last second, preferring to finish me off with her hand instead. And yet, here she was, talking about how she'd taken another man's cum in her mouth like it was nothing.

Lucy's smirk deepened, and she leaned in closer, her lips brushing against my ear as she whispered, "Well... maybe his just tasted better."

The words sent a jolt of jealousy and arousal straight through me. My mind reeled as I tried to process what she'd said. A mix of emotions swirled inside me—anger, surprise, arousal— all tangled together, making it impossible to think straight.

"You really... swallowed for him?" I asked again, my voice shaky with disbelief.

Lucy pulled back slightly, looking into my eyes with a teasing glint. "Yes, I did. And you know what?" she purred. "I loved every second of it."

"Then I texted you and asked if I could fuck him," Lucy continued, her hand still gently fondling my balls, while my own hand worked steadily. "As soon as I hung up with you, I literally jumped on his big cock. I just couldn't wait. I rode him like that for a while, face to face, kissing him, grinding on him as hard as I could."

My breath hitched as I imagined the scene—the thought of Lucy, my wife, straddling another man, riding him with that same eagerness she used to reserve for me. My hand picked up speed, but I tried to keep my focus, listening intently.

"Then he spun me around," she added, her grin widening. "I kept riding him in reverse, and he couldn't keep his hands off my ass. Gripping, groping... I think he must have a thing for asses, because he seemed obsessed with mine."

She laughed softly, clearly enjoying the memory, while my heart pounded in my chest. The image of her riding him, his hands all over her ass, sent a surge of jealousy and arousal through me. I could barely hold myself back.

"I rode him like that for about half an hour," she continued, her voice growing more breathless. "But I didn't cum." She glanced at me, biting her lip, clearly enjoying how much this was getting to me.

"And then," she said with a sudden, exhausted laugh, "out of nowhere, he turned me around, picked me up, and started bouncing me on his dick."

My hand faltered for a moment. He picked her up? Again? I could barely wrap my mind around it. She was 155 pounds, with that gorgeous, thick ass—and this guy was just tossing her around like she weighed nothing. The shock of it made my stomach twist with a strange mix of jealousy and awe.

Lucy let out a soft moan, as if reliving the moment. "That's when I came," she whispered, her voice heavy with satisfaction. "He bounced me up and down on his cock, and I just couldn't hold back anymore."

I took over the jerking from her, needing to feel some control again, while her hand slid back to my testicles, gently massaging them as she continued her story.

"He bounced me for a while," she said with a breathy laugh. "I still can't believe how long he kept going—and he didn't struggle at all."

She glanced at me, her eyes gleaming with something I couldn't quite place. Was she teasing me? Letting me know just how much stronger this guy was? It hit me hard. I could feel the difference—this man had strength I couldn't match.

"I think I have a new favorite position," she added, a teasing smile playing on her lips.

The thought of her discovering something new with him, something I hadn't given her, sent another surge of jealousy through me. I could barely hold back anymore, my hand moving faster, but I forced myself to slow down. I wanted to hear everything.

"When he finished bouncing me," she continued, "he sat me down, turned me around, and slid his big fucking cock inside me again, bending me over." Her voice lowered, growing more intense. "He pumped me that way for a bit, and then he motioned for me to get on all fours. I lustfully accepted."

I groaned softly, the image of her on all fours, this guy taking her from behind, filling my mind. It was almost too much.

"We did 'normal' doggy-style for a while," she said with a grin, "but then he did something really cool. He stood up—over me—and kept fucking me while I was still on all fours."

I blinked, trying to picture it, but before I could process, Lucy got up from the couch and dropped to the floor, getting on all fours to demonstrate. She looked up at me, laughing softly. "I don't think I'm explaining it right," she said, positioning herself. "See, he's really tall, like 6'4", and his dick is pretty long. So he just stood over me while I stayed on all fours."

I stared at her, watching her body move as she tried to show me what he had done. My heart pounded in my chest, the image burning into my mind. It was something I had never even thought to try, and now she was showing me how this other man had done it.

"And he kept fucking me like that," she added, still on the floor, her eyes gleaming. "It was amazing."

"So… you came from the bouncing, huh?" I asked, trying to lead her back to that moment, wanting to hear more about it.

Lucy's eyes lit up, and she grinned widely. "Oh, hell yes," she said, her voice filled with excitement. "I loved it! I've never felt anything like that before—just being lifted like that, bounced up and down on his cock. The way he held me, how strong he was… it was insane. I came so hard."

My heart pounded as I listened, my hand slowing its movement again. The image of her losing control, of this guy giving her something I couldn't, was pushing me to the edge. But then she went on, and I could feel the intensity of her story rising.

"And I came again when he was standing over me," she added with a sly smile. "That was already amazing. By far, the best sex I've ever had." She paused, watching my reaction, clearly loving how much this was getting to me.

"We were both dripping with sweat," she continued, "and I could tell he wanted to change things up again—try something else. But I stopped him."

I blinked, caught off guard. "You stopped him?"

"Yeah," she nodded, her grin widening. "He was standing over me, right? So I positioned myself under him, got on my knees, and started sucking his dick."

My breath caught, and I groaned softly as I pictured her on her knees, taking him into her mouth. The jealousy flared again, but so did the arousal, making it hard to think straight.

"It took a while before he came," she said, her voice lowering as she leaned in closer. "But it was so hot. He was pulling my hair, fucking my face… you know how much I love that."

I could barely breathe as she spoke, my heart racing in my chest. I had never imagined her with another man like this—taking control, but also being completely taken by him.

"And then," she said with a soft moan, "he just shot his cum down my throat. He held my head and made me swallow."

I tensed, the shock hitting me again. She had swallowed for him twice? He didn't even need to ask her! My mind whirled with the implications, with the fact that she had never done that for me in years, yet here she was, talking about it so casually, like it was something she craved.

"After that," Lucy continued, her voice softening, "we stopped for a while. Just laid together, catching our breath. I told him how amazing he was."

I could only imagine that moment, the two of them lying there, naked and tangled together. My stomach twisted with jealousy, but I couldn't deny how much it was turning me on.

"He said, 'was?'" she laughed, shaking her head. "Like, as if to say, we're just getting started."

Her eyes glinted with amusement as she recalled the moment, and I could tell how much she had enjoyed every second of it. She leaned in closer, her breath warm against my ear. "And I was melting by then. I looked at the clock, and it was already two in the morning. I told him I should probably go soon, but..." she paused, biting her lip. "He wasn't done yet."

I groaned again, my hand moving faster as I hung on her every word.

"He went down on me again," she whispered, her eyes darkening with the memory. "I didn't expect it. He was so good at it, I couldn't resist. And then we started fucking again. We just kept going."

I swallowed hard, barely able to keep control. "How many times did he…?"

Lucy grinned. "He came three times. Once when I swallowed, once when I gave him a blowjob on the couch, and the last time… missionary."

I couldn't stop myself anymore. The jealousy, the shock, the arousal—it all crashed over me, and I groaned as I finally let go, the tension breaking.

Lucy smiled, watching me with a satisfied look, knowing exactly how much her story had affected me.

I sat up a bit, the thought suddenly hitting me. "I didn't even ask… did you guys use a condom?"

Lucy hesitated for a moment, her expression shifting slightly. "Uh… no," she said, her voice a bit softer, and I could see a flash of guilt in her eyes. "Are you mad about that?" she asked, her fingers gently brushing my thigh. "You know I'm on birth control, so I just figured it would be OK, and that you wouldn't mind. Actually," she added with an awkward laugh, "I didn't even think about it at first… we just sort of jumped into the whole thing. After the first round, I realized we hadn't, but by then… well, it felt too late."

I paused for a moment, processing what she said. Part of me was surprised, but the other part—the part that had been turned on all night—felt a thrill at the idea. I shook my head, letting the tension drain from my body.

"No," I said, my voice thick with arousal. "I'm not mad. Honestly, I think it's pretty hot."

My hand moved faster as Lucy's guilt turned into a small smile, clearly relieved. She continued, sensing how much the story was affecting me, trying to wrap up the night's events.

"He pushed my legs up over his shoulders, almost over my head —my back was barely on the ground," she said with a soft laugh. "Then he got on his knees and fucked me so deep, I couldn't believe it. I came again, of course."

I groaned softly, picturing it—the way he must have looked over her, thrusting into her as she was folded beneath him. My stroking grew faster, the tension building again.

"He rolled me onto my side after that," she continued, "and we scissored for a bit. He lifted my leg as high as it would go, and god, it felt so good. Then we went back to normal missionary, but this time he had my legs over his arms."

The thought of them moving through these positions, of him controlling her body like that, filled my mind. I could barely hold back.

"I could tell he was getting close again," she said, her voice dropping slightly, "and then he asked me... where I wanted him to cum."

My heart pounded at her words, my hand moving furiously now as I waited for her next line

"It was so fucking good," she continued, her breath hitching as she spoke, "that I didn't even hesitate. I told him I wanted it inside me."

That hit me like a shockwave. I groaned as the image of her telling him that, the moment of her asking for his cum, seared into my mind.

"As he shot that last load into my pussy," she said, her voice heavy with satisfaction, "I came the hardest I had all night."

I couldn't hold back anymore. With a deep groan, I shot my load, feeling more intensity than usual. It was overwhelming —knowing that Lucy had spent the night with this muscular, hung, nine-inch stud, that she had let him cum inside her. The jealousy, the arousal—it all exploded at once.

Lucy smiled, satisfied, as she watched me come down from the high. We headed upstairs to go to bed, and as we walked, a final thought struck me.

"Oh, I almost forgot," I said, glancing at her. "You never mentioned—and I was wondering—did you leave your shoes on the whole time you fucked?

She looked at me, a sly grin spreading across her face. "Yes, I did," she said with a soft laugh. "When we finished the first time, I noticed they were still on and actually thought of you because of that." She paused, looking at me with that playful glint in her eye. "I thought you'd like that part."

A rush of heat went through me again, even after everything. It was such a small detail, but it felt like the final touch to an already unforgettable night.

"It sounds like it was truly a memorable night," I said softly, smiling back at her. Then, after a beat, I added, "And you can see him again... whenever you want to."

Lucy's smile grew, and I could tell she was already thinking about the possibilities.

SERVING THE WAITER

I t had been several weeks since Lucy's night with her coworker, and while nothing major had happened since, the stories from that night had been enough to keep us both going. She told me that the flirting at work had gotten heavier —some inappropriate touches here and there when no one was around, and a few goodbye kisses at the end of the day. But no new encounters, no new stories. I could tell she was still holding on to the excitement from that night, just as I was.

But then one day, Lucy came home from work with a noticeable spring in her step. There was something different about her, an extra bit of happiness that caught my attention. As we sat at the kitchen table, I couldn't help but ask, "How was work today? Did something happen I should know about?"

Lucy gave a little laugh, her eyes flicking away for a moment before returning to mine. "Well, actually... I do have something to share."

My pulse quickened immediately. I leaned in, already eager to hear what fresh news she had. "Is it something with Jordan?" I asked, expecting her to have made new plans with her 'fuck buddy.'

She shook her head, that teasing smirk forming on her lips. "Actually, no," she replied, her voice dropping just a little. I could see the playfulness in her eyes as she leaned in closer. "I know we've never talked about this, but... how would you feel if it was someone else?"

Her question caught me off guard, and I raised an eyebrow, feeling a mix of surprise and curiosity. For as long as I could remember, I had wished Lucy would fully embrace her sexuality —let go of any inhibitions and explore whatever turned her on. She had mentioned a few times how she wished she had played around more when she was younger, before we met. I had always reassured her that no matter what she did, I would always love her, and none of it would change how I saw her. If anything, it made me more excited to see her embrace new experiences.

"I wouldn't mind at all," I replied quickly, my curiosity piqued. "In fact, I think it would be hot."

Lucy smiled, leaning in closer, her chin resting on her palms as she looked at me with a glint in her eye. "Well... Steve, the waiter at the restaurant the girls and I go to for lunch," she began, "I decided to start flirting with him. You know, in light of everything with Jordan."

I felt a sudden stirring in my pants as I leaned in even closer, our noses just a few inches apart. Her giggle only fueled my excitement. "Really? That hot young guy you've been checking out for a while now?" I asked, my voice growing more eager.

"Yes," she said with a smirk. "That's the one."

My mind raced at the thought of Lucy flirting with Steve. I had seen him a few times when we went out to eat—tall, fit, with that youthful confidence. And now she was telling me she had taken it further. It was almost too much to process.

"I was more nervous to flirt with him, though," she admitted, biting her lip slightly. "He's so much younger than me... only twenty-five."

I raised my eyebrows, both surprised and aroused at the idea.

"Twenty-five?" I echoed. "Well, you can be a cougar," I joked, leaning back with a grin. "Young guys love that. An older woman who takes charge and teaches them the ropes."

Lucy chuckled at my reply, her eyes glinting with amusement. I leaned in, unable to hide my eagerness. "So... how did the flirting go?" I asked, the anticipation clear in my voice.

She sat back in her chair, crossing her legs as she got comfortable. "Very well, actually," she said with a smile. "We were only there for lunch, so it wasn't anything over the top. I wasn't sure how the girls would react if I suddenly started flirting with a young hunk out of the blue."

I laughed at that, shaking my head. We had agreed not to 'come out' to our friends or colleagues about this new dynamic between us—most people wouldn't understand it. Lucy rolled her eyes playfully, clearly amused by the thought of her friends catching on.

"Did any of them say anything?" I asked, curious how close she'd come to getting caught.

"Well," she began with a grin, "Pam did say I was 'being a dirty girl,' but she laughed about it, so I don't think she was reading too much into it."

I chuckled, but my mind was racing, imagining Lucy flirting with Steve while her friends were none the wiser. It was exciting, knowing she was exploring this new side of herself.

"And then," she continued, her grin turning a little more wicked, "as we were leaving, I purposely forgot my purse at the table. The girls were already heading out the door, so I went back to get it. Steve was there, clearing the table, and as I crept up behind him... I couldn't resist."

I raised my eyebrows, surprised by her boldness. "What did you do?"

"I squeezed his butt," she said with a sexy grin, her eyes sparkling with mischief.

"Wow," I said with a laugh, clearly impressed. "How forward of you."

Lucy chuckled, leaning forward slightly. "Oh, he didn't mind," she replied, her voice lowering a bit. "He shot me a smile and bit his lip. It was actually pretty hot."

I could feel my pulse quicken at the thought of Lucy, my wife, flirting so openly with this young waiter. The idea of her making the first move, feeling confident enough to touch him like that, sent a surge of excitement through me.

"And then," she continued, her expression turning almost bashful, "I faced him and said, 'Look, I want to get to know you better... can I have your phone number?'" She gave me a playful, exaggerated look. "I know, totally lame, right? I haven't hit on anyone in over ten years—I'm rusty."

I laughed, shaking my head. "Well, it seems like it worked," I teased, leaning in closer.

"It did," she said with a grin. "He quickly wrote down his number on his notepad and handed it to me. I smiled at him and told him I'd be in touch, then walked out of the restaurant like it was nothing."

I was getting even more excited now, the possibilities swirling in my mind. Lucy was going to take a second lover—and this one was younger, someone we had even fantasized about. We'd talked during sex about the idea of her being with younger men, how much she enjoyed the possibilities. So far, it had only been famous actors she pointed out when we watched TV. But now? Now it was real.

"So," I asked, my voice a little breathless with anticipation, "was that all?"

"For today, yes, that was it," Lucy said, leaning back on the table with a relaxed smile. "I went back to work and finished my day, but I kept thinking about it. Even on the drive home, he was on my mind." She bit her lip thoughtfully. "Should I call him tonight? Or maybe just start with texting? Yeah, I think texting first would be better."

She paused for a moment, her expression playful. "But isn't there some kind of two or three day rule when calling someone? Or is that just for guys?" She gave me an honest smile, her eyes sparkling with mischief.

I laughed, shrugging it off. "That rule only really applies in the movies. I've never followed it."

"Good," she said with a grin, pulling out her phone and sliding open the keyboard. "Then I'll go ahead and text him."

I watched as she typed for a few moments, her fingers moving quickly over the keys. Then she slid the phone across the table toward me. The message read: "Hey there, sexy."

I raised an eyebrow, feeling a rush of excitement at the sight of the text. It was casual but suggestive enough to get the ball rolling. She was clearly hinting at her interest in him, and it was turning me on more than I cared to admit.

"That'll definitely break the ice," I said, my heart racing.

It didn't take long for her phone to vibrate on the table. Lucy picked it up, and as soon as she read the message, she chuckled softly, a smile creeping onto her face. Without a word, she began typing her reply, her smile growing as her fingers danced over the keyboard.

I leaned in, eager to know what Steve had said. But Lucy just slid the phone shut, tucked it into her pocket, and stood up from the table.

"What did he say?" I asked, curiosity getting the better of me.

She glanced back at me with a teasing smile, her eyes glinting. "You'll just have to wait and see," she said, her voice playful.

I watched her walk out of the room, my mind buzzing with curiosity and excitement. A few minutes later, I heard the faint sound of the shower starting upstairs.

Unable to contain my curiosity, I quickly ran up the stairs. When I reached the top, I saw that the bathroom door was open, so I decided to walk in. The shower curtain was drawn, but I could tell from the soft sound of water splashing that Lucy was lying down in the tub, letting the shower pour over her.

I slid the curtain aside quietly, and what I saw made my breath catch. Lucy was stretched out in the tub, her body glistening under the water. In one hand, she held her vibrator, gently pressing it against herself as she moaned softly, completely lost in the moment.

I stood there for a second, watching her, feeling my heart race as I took in the sight of her pleasuring herself under the spray of the water. The soft hum of the vibrator filled the bathroom, mixing with the sound of the water hitting her skin.

I flashed a big grin at Lucy and slouched down, lowering myself so our heads were level. "Whatcha doin'?" I asked playfully, my voice barely hiding my growing excitement. She flashed a grin back at me, her eyes closing briefly in pleasure.

Just then, she slid her vibrator deeper, moving it in and out of her dripping wet hole, her soft moans filling the small, steamy bathroom. I could barely contain myself as I watched her— so relaxed, so completely in control of her pleasure. My hand instinctively moved to my pants, and before I knew it, I was jerking off, my eyes glued to her as she masturbated.

Watching her pleasure herself, knowing she had Steve on her mind, drove me wild. It wasn't long before I came, my breath ragged as I finished. I quickly readjusted my pants, feeling the rush of what had just happened.

Lucy smiled at me as she reached over and slid the curtain closed again, her soft laugh teasing me as she resumed her shower. I stepped out of the bathroom, still buzzing from the moment, and made my way to the bedroom. I sat on the bed, waiting for her return, my mind racing with thoughts of what she might say next.

A few minutes later, the sound of the water shutting off echoed through the house. She emerged from the bathroom, her skin glistening as she wore only her robe. She grabbed her hairbrush off the vanity and sat next to me on the bed. As she brushed her damp hair, she gave me a sidelong glance and said, almost nonchalantly, "Okay, yeah... I want to fuck him."

My jaw dropped. "Really?" I asked, my voice filled with a mix of surprise and excitement. "You decided that quickly, or have you been thinking about this for a while?"

Lucy giggled, her voice light as she brushed out her hair. "Oh, I've thought about it," she said with a grin. "But he kept popping into my mind while I was in the shower. I just have to find out what it's actually like, instead of just fantasizing about him."

Her words sent a jolt of arousal through me. The idea of her wanting Steve, not just as a fantasy but in reality, was thrilling. I leaned in closer, unable to stop myself from asking, "So... are you going to tell me what he texted back?"

Just as I asked, her phone rattled on the dresser, vibrating with a new message. Lucy stood up, grabbing the phone with a slight frown. "Aw, two missed texts," she said, pouting her lips as she read them.

I watched her, the tension building as I waited to hear what he had said. After a few moments, she finished her reply and returned to the bed, sliding the keyboard closed.

"He just said he's doing good," she explained, "trying to find something to get into tonight, and asked if I was busy."

"And... what was your answer?" I asked, leaning forward, my pulse quickening with anticipation.

Lucy grinned, enjoying the tension in the air. "I told him I'd ask what you thought and try to make plans with him tonight."

I raised an eyebrow, surprised. "Really? You mentioned me already? I honestly thought he was under the impression you were stepping out behind my back and you were going to play it that way."

She stood up from the bed, and as she slid her robe off, revealing her naked body, I couldn't help but admire her. My wife looked incredible—her figure perfectly balanced with ample tits, not too big but just right, about a C cup. Her hips were wide, her waist narrow, and her juicy, bitable ass was always a sight that drove me wild.

As she slipped into a dress, she glanced over at me. "Well, we'll see if he's cool with knowing the truth," she said, smoothing the fabric over her curves. "I'll see how he reacts. If he's okay with it, I'll tell him that you know and that you get off on me fucking other men. If not..." She paused with a teasing smile. "I'll just tell him it was a joke, that you don't know, and I won't tell."

Lucy sat back down on the bed, her confidence radiating from every movement. The sound of her phone vibrating pulled our attention, and she giggled as she slid out the keyboard to respond. After a few taps, she looked back at me, noticing my eagerness.

"He said 'okay' and to let him know if you care whether I meet up with him tonight," she said with a smile, watching my reaction closely.

The words hit me with a surge of excitement, and without thinking, I blurted out, "Tell him yeah!"

Lucy laughed, shaking her head at my enthusiasm as she typed out her response. Once she sent the message, she stood up, a playful glint in her eye. "Well, I guess I should start picking out my clothes," she said. "I told him to give me an hour, then come and pick me up. I'll send him our address and get ready."

I watched her as she moved around the room, excitement buzzing through me. As the hour passed, Lucy transformed before my eyes, turning herself into the picture of seduction. She looked absolutely stunning—her blonde hair slightly curled, with soft waves framing her face and part of it flowing over one eye in a way that made her look effortlessly sexy.

Her outfit was designed to turn heads. She had chosen a black thong with a mesh front that offered a tantalizing view of her neatly trimmed pubic hair, a small patch just above her clit. The thong was perfectly paired with a tight black mini skirt, revealing her toned legs, and an equally suggestive sheer black top that showed off her black bra underneath. The whole ensemble screamed confidence.

But it was her shoes that truly did me in. She wore black high heels, open-toed with sleek silver buckles on the sides, revealing her perfectly pedicured toes. Her nails were painted a vibrant pink, a shade that made them stand out beautifully against the dark leather of the shoes. The sight of her feet in those sexy heels —her favorite, and mine—was enough to push me to the edge of arousal all over again.

"Well, how do I look?" Lucy asked, her voice filled with playful anticipation. I stared at her, mouth open, jaw dropping as I took her in—every detail of her outfit, her confidence, her sex appeal. My eyebrows shot up as I tried to find the words.

"Hell yes! I want to fuck you right now, actually," I blurted out, barely able to contain myself.

Lucy giggled at my reply, her eyes sparkling with amusement as she grabbed her purse and headed downstairs. She moved with a confidence that made my heart race. Just as she reached the final step, her phone buzzed with an incoming text. She slid it open and walked over to the couch, her expression shifting into one of anticipation as she read the message.

"He's on his way," she said, her voice tinged with a hint of surprise. "He said it'll only take him about five minutes." She glanced up at me, raising an eyebrow. "Either he drives really fast, or he lives closer to us than the restaurant."

She walked over to the door, opening it and looking out into the night. I followed her, my excitement growing with every passing second.

"Do you have any idea what you're going to do tonight?" I asked, standing just behind her, my voice low with curiosity.

"Oh, I don't know," she replied, her gaze still fixed outside. "Maybe we'll get a drink… or find a club. We'll see."

I crept up behind her, sliding my arms around her waist, feeling the warmth of her body through her clothes. "Are you going to try to fuck tonight?" I whispered, my lips close to her ear.

Lucy laughed softly, leaning back against me. "Probably not," she said, her voice teasing. "But then again… you never know." She turned her head slightly, giving me a mischievous grin. "The 'new' me is a bit of a slut, isn't she?"

Her laugh was light, but the words sent a surge of excitement through me. She was embracing this new side of herself, teasing me with the possibilities of what might happen tonight.

Before I could respond, she turned and gave me a quick kiss on the cheek just as a blue sports car pulled into the driveway. "Well… that's him," she said, a hint of nervous excitement in her voice as she opened the screen door.

I watched her, feeling a mix of anticipation and arousal as she prepared to leave. She glanced back at me one last time, her smile softening.

"I shouldn't be too late tonight," she said. "But if it starts to look like it's going to be a late night… like last time," she added with a wink, "I'll text you."

She gave me a wave as she walked down the path to the car, her hips swaying with confidence. I stood in the doorway, watching her leave, but then my eyes shifted to Steve. This was the first time I'd actually seen him, and my heart gave a strange, excited lurch.

He was young—definitely younger than us—and undeniably attractive. That only added to the excitement, knowing that my wife was with someone like that. It was one thing to hear her talk about him, but seeing him for myself? It was something else entirely. He had that kind of look, the kind that could make any woman swoon. His sandy brown hair was cut short and faded up to a messier top, giving him a casual, effortlessly cool look. And judging by the way he was sitting, arm resting casually out of the car window, it was clear he was built too. I could see the definition in his arms, his shoulders broad even in that seated position. Lucy had told me he was over six feet tall—probably about six-one. Me? I was only five-eight, equal height with Lucy.

I couldn't help but feel a rush of arousal at the thought. I knew Lucy had a thing for tall men, and now she was out with one— young, fit, and confident. It turned me on even more, knowing that the guy she wanted to fuck was someone I could admire too. I watched as they drove off together, Steve's car disappearing down the street, before I closed the door.

The evening dragged on slowly after that. I flipped through random television shows, trying to distract myself, but my mind kept drifting back to Lucy. What was she doing? Was she thinking about me? Was she going to fuck him tonight?

It wasn't until around seven o'clock that my phone buzzed,

pulling me out of my thoughts. I grabbed it off the coffee table, my heart quickening as I saw it was a text from Lucy.

"Just sitting and talking at the bar. Going to the park next," the message read.

I stared at the text, my mind spinning. The park? In the dark? Did that mean she was going to have sex with him tonight? I tried not to read too much into it—if that was the case, the waiting would only feel longer. Instead, I quickly typed back a reply: "Got it. Call or text me if plans change or run late."

But after sending the message, I didn't get a reply. The minutes ticked by, and as half-past eight rolled around, I heard the sound of a car pulling into the driveway. My heart leaped. I jumped up from the couch, peeking through the curtain to see her stepping out of Steve's car and walking toward the house.

She's back already? I thought, surprised. That wasn't long at all. Maybe she was right—they didn't fuck tonight.

I opened the door just as she reached the front steps, my excitement barely contained. Lucy smiled at me as she walked into the house, her eyes sparkling with amusement.

"Well, hello there," she said, her voice teasing as she kicked off her shoes. "Aren't we excited tonight?"

I shook my head, trying to act casual but unable to hide my eagerness. "And... should I be?" I asked, my voice filled with anticipation. "I'm eager to hear what kind of activities you got into tonight."

Lucy laughed softly, walking past me as she headed into the living room. I followed her, my heart racing as I waited for her to fill me in.

"I'm sorry to disappoint you, but I didn't have sex tonight," Lucy said as she took off her coat, her voice teasing but gentle. I could feel my heart drop slightly at her words, though I tried to hide it.

She hung her coat on the rack, and as she did, I watched her hike up her skirt. My breath caught as she slid off her panties—those sexy black mesh thongs that had been driving me crazy since she put them on. She didn't stop there, though. She unfolded them slowly, holding them out in front of her as she stood in front of me.

Lucy stepped closer, holding the crotch of the thong right up to my face. "But look how fucking wet I got, though," she said, her voice dropping to a sultry whisper. She pressed the damp material against my nose, letting me take in the scent of her pussy. The smell was unmistakable—intense and intoxicating.

I grabbed the panties from her hand, feeling the slickness of her arousal, but my mind was still spinning from her earlier words. She hadn't fucked Steve. As hot as this was, I couldn't help the slight wave of disappointment that washed over me. I followed her to the couch, the mesh panties still clutched in my hand.

Lucy must have noticed my expression, her eyes softening with a playful grin. She sat down on the couch, patting the seat next to her. "Come sit down, you," she said, her tone gentle but teasing.

I hesitated for a moment, still processing everything, but her smile drew me in. I sat beside her, feeling the tension in the air between us. She leaned in closer, her warmth radiating, and I could tell she was enjoying this moment—playing with my anticipation, teasing me with the possibilities of what could have happened.

I sat down beside Lucy on the couch, still processing everything she'd said and done. Without missing a beat, she tugged on my belt, her fingers deftly working at the buckle. "Undo your pants," she said softly, her voice low and laced with intent.

Her command caught me off guard, but I complied, fumbling with my belt and undoing the buttons. As I parted the zipper, she was already sliding her hand beneath my boxer shorts, her fingers brushing against the sensitive skin just above my cock. The sensation made me twitch slightly, my anticipation growing with every touch.

"Care for a blowjob?" she asked, her voice teasing, as her fingers wrapped around my shaft, gently massaging me to full hardness.

I hesitated for a second, taken by surprise. "Uh... sure," I stammered, feeling my cock stiffen even more in her grip. I wasn't expecting this at all. She'd already told me they didn't have sex tonight, so I figured there was no story to tell. Maybe this was her way of giving me a preview of what could come—something to tide me over until her next night with Steve.

Lucy smirked, her eyes glinting with mischief as she slowly, deliberately, pulled my cock out of my boxers. She didn't rush it. Instead, she took her time, savoring every moment as she exposed me to the cool air, letting her fingers glide over my length. My cock was already hard, but her teasing touch made me pulse in her hand, the tension building as she stroked me lazily.

"I wouldn't want to be rude," she said with a wicked grin, giving my cock a playful squeeze. "After all, it wouldn't be fair to you if I only sucked his dick tonight."

Her words sent a shiver down my spine, the mixture of jealousy and arousal swirling inside me. I could barely process it before her tongue flicked across the tip of my cock, sending a jolt of pleasure through me. She was slow, deliberate, her tongue tracing circles around the sensitive head, just enough to make me ache for more.

She met my eyes, her lips curled into a teasing smile. "You like that?" she whispered, barely above a breath, before dipping her head lower, running her tongue along the underside of my shaft. Her touch was feather-light, designed to tease, to drive me wild without giving me what I wanted.

I groaned softly, my body tensing in response to her playful teasing. She kept me on edge, licking slowly along the length of my cock, but never fully taking it into her mouth. Her hand gripped me lightly at the base, stroking me just enough to keep me throbbing in her palm.

Then, without warning, she finally slid her lips over the head of my cock, the warmth of her mouth making me shudder. Inch by inch, she took me deeper, her tongue pressing against the underside as she hollowed her cheeks, creating just the right amount of pressure. I let out a low groan, my hand instinctively moving to the back of her head as she took me further.

But Lucy wasn't in any hurry. She moved at her own pace, her mouth gliding down my shaft before pulling back up, her tongue teasing the head with each slow, deliberate bob. She moaned softly around my cock, sending vibrations that made my toes curl. Every time I thought she was going to pick up the pace, she slowed down again, keeping me teetering on the edge.

A few more slow, teasing bobs of her head had me groaning aloud, the tension building unbearably. But before I could even think about losing control, I reached down, gently pulling her up toward my face. I needed to feel her closer, to kiss her, to taste her after everything she had done to me.

I pulled Lucy up to me, kissing her deeply, savoring the taste of her lips. The kiss was full of hunger, a mix of desire and jealousy swirling inside me. When I pulled back slightly, I looked into her eyes, searching for a sign of what had happened tonight.

"So," I whispered, my voice thick with anticipation, "you sucked him off tonight?"

Her lips curved into a teasing smile, and she kissed me back, slow and deliberate. As she pulled her lips away, she traced my mouth with her tongue, her breath warm against my skin. "Yes," she said softly, her words dripping with satisfaction.

"Completely."

The way she said it, with that sly grin, sent a wave of jealousy through me. Before I could react, she slid back down to her previous task, her hand stroking my cock as she hovered just above it. Just before she took me into her mouth again, she added, almost casually, "And he came so fucking much... I wound up swallowing a lot of it."

The words hit me like a punch to the gut. The reminder of what she had done, what she had given to him—what she never gave to me—had my mind spinning. I groaned softly, feeling my cock throb harder as she wrapped her lips around me again, taking me deep into her mouth. Her movements were slow, deliberate, every stroke of her tongue designed to drive me wild.

As she worked me, I felt my orgasm building, the tension coiling tight inside me. My breathing grew ragged, and I gave a soft grunt, tapping her head to let her know I was close. "Wait," I managed to say between gasps, "let me lick you... before I cum."

Lucy arched her head toward me, her lips still pressed gently against the head of my cock. She looked up at me, her eyes gleaming with that same teasing glint. "He already took care of me," she whispered, her voice low and full of satisfaction.

The words stung, a reminder that another man had already pleasured her. Still, she didn't stop. She didn't even miss a beat as she turned back to continue sucking my cock, her mouth gliding up and down the length of me with practiced ease.

As Lucy's mouth worked me, I felt the tension building, my body tightening as I neared the edge. Her lips moved expertly along my shaft, her tongue swirling around the head of my cock, teasing me mercilessly. My breathing grew ragged, and I felt that familiar rush of pleasure cresting.

I was so close—just a few more strokes and I would've lost control entirely.

But then, just as I was about to cum, Lucy suddenly pulled her mouth away. I gasped, my body trembling as the sensation ebbed, confused and aching for release.

She sat up slightly, her lips glistening as she looked me dead in the eye, a teasing smirk curling on her face. "No cumming in my mouth," she said simply, her voice low but firm, leaving no room for negotiation.

Her words sent a jolt through me, stinging with the sharp reminder of what she had done earlier. She had swallowed for him, but now, here she was, refusing to do the same for me. The jealousy flared up even hotter, mixing with the overwhelming desire still pulsing through me.

Before I could respond, she wrapped her hand around my cock, stroking me with quick, deliberate movements, pushing me right back to the edge. There was no stopping it this time. My body tensed, and with a deep groan, I exploded, my cum spilling into her waiting hand.

She watched me with that same smirk, satisfied as I finally released into her grip. When it was over, she wiped her hand clean, standing up from the couch with casual ease, as if the moment was nothing more than an afterthought.

"Okay, I have to work in the morning... and so do you," she said, her tone light and teasing. "We should get to bed."

I stood up slowly, the aftershocks of the orgasm still tingling through me, but my mind was spinning. I leaned down, pressing a soft kiss to her forehead, but the frustration still clung to me. "But... you didn't get off tonight," I murmured, trying to catch her eye.

She chuckled, her grin widening as she gave me a playful look. "Who said that?" she replied, batting her eyelashes as she turned and headed up the stairs, leaving me standing there, a mix of jealousy and arousal still coursing through me.

INTRODUCING
THE BITCH

About a week had passed since Lucy's second outing—this time with Steve, the 25-year-old waiter. I had been turning it over in my mind ever since, but today, over Saturday morning breakfast, I decided to ask her a few more questions.

"Have you girls been back to that restaurant since your 'date'?" I asked, my tone casual as I took a sip of my coffee, though my curiosity was anything but casual.

Lucy sat across from me at the kitchen table, fork in hand as she worked through her pancakes. She looked up with a mouth half full of food and nodded. "Oh sure, we've been back there like twice, I think," she said, swallowing before continuing. "He's cool with the secrecy part, though. Doesn't treat me any different in front of the other girls."

I nodded, listening carefully as I took another sip of coffee. "That's good," I replied. "And you guys are still talking?"

Lucy smirked, giving me a sideways glance. "Yeah, we text like every day now," she said, shrugging. "I think he's starting to understand our arrangement."

There was something in her tone, something light and

nonchalant, but it piqued my interest even more. "Have you two made any more plans to see each other?" I asked, leaning in slightly.

She paused mid-bite, setting her fork down as she looked at me with a slightly puzzled expression. "Actually, no," she said, her brow furrowing slightly as if the thought had just occurred to her. "He hasn't even asked to see me again." She glanced up at the ceiling, as if searching for an answer there. "Oh well," she shrugged. "Maybe he just wanted some head and that was it. You know, other than the blowjob, we didn't really do anything but kiss."

I raised an eyebrow, unable to stop the chuckle that escaped my lips. "So fingering another man's wife is 'nothing'?" I asked, grinning as I teased her.

Lucy rolled her eyes, but she smiled as she leaned back in her chair. "Well, you know what I meant," she said with a playful shrug. "We didn't, like… fuck, you know?"

She finished the last bite of her pancakes, pushing her plate to the side. I watched her, my heart swelling a little at the casual way she spoke about this new dynamic between us. It felt so natural now, yet still so thrilling.

I set my cup down, leaning forward as I looked at her. "I love you, Lucy."

She looked up at me, a little surprised. "What was that for?" she asked, her brows knitting together. "I mean, I know you love me —you're my husband." She gave a little laugh, standing up to take her plate to the sink. "Besides, you better love me," she called over her shoulder. "After all, I'm fucking all these guys for you."

Her laughter filled the kitchen, and I couldn't help but laugh along. "You're fucking them for me?" I said, my tone teasing. "Like you're not having fun? And let's be honest—it was only one guy you actually had sex with."

Lucy placed her plate in the sink, turning around to face me with a grin. She leaned back against the counter, putting her head back dramatically as if to exaggerate a sigh. "Oh yes, you're right," she said, her voice dripping with playful sarcasm. "I do like it. Love it, in fact."

Her words sent a jolt of excitement through me, but before I could respond, she lifted her head, her eyes sparkling with mischief. "Do you want to meet Jordan?" she asked, her tone tricky, teasing.

I blinked, caught off guard by her sudden question. "Meet Jordan?" I echoed, unsure of where she was going with this.

Lucy leaned forward, her grin widening. "Yeah," she said, her voice low and playful. "I think it'd be interesting... don't you?"

I thought about it for a second before answering. Meeting Jordan —this man who had given Lucy the best sex of her life—was something I wasn't sure I was ready for. It was one thing to hear about her adventures, to know that she was with other men, but to meet him face-to-face? That felt like a different level entirely.

"I'm not sure," I told her, my voice uncertain.

Lucy smiled, her tone playful as she slowly walked back toward the table, a seductive sway in her step. "Oh, come on," she teased. "You'd really like him, baby." Her voice was soft but full of confidence. "You guys actually have a lot in common."

I raised an eyebrow, smirking. "Oh yeah? Like what?" I asked, half-joking. "Definitely not condom size, I know that much."

She burst into laughter, sliding back into her chair. "No, silly!" she said with a grin. "I mean like normal stuff. You know, stuff that 'normal' people do."

I laughed, shaking my head. "Normal people?" I teased. "As in, guys who don't jerk off to the stories their wives tell them about who and how they fucked the night before?"

"Exactly!" she said with a wide smile, clearly enjoying the banter.

I leaned forward, my heart racing with a mix of excitement and nervousness. "Okay, if you want me to meet this Greek sex god," I said, throwing in a bit of humor to mask my hesitation, "I guess I will… for you, dear."

I leaned over the table to kiss her, but to my surprise, she pulled back, a sly smile on her lips. My brow furrowed in confusion as she stood up, making her way back to the counter.

"I've been doing some reading," she said, her voice softening, as if she was about to reveal something important. "About what we're doing, I mean."

I watched her closely, intrigued. "Reading?"

She turned, leaning against the counter as she propped herself up, her eyes glinting with a mixture of excitement and mischief. "You know, there's a term for this kind of thing," she said, almost teasing.

"Uh… yeah," I replied, my voice hesitant but curious. "Of course I know. How do you think I find my porn?"

Lucy chuckled, shaking her head as I stood up and walked toward her. "Cuckold," she said, her voice dropping to a low whisper as I moved closer. She opened her arms, inviting me in, and wrapped them around my shoulders as soon as I was within reach. Her lips grazed my lower lip, sending a shiver down my spine.

"So…" she whispered, her forehead pressing against mine, her breath warm on my skin. "You are now my bitch boy." Her voice was devious, her eyes dancing with amusement as she pulled me even closer.

I pulled my head back slightly, still holding her waist, my expression a mix of surprise and awkwardness. "Um… excuse me?" I said, my voice incredulous but intrigued. "What exactly have you been reading?"

Lucy giggled, pulling me back in, her arms tight around my shoulders. "Just some websites," she said, her tone casual as she kissed me again, her lips soft and teasing. "You know, random websites.

I chuckled, leaning into her kiss but still curious. "Random websites, huh?" I asked, my voice teasing. "What kind of randomness are we talking about?"

Her kisses deepened, her lips trailing along my jaw as she whispered in my ear. "I found this site about 'how to cuckold your man' the other day when I was surfing at work," she said, her voice dripping with seduction. "And I have some ideas of what we're going to do... and what we're not going to do."

The words sent a shiver of both excitement and apprehension through me. "Not do?" I asked, my heart racing as my mind scrambled to figure out where this was going. Part of me feared she might be getting into something deeper than I was ready for —but who was I kidding? I would do anything this woman asked me to.

Lucy's eyes gleamed with excitement, a new energy radiating from her as she stood before me, her arms still loosely draped around my neck. "Well, you get off on me fucking other guys and hearing all the naughty details," she said, her voice soft but assertive. "And you're the one that got me interested in this 'lifestyle'. But now..." she paused, a glint of mischief in her eyes, "I'm taking the reins, just like all the other women I've been reading about."

Her words hung in the air, heavy with meaning. I swallowed, suddenly feeling a shift I wasn't sure I was ready for. She leaned in closer, her voice lowering, filled with excitement. "So... you're going to do what I tell you to do."

I blinked, puzzled by her sudden shift in tone. Sure, I got off on hearing about her sexual adventures, knowing all the details about what she did with other men. But now, this felt different.

The way she said it, the control she was assuming—it threw me off balance. I had watched plenty of cuckold porn, but I wasn't sure if I was ready to live that out fully.

Still, I trusted her. I always had. And deep down, the excitement of letting her take control stirred something inside me. I figured I'd go along with it. "Okay," I said hesitantly, my voice catching in my throat. "I'll do it."

Before I could even process what was happening, Lucy's hand flew up, slapping me hard across the face. The sting of it left me reeling, my cheek burning as I stumbled slightly, shocked by the sudden aggression. I reached up to rub my face, looking at her with wide eyes.

"Yes, you will do it," she said coldly, her lips curling into a smirk. "Say it… my queen."

I hesitated for a moment, the words foreign on my tongue. But I could see the challenge in her eyes, the dominance she was asserting over me. It sent a thrill of both fear and arousal coursing through me. "Yes," I said, purposefully pausing before lowering my gaze. "Yes, my queen."

She smiled, satisfied, before stepping forward and wrapping her arms around my neck again, pulling me close until our noses touched. "Jordan is coming over tonight," she whispered, her tone casual, as if it didn't matter what I thought about it.

I stiffened at her words. This wasn't just a game anymore. I was going to be her cuckold—not just hearing about her sexual outings after the fact, but living through it. The realization hit me hard, and I could feel my stomach knot with a mix of dread and excitement.

"Okay…" I stammered, unsure of what else to say. "Are you going to be acting like this when he gets here?" The thought of her treating me this way in front of Jordan made me uneasy. He was taller than me, more muscular, and from everything Lucy had said—far larger where it mattered. I wasn't sure I could handle that dynamic being out in the open.

Lucy pouted her bottom lip, feigning sympathy. "Aw... would that make you sad, bitch boy?" she asked, her voice dripping with mock concern. I cocked my head, confused by the mix of teasing and seriousness. I could no longer tell when she was playing and when she was being real.

She leaned in closer, her breath hot against my skin. "Tell you what," she whispered, her lips grazing my ear. "If you're good while he's here... he won't see a thing."

With that, she gave me a gentle shove to the side, her playful smirk never fading. She walked past me, her hips swaying confidently as she left the room. I stood there, rubbing my cheek, still feeling the sting of her slap, and realized that a part of me was scared—scared of what was going to happen tonight.

But the other part? The other part was more than excited.

After I finished the dishes, I heard the soft sound of Lucy's footsteps descending the stairs, and I instinctively made my way to the living room to meet her. When she appeared, my breath caught for a moment. She was wearing her white silk nightgown, the one that clung to her curves in all the right ways. It was usually tight enough to reveal the faint lines of her panties beneath, but tonight, there were none. My heart skipped, a mixture of excitement and dread brewing deep inside me.

She moved with a quiet confidence, her bare feet padding softly across the hardwood floor as she crossed the room. She didn't stop or acknowledge me at first—just walked to the door and slowly unlocked it. Her movements were deliberate, almost taunting.

"Jordan is on his way over," she said casually, her voice low, with an air of control that made my stomach flip.

My mouth went dry. "Are you going to be wearing that?" The question slipped out before I could stop myself.

Lucy stopped mid-step and slowly turned to face me. Her eyes glimmered with amusement, a sly smile playing at the corners of her lips. Without saying a word, she bent down, her fingers gripping the hem of her nightgown, and in one swift motion, she lifted it up to her waist. The silk gathered around her hips as she exposed her freshly shaved, glistening pussy to me.

My heart raced, and I felt the blood surge to my groin. She had never looked so bold, so uninhibited. "Yes," she replied with a teasing lilt in her voice. "Why, do you have a problem with my lover seeing me like this, bitch boy?"

The words hit me like a slap. Her tone, her words—they were meant to cut, to remind me of the dynamic that had shifted between us. I swallowed hard, the arousal tightening in my pants despite the whirlwind of emotions twisting inside me. Her shaved pussy caught me off guard. We'd talked about it before, but she'd always refused. The surprise must have shown on my face because Lucy's grin widened.

"You shaved," I managed, my voice rough.

"Well, yeah," she said with a light chuckle, clearly amused by my reaction. "Jordan asked me to for the next time we fuck." The way she said it, so nonchalant yet dripping with anticipation, sent a fresh wave of heat through me.

She stood there, still holding her nightgown up, watching me, waiting for my response. Her confidence was palpable, radiating off her in waves. I was torn. My instinct was to push back, to challenge her, to reclaim some semblance of control. But I knew better. If I protested too much, if I pulled away from this game we'd started, it might all come crashing down, and Lucy would stop sleeping with other men altogether. The fantasies would end, and the carefully constructed reality we'd built would dissolve.

But if I went along with it… If I leaned into this new version of Lucy, bolder and more confident with each step she took outside the bounds of our marriage, would I regret it? Would I lose even more of myself in the process?

Lucy's eyes stayed locked on mine, her grin now a challenge. She was testing me, seeing if I could keep up with her pace. There was no turning back.

"No, no problem," I said finally, forcing my voice to sound steady even though I could feel the tension thickening in my throat. "You look... perfect."

Her grin softened into something darker, more intimate. "That's what I thought," she said, letting her nightgown fall back into place, the silk brushing over her bare skin like a whispered promise. She turned back toward the door, leaving me standing there, half-hard, half-tormented, and wholly under her control.

As I watched her, I realized just how far this had gone. And yet, the ache of anticipation stirred within me, a constant reminder that I had willingly opened this door.

As headlights swept across the living room curtains, signaling Jordan's arrival, Lucy leaned in close to me. Her breath was warm against my ear, her words both soothing and commanding at the same time. "Our safe word will be 'red' if it's too much, and 'green' if you're okay with things. I read them on that site."

Her tone was soft but deliberate, a subtle reminder of who was in control tonight. The reassurance of a safe word relaxed me—if only for a moment. Still, uncertainty gnawed at the edges of my resolve. I had no idea how far things would go. The reality of it all loomed, heavy and thrilling.

The sound of Jordan's car door closing made my chest tighten. Lucy's smile widened as she opened the front door, her movements fluid and confident. "Hello, Jordan," she greeted him, her voice suddenly light and playful as she waved him in.

I stood frozen, watching as she shut the door behind him and then, without hesitation, wrapped her arms around his shoulders. I hadn't expected her to go so quickly from greeting to touching, but here she was, standing on her tiptoes to kiss him. And not just a peck—their lips met with an intensity that caught me off guard. Tongues swirled, mouths hungry. The sight of it stirred something deep in me, and yet, instead of softening, my erection only hardened further.

I couldn't look away, even though my stomach twisted. His hands roamed down to her ass, gripping her like it belonged to him. And the kiss... the kiss didn't stop. It was heavy, intense, a display of ownership. Was he going to fuck her right here in the doorway?

The thought sent a pulse of heat through me. I tried to brace myself for what would come next.

But Lucy, ever in control, finally pulled back and lowered herself flat-footed. Jordan's hands dropped from her, but he kept one arm possessively around her waist as she turned to face me, her eyes gleaming with mischief.

"Jordan, I'd like you to meet 'bitch boy,'" she said with a wicked grin, pointing at me like I was nothing more than an afterthought, an accessory to her evening's plans.

Jordan's gaze flickered over me, sizing me up with an amused smirk tugging at his lips. "Hey man, what's up?" he asked, casual, as if the situation were normal.

My mouth was dry. I managed a weak, "Uh... not much, I guess." Lucy laughed—bright and genuine, as if we were all sharing a joke, though I wasn't quite sure I got the punchline. Jordan forced a chuckle too, his hand sliding behind her to give her ass another squeeze. Was he as comfortable with this as he seemed? Or was he playing a role, just like me?

Lucy didn't let the moment linger. She took Jordan's hand and led him over to the couch, guiding him like she was taking her rightful place beside him. I stayed rooted where I stood, unsure of what was expected of me now. My legs felt heavy, my thoughts jumbled.

When they sat down, she swung one leg over his lap, her body draped casually across him, as if this were the most natural thing in the world. His hand moved instinctively to her thigh, resting possessively on her bare skin, and the tension between them was palpable.

"Hey, bitch boy…" Lucy's voice cut through my haze, her eyes locking on mine with an intensity that made my pulse quicken. She pointed to the floor beneath her feet. "Get down there, now."

I hesitated. Her gaze sharpened, eyebrows raised, her lips forming into a pout, exaggerated and mocking. She tapped the floor impatiently with her finger. Every second stretched painfully until, finally, I obeyed. My legs felt weak as I knelt in front of them, the weight of my submission heavy in the air.

"Jordan," Lucy said, her voice light again, playful, "Do you think our carpet is too green?" Her words hung in the air for a beat. The carpet was blue, a deep blue—this was a test, a way to see if I'd intervene or question, a way to keep me teetering on the edge.

Jordan looked momentarily confused but played along. "I think it's blue," he said, his brow furrowed slightly.

Lucy smiled, a devious glint in her eyes as she turned her attention back to me. "You're right. It isn't very green at all."

Without warning, she leaned forward and began unbuckling her shoes, her fingers working slowly, deliberately. She slid one foot out of its sleek black heel, revealing her pink-painted toes. She held her foot out in front of me, just inches from my face. "Want to show Jordan what my bitch boy likes to do?"

Before I could process what was happening, her big toe pressed against my lips, firm and demanding. Instinctively, I opened my mouth, and she shoved it inside. The taste of her skin filled my mouth as her toes slid past my lips, and I could feel the weight of her foot pressing against my tongue.

As I sucked, Lucy's gaze never left mine, even as she leaned back into Jordan, her lips seeking his once more. Their mouths collided with the same intensity as before, tongues tangling as I knelt beneath them, my mouth full of her toes. Each kiss they shared felt like a punch to my gut, a reminder of where I stood— literally and figuratively.

And yet, the ache between my legs only grew stronger.

Lucy's foot moved with deliberate precision, each toe gliding in and out of my mouth, giving every one equal attention. The slickness of her skin against my tongue, the way she controlled the rhythm, made me feel even more helpless under her control. My pulse quickened with every subtle shift of her foot, and as I sucked and licked, a fresh wave of arousal washed over me. The taste of her skin, the soft curve of her arch—I couldn't help it. My foot fetish was being exploited, and Lucy knew exactly what she was doing.

Above me, her hand slid down Jordan's chest, her fingers tracing the lines of his muscles through his shirt as they kissed. Their tongues moved in tandem, swirling and twisting, their kiss heavy with the intent of putting on a show for me. I could tell Lucy was controlling the pace, making sure I had a clear view of their intimacy, each kiss like a dagger twisting in my chest —and yet, I couldn't deny how hot it all was. Every move was deliberate, meant to keep me firmly in my place.

Her hand traveled lower, fingers now grazing the edge of his belt, teasing me with what would come next. The anticipation was thick in the air, my heart pounding in my ears as I watched her pause. She broke the kiss, her foot still hovering in the air near my mouth, her toes shiny with my saliva. Her eyes, dark and commanding, locked onto mine.

"Would you like to see this massive cock that I fucked?" she asked, her voice thick with the promise of humiliation.

My throat tightened. It was a simple question, but one loaded with expectation. She wasn't asking me as her husband; she was asking me as her submissive. And I knew I had to respond accordingly.

"OK," I murmured, my voice uncertain.

Without missing a beat, Lucy's foot swung gently but swiftly, delivering a light slap across my cheek. The sting was more shocking than painful, but it sent a jolt through me. Jordan let out a snicker, clearly amused by the power dynamic unfolding in front of him.

"Excuse me, bitch boy," Lucy said, her voice sharp and demanding. "What was that?"

I froze for a moment, my mind racing. This was the game, and if I didn't fully lean into it, none of us would have any fun. She had laid the groundwork with the safe words, and a small part of me felt secure knowing I could stop this if it went too far. But it hadn't yet. Instead, I found myself more intrigued, more curious about what was coming next.

I took a breath, deciding to play along fully. "Yes, my queen," I said, my voice low and reverent. "I'd love to see it."

Lucy's grin widened as she turned her attention back to Jordan. Her fingers deftly unbuckled his belt, pulling it free from his waist with a slow, deliberate motion. The sound of the leather slipping through the loops was somehow erotic in its simplicity. She undid the button of his dress pants, her eyes still on me, her lips parting slightly as she slid her hand inside.

"Oh..." she murmured, her fingers curling around his cock. She opened her mouth, her eyes lighting up with a mix of excitement and teasing malice. "It's already so much bigger than yours—and he's not even hard yet."

I swallowed hard, the reality of her words hitting me. I had heard her talk about Jordan's size before, her breathy descriptions that had both aroused and unsettled me. But now, seeing it was another matter entirely. She slowly slid his pants down, revealing inch after inch of thick, dark flesh. When she finally pulled him free, her hand wrapped around a cock that was, indeed, large—and only growing harder under her touch.

She began to stroke it with slow, steady movements, her grip firm, her gaze never leaving mine. Her thumb slid over the tip, a bead of precum glistening in the dim light as she flicked it with her fingers. She seemed to revel in my discomfort, watching me as I knelt there, powerless and entranced.

"Don't you think the carpet is green, darling?" Lucy asked, her tone light, but her eyes still locked on me, challenging me, daring me to break. With each word, she thumped Jordan's cock up and down in her hand, the heavy sound filling the room.

The question hung in the air, another test of my submission. The carpet wasn't green, and we both knew it. But I understood the meaning now. It wasn't about the color—it was about control. It was about me agreeing to the lie, accepting the reality Lucy was creating for all of us.

"Yes, my queen... it is sort of green now that you mention it," I replied, my voice low, submissive. The words felt strange in my mouth, but they served their purpose. The flicker of approval in Lucy's eyes was enough to make my heart race.

Without missing a beat, Lucy leaned down, her lips parting as she took the head of Jordan's cock into her mouth. The sight was mesmerizing—her tongue sliding out, swirling around the girth of him, wet and eager. A soft, pleased moan escaped her lips, vibrating around his length as she took him deeper. Inch by inch, her mouth stretched to accommodate his size, and I could only watch in awe, my pulse pounding in my ears.

"Mm mm..." she hummed, her eyes half-lidded in pleasure as she pushed her mouth further down his thick shaft.

Jordan's hand found its way to the back of her head, his fingers threading through her hair. At first, it seemed like he was simply following her movements, but then his grip tightened. His other hand came up, steadying her as he pushed her head down with more force.

"Oh yes... suck that dick, you little slut," he growled, his voice thick with dominance.

I watched, transfixed, as Lucy struggled to take more of him into her throat. Despite the difficulty, she was trying—trying to deep throat a cock that was far larger than anything she'd taken before. She gagged slightly, her eyes watering, but there was a determination in the way she continued. The sound of her wet, eager mouth, the way her lips stretched around his girth, sent waves of arousal through me.

Then came the smack—Jordan's hand came down hard on her ass, the sound sharp in the otherwise quiet room. Lucy grunted around his cock, the noise rough and needy. The slap left her ass cheeks red and stinging, but her moan was one of approval, not discomfort.

"You like that, don't you?" he asked, his voice dripping with authority.

She grunted again, nodding as best she could with his cock halfway down her throat. The sight of my sexy wife, on her knees, sucking this massive cock just a few feet in front of me —it was intoxicating. Every part of it. The way Jordan's body dwarfed mine in every way, the raw physicality of his presence, was undeniable. The size of his dick alone was something to marvel at, but it wasn't just that. It was his sheer dominance over her, over the situation, and, by extension, over me.

As Lucy's head bobbed up and down his length, she stretched one leg out and shoved her foot back into my mouth, her toes grazing my lips in a commanding gesture. Instinctively, I opened my mouth and sucked on her toes, the taste of her skin mingling with the heat of the moment. My cock was throbbing, pressing hard against the fabric of my pants, desperate for release. I couldn't help it—I reached down, fingers trembling, and began to undo my own belt.

But just as I unbuckled it, her foot slid out of my mouth, and she delivered a swift, stinging slap to my cheek with it. This one was harder than the first, more forceful, but still just on the edge of playful. I froze, unsure of what I'd done wrong. She pulled her mouth off Jordan's cock with a wet pop, her lips swollen and glistening.

"What do you think you're doing, bitch boy?" she asked, her voice dripping with mockery. She cocked her head to the side, her foot still resting near my mouth. "You're not thinking of playing with your dick, are you?"

I hesitated, my hands still at my belt, but unmoving. My mind raced. Should I ask permission? Should I apologize? I had no idea how far she wanted to take this. My eyes darted to Jordan, whose smirk only deepened. He was enjoying this—the power, the show. And so was I. The tension in the room was thick, each second stretching on as I considered my next move.

"May I please touch myself, my queen?" I asked finally, the words shaky but sincere.

Lucy's grin widened, a knowing gleam in her eyes. She resumed stroking Jordan's cock with slow, deliberate movements, her fingers gliding over his length. "Aw, does watching me suck this big fucking cock excite you, honey?" she cooed, her voice sickly sweet, almost patronizing.

It was everything I'd ever fantasized about, and yet it cut deeper than I expected. As I knelt there, watching Lucy in control of Jordan's body, I felt a mixture of arousal and humiliation swirl inside me. This was my fantasy coming to life, and I had no choice but to embrace it. I'd always imagined her with a man like Jordan—bigger, taller, more dominant—and now, it was happening right in front of me.

"Oh god, yes, my queen!" I exclaimed, almost forgetting to add the title in my excitement. The words felt foreign, yet strangely liberating. This wasn't our usual banter. We had never gone this far before.

Lucy smirked, her eyes glittering with power. "I bet you do, bitch boy," she said, the words dripping with condescension. She leaned down, wrapping her lips around the head of Jordan's cock again, her tongue swirling over the swollen tip as she took him into her mouth. The way her mouth stretched around his thickness, the way her jaw worked to accommodate his girth —it was mesmerizing. She sucked him with slow, deliberate movements, her lips gliding up and down his shaft.

After a few deep strokes, she pulled back and glanced at me, her lips swollen and glistening. "Not yet," she teased. "I have other ideas for tonight, and I know you won't be able to last if you start jerking that little dick right now."

Her words stung, but they also sent a thrill down my spine. My erection strained against my pants, desperate for release, but I obeyed. Her foot slid out of my mouth and back to the floor as she sat up, still stroking Jordan's cock with a lazy, sensual rhythm. She motioned for him to stand, and as he did, she began to lower his pants. When they pooled at his ankles, she had to stretch up onto her tiptoes to lick the tip of his dick.

He stepped out of his pants, and Lucy tossed them aside before pushing him back onto the couch. Standing tall, she raised her arms above her head, like a queen waiting to be served. "Bitch boy, remove my gown," she commanded.

I scrambled to my feet, eager to please, my hands reaching for the hem of her silk gown. But as I started to lift it over her hips, her sharp voice stopped me.

"No," she said, turning her head to look at me with a smirk. "Get down and slowly pull it up."

Without hesitation, I dropped to my knees again, my face inches from her legs. Slowly, reverently, I picked up the bottom of her gown, lifting it inch by inch, the silk sliding smoothly over her skin. When I reached her thighs, the fabric clung to her curves, and I trembled as I exposed her further. When the gown reached her ass, Lucy stopped me with a firm hand on the back of my neck.

"Look at you," she teased, her voice low and mocking. "On your knees, just like you belong."

She bent forward slightly, arching her back and shoving my face into her ass. The scent of her arousal was overwhelming, her skin soft and warm against my lips. "Lick my asshole, bitch boy," she ordered, her voice dripping with authority.

I obeyed, my tongue flicking out to taste her. Her hips began to move, grinding against my face as I worked to please her. She moaned softly, her body writhing in pleasure, but her focus wasn't on me for long. With her free hand, she beckoned Jordan closer.

When he stood, his cock was fully erect, pointing directly at her face. She gripped him with both hands, her fingers barely able to wrap around his thickness. "Now this," she said, glancing down at me with a wicked smile, "this is a real cock, bitch boy. Just look at the size of it. So much bigger than yours, isn't it?"

Her words hit me like a punch, but I couldn't deny the truth. Jordan was bigger—much bigger. And she was reveling in that fact.

She ran her tongue along his shaft, teasing him, before taking him back into her mouth. Jordan groaned, his hands finding their way to the back of her head, gripping her hair tightly as he began to fuck her face. The sound of her wet, eager mouth filled the room, her moans vibrating around his cock. I could hear her gagging slightly as he pushed deeper, his size too much for her to take fully.

"God, I bet you wish you had a cock like this," Lucy said, pulling back to catch her breath. "But you don't, do you? No, your little dick couldn't even compare." She shoved him back into her mouth, taking him as deep as she could, while her hips ground harder against my face. "I love sucking this big cock... it's so much better than yours."

My cock twitched at her words, aching to be touched, but I didn't dare move. Her taunts cut through me, humiliating and arousing me all at once. This was exactly what I had wanted— Lucy fully embracing her role, making me feel small, inferior. And yet, it stung more than I had anticipated.

Jordan was relentless, thrusting into her mouth with force, his hands guiding her head as she gagged and moaned. "Oh yes, baby, you love this cock, don't you?" he growled, pulling her hair harder as he slammed into her.

Lucy moaned around him, her body trembling with arousal. I could feel her wetness dripping down her thighs, coating my lips as I licked her eagerly. She was getting off on it—on being dominated, on having a man so much bigger and stronger than me fuck her like this.

"See how much I love this, bitch boy?" Lucy said, pulling back from Jordan's cock long enough to look down at me. "I never moan like this when I suck your little dick."

Her words sent a fresh wave of heat through me. I could feel the humiliation tightening in my chest, mixing with the arousal that was now unbearable. My cock throbbed painfully, desperate for release, but I knew better than to touch myself without her permission.

"You could never make me feel like this," she continued, her voice soft but cutting. "But Jordan... Jordan knows exactly how to handle a woman. Isn't that right, baby?"

Jordan grunted in response, thrusting back into her mouth with more force, his cock disappearing between her lips. The sight was almost too much to bear. I could only watch, licking her asshole, as she took him deeper than I'd ever seen her take anyone. It was everything I'd ever fantasized about—and more.

Lucy moaned louder, her body shuddering as Jordan fucked her face with abandon. And all I could do was kneel there, tasting her, while she made it clear just how much better Jordan was.

Jordan stopped thrusting into Lucy's mouth, gripping her hair tightly as he pulled her up, forcing her to stand on her tiptoes. Her ass lifted from my face as he yanked her closer, their lips crashing together in another deep, hungry kiss. I sat there, my view shifting to an impeccable angle, staring up at my wife's perfect, round ass and the glistening folds of her pussy, still wet from the intensity of the moment.

His large hands moved with deliberate confidence, sliding down her back before gripping her ass with both hands. He squeezed her cheeks firmly, possessively, and then, with a show of raw strength that made my heart race, he lifted her as though she weighed nothing. Her legs instinctively wrapped around his waist, her heels digging into his lower back as she clung to him, their kiss unbroken.

I watched, spellbound, as Lucy reached between their bodies with one hand, her fingers guiding his colossal cock to her waiting pussy. The moment his thick head pressed against her opening, I could see the anticipation on her face, a flicker of excitement mixed with need. She shifted her hips, adjusting herself slightly, before lowering her body onto him. Slowly, inch by inch, his massive cock disappeared inside her, filling her in a way that made my breath catch.

The sight was surreal—her pussy, which had always seemed perfectly normal to me, now stretched impossibly wide to accommodate him. The contrast was stunning. I could see her folds straining to take all of him, her wetness glistening in the dim light, and it was like watching my wife in a completely new way.

Jordan began to bounce her on his cock, his hands firm on her ass as he lifted her up and down with ease. Each time he raised her, I could see all nine inches of him, thick and glistening with her juices, before he slammed her back down onto his lap, his cock disappearing into her until her ass hit his sack. The sound of their bodies colliding filled the room, mixed with Lucy's moans of raw pleasure.

"Oh, fuck yes, Jordan... fuck me!" Lucy screamed, her voice high and breathless. With each powerful thrust, she let out a loud moan, her body trembling in his grip.

I lay there beneath her, watching from the perfect angle as she was bounced on this massive cock. Her toes curled and pointed as her legs clung to him, her feet intertwined below his knees. Each time he lifted her, I could see the way her pussy tightened around him, her juices beginning to seep out, coating his cock and clouding the view as they moved together.

Lucy's head tilted back, her mouth hanging open in ecstasy. "I'm coming!" she cried, her voice shaking with pleasure.

My heart pounded in my chest, my cock throbbing with arousal, but I couldn't touch myself. Not yet. She was right—I wouldn't have been able to last. Watching her take him, seeing her body react to his size, it was all too much. I could feel my pulse racing in my throat, the ache of my erection almost painful now as I sat there, helpless and consumed by the sight.

Jordan didn't slow down. He kept bouncing her up and down, thrusting into her with long, deep strokes, his cock glistening with her wetness. Every time he pulled her up, I could see the slippery white juices dripping from her pussy, coating his cock as he plunged back into her. The rhythm of their movements became more urgent, their bodies slick with sweat as they moved together, Lucy's cries of pleasure echoing in the room.

"Oh, fuck yes!" Lucy moaned, her legs trembling as her toes pointed, her orgasm crashing over her. Her body shook in his arms, her fingers digging into his shoulders as she clung to him, lost in the overwhelming pleasure.

"Fuck me, fuck me, fuck me!" she chanted, her voice breaking as Jordan continued to slam into her, his hands gripping her ass tighter, lifting and dropping her with an intensity that made her body quake.

I wanted nothing more than to touch myself, to relieve the unbearable pressure between my legs, but I knew better. My role was to watch, to wait. My queen had plans for me, and I couldn't break her rules now. Not when she was finally becoming everything I had ever dreamed of—a woman who reveled in being taken by a man so much bigger, so much stronger than me.

And I loved her for it.

Jordan's grunts became more urgent, his thrusts deeper and more forceful as he held Lucy tightly in his arms. Each bounce brought her higher before he slammed her back down, impaling her on his massive cock. The sounds of their bodies colliding filled the room, and Lucy's moans grew louder, more desperate.

"Whose pussy is this, Lucy?" Jordan growled, his voice rough with lust as he continued pounding into her.

Lucy's head snapped back, her mouth hanging open in pure ecstasy. "It's yours, Jordan!" she screamed. "It's all yours!" Her voice trembled with each word, her body shaking in his arms as she clung to him. "Only yours, baby!" she moaned, her hands gripping his shoulders for support. "Oh god, I love your dick!" she cried, her eyes rolling back as he drove into her harder, her wetness coating his cock.

The words sent a jolt through me, a mixture of arousal and disbelief swirling in my chest. Lucy had never sounded like this with me, never been this vocal about anyone owning her. And yet here she was, giving herself over to Jordan completely, her body and her voice drenched in submission.

"Cum in my pussy, baby!" she suddenly screamed, her voice raw with need. "Fill me up!"

As soon as the words left her mouth, Jordan's pace became erratic, his grunts louder, more animalistic. I could feel the tension in the room shift, the energy heightening as he reached the edge.

"I'm cumming, you fucking slut," he growled, his voice deep and commanding. His fingers dug into her ass as he held her tightly against him. "Your pussy feels so good, I'm going to fill it up for you and bitch boy."

The words hit me like a slap. For me? He was cumming for me too? What did that even mean? My mind spun, trying to make sense of it. The idea that he was including me in his pleasure, that he was somehow dominating both of us, left me breathless. It was as though he was asserting his claim not only over Lucy but over our entire relationship, our dynamic, and even my role in it.

Jordan pumped her up and down a few more times, his body shuddering as he reached his peak. Then, with a final, powerful thrust, he stopped, pulling her flush against him as he filled her with his cum. His head dropped to her shoulder, and they shared a deep, lustful kiss, their tongues tangling together as his cock pulsed inside her.

Lucy let out a soft whimper, her body trembling from the aftershocks of her orgasm. "Thank you," she whispered against his lips, her voice breathy and full of gratitude. "You're so amazing. I just love fucking you."

They stood there for a moment, wrapped in each other's arms, before Lucy slowly turned her gaze down to me. Her eyes sparkled with satisfaction, and a wicked smile curled her lips. "Hey, bitch boy," she said, her tone playful and commanding. "Take your pants off."

I didn't hesitate. The sight of my wife being fucked so thoroughly by another man was still fresh in my mind, and the arousal that had been building inside me all night was unbearable. I stood quickly, fumbling with my pants, my hands shaking as I stripped them off.

"Now, lay down," she commanded, pointing to the floor in front of her.

My heart pounded as I obeyed, laying flat on the ground beneath her. My erection throbbed painfully, my mind swirling with the images of what had just happened. I knew I could easily cum just from thinking about it, but I was determined to hold back.

Jordan gently lifted her off his cock, the sound of her wetness and his cum slipping free filling the air. She moved above me, positioning herself with a leg on either side of my head, her swollen pussy and slick ass hovering inches from my face. I could smell the musky mixture of her arousal and Jordan's cum, and the heat between her legs was overwhelming.

I stared up at her, lost in the moment, but as I reached down to finally stroke my aching cock, she slapped my hands away with a sharp, decisive movement. "No," she said firmly, her voice full of authority.

I froze, my hands trembling at my sides. The frustration of not being able to touch myself was almost unbearable, but I knew better than to disobey her. My queen had spoken, and her command was law.

Lucy lowered herself, her ass pressing against my face, her wetness smearing against my skin. I could feel the mixture of her juices and Jordan's cum coating my lips as she began to grind against me, her hips moving in slow, deliberate circles. Her moans filled the room again, soft and low this time, as she reveled in her power over me.

I couldn't see much beyond the curve of her ass and the glistening folds of her pussy, but I could feel everything—the weight of her body, the heat of her arousal, and the sharp sting of denial as my cock throbbed, untouched. All I could do was lie there, my tongue working eagerly to please her as I tasted the remnants of her ecstasy, while my own release remained just out of reach.

Lucy's voice cut through the room like a blade, her tone dripping with authority. "Now, I want you to eat all of his wonderful cum out of my pussy."

The words sent a chill down my spine, and for a moment, I froze. My heart pounded in my chest, a mixture of shame and arousal swirling in the pit of my stomach. I didn't want to do it. The thought of licking another man's cum out of her—Jordan's cum —turned my stomach. The bitter taste, the undeniable proof that I couldn't compete with him, was more than I could bear. And yet, I couldn't deny the command in her voice, the way she so easily controlled me. I was completely under her power.

Before I could fully process what was happening, Lucy's body lowered onto my face. The weight of her, the heat of her dripping pussy, filled my senses. She was wet—so wet—and it wasn't just from her own arousal. Jordan had just finished inside her, and now it was my job to clean up the mess.

As her pussy pressed against my mouth, I could feel the slickness of Jordan's cum, thick and warm, oozing from her. My instincts told me to pull away, to resist, but Lucy's hips moved with a brutal rhythm, grinding her pussy against my lips and nose, leaving me no choice. I opened my mouth, and the taste of him flooded my senses. It was bitter, salty, and humiliating.

I gagged slightly, my body recoiling from the taste, but Lucy was relentless. She moaned softly, her hips undulating as she smeared herself all over my face, moving from the crack of her ass to her swollen clit. Every part of her was coated with Jordan's cum, and with each grind of her hips, more of it filled my mouth.

"Lick it up," she demanded, her voice firm. "Clean me out, bitch boy."

I obeyed, my tongue working against her slick folds, tasting the mix of her juices and his cum. My mind spun with the humiliation of it all—Jordan's cock had stretched her so wide, and now I was the one left to finish the job. I could never fill her like he did, never satisfy her the way his much larger cock could. I was nothing more than an afterthought, a cleanup crew. The realization hit me like a punch to the gut.

But even in the midst of the shame, there was something else— something I didn't want to acknowledge. A strange satisfaction bubbled up inside me as I felt her body respond to my tongue. Her moans grew louder, her hips grinding harder against my face. I could feel her clit swelling under my mouth, and despite the bitterness of Jordan's cum, there was a twisted pleasure in knowing that I was still making her cum. My mouth, not his cock, was bringing her to this edge.

Lucy's moans grew more frantic, her hips moving in desperate, needy circles. "Oh fuck, yes," she gasped. "That's it. Keep licking, keep eating his cum."

Her words were like daggers, sharp and cutting, but they only fueled my arousal. My cock throbbed painfully, desperate for release, but I knew I couldn't touch myself. Not yet.

As I continued licking, I felt her body tense, her breathing hitching as she reached her climax. "Oh god," she moaned, her fingers tangling in my hair as she pressed herself harder against my face. "I'm cumming, I'm cumming."

Her hips bucked wildly, her thighs squeezing my head as she came, her juices mixing with Jordan's cum in my mouth. The taste was overwhelming, but the sound of her pleasure, the way her body trembled on top of me, was strangely satisfying. Despite the humiliation, I had made her cum.

And then, just as I thought I could take no more, Lucy reached down and grabbed my cock. Her fingers wrapped around me, stroking me slowly as she continued grinding on my face. My body jolted at the touch, the overwhelming need for release surging through me.

"You can cum now, bitch boy," she purred, her voice thick with mockery. "I think you've earned it after eating all of his cum."

Her words sent a shockwave through me. I was so close, so

painfully close, and her hand on my cock was all it took to push me over the edge. I could feel the pressure building, my entire body trembling with the need to explode.

But just as I teetered on the edge, Lucy leaned down, her lips brushing against my ear. "It's funny," she whispered, her voice dark and cruel. "Jordan's cock stretched me out so much that I doubt I'll even be able to feel you anymore. Such a tiny little thing, aren't you?"

Her words hit me like a slap. The brutal honesty, the mockery, shattered whatever remained of my pride. I couldn't compete with him—not with his size, his strength, or his ability to satisfy her. I was small, insignificant, and completely at her mercy.

And with that final blow, I couldn't hold back any longer. My cock twitched violently in her hand, and I came harder than I had in a long time. The orgasm ripped through me, uncontrollable, and I exploded all over myself. Cum shot across my stomach, splattering onto her hand, her arm, and even the floor. It was messy, desperate, and humiliating—just like everything else that had happened tonight.

Lucy pulled back, her body sliding off mine as she rolled onto her side. She looked down at the mess I had made, her eyes gleaming with satisfaction. "Oh, look at you," she teased, her voice dripping with condescension. "You really couldn't hold it in, could you?"

I lay there, panting and spent, my face sticky with her juices and Jordan's cum, my body trembling from the force of my orgasm. Lucy leaned over me, her lips pressing against mine in a deep, wet kiss. I could taste everything—her, Jordan, and myself —all mingling together in a bitter cocktail of submission and surrender.

She pulled back, her eyes locked onto mine. "See," she whispered, her breath warm against my lips. "Doesn't he taste good?"

I couldn't respond. My mind was a blank, overwhelmed by everything that had just happened.

"This wasn't so bad, was it?" she asked, her voice soft but

commanding. "Do you care if he spends the night?"

Her smile, seductive and teasing, left me speechless. My head spun, my thoughts jumbled, and before I could even think, I heard myself say, "Sure, I guess."

THE MORNING AFTER

I woke up early the next morning, my back stiff from a night spent on the couch. The sunlight was just beginning to filter through the curtains, casting long shadows across the room. For a few moments, I lay there, my mind replaying the events of the night before. The intensity of it all—the sounds, the sights, the overwhelming mix of arousal and humiliation—still lingered in my body like a hangover. I shifted, feeling the ache in my chest, a strange emptiness that I couldn't quite place.

I decided to head upstairs to check on Lucy, hoping to see her alone for a moment, to talk, to make sure everything between us was still the same—or at least, that it hadn't changed too much.

As I reached the top of the stairs, the house was quiet. Too quiet. My breath caught in my throat as I crept down the hallway, each step feeling heavier than the last. The bedroom door was still ajar, left open from the night before. Slowly, I peered inside, unsure of what I would find.

Lucy was lying on the bed, still completely naked, her leg draped possessively over Jordan, who was also naked. They were both fast asleep, their bodies entwined in a way that seemed too intimate, too familiar. My heart clenched, and for a brief moment, I wasn't sure what to feel. Jealousy? Regret? Or maybe something else, something I didn't want to admit.

"What am I supposed to do now?" I thought to myself, the knot in my chest tightening. "Do I wake them? Or just let them sleep?"

The sight of them together stirred that old feeling deep inside me, the one I'd felt when Lucy first told me about her night with Jordan. That same knot of uncertainty, a mix of excitement and fear, was back. I wanted to talk to her. Not to relive the details of the night, but to reassure myself—to know that our marriage, our connection, was still intact. I needed to hear her say it, to feel it.

But I hesitated. After all, I was the one who pushed for this. I begged her to sleep with another man. I wanted to know every detail, every whispered word and moan, even though the reality of it had shaken me. I had fantasized about it for so long, even dreamed about being in the same room while she fucked someone else, and yet, now that it had happened, I felt... unsteady. I wasn't sure if I had truly prepared myself for what this would mean.

With a sigh, I turned and headed back downstairs, leaving them to their sleep. My mind raced with a thousand questions. I'd seen a lot of what had happened last night, but I knew there were things I hadn't witnessed—things that nagged at me now. What did they talk about before they started? What did they say to each other after I left the room? Did they laugh? Did they share something deeper than just sex? The questions gnawed at me, the unanswered moments filling my mind like static.

I needed a distraction.

Deciding to stick with the routine, I grabbed my keys and headed to the corner store for donuts, like I did most Sunday mornings. The drive gave me time to breathe, but the questions followed me like a shadow. I couldn't shake the images from my head, and worse, I found myself analyzing the young man behind the counter as I paid for the donuts. He was clean-cut, well-built, the kind of guy Lucy might find attractive. Would she want to fuck him? Was he the type she would be drawn to now

I caught myself, shaking my head as I pushed the thoughts away. What the fuck is wrong with me? My mind had spiraled, and now I was wondering about the size of this guy's cock, whether Lucy would find him more satisfying than me. I felt ridiculous, but the nagging insecurity lingered.

When I returned home and opened the door, I was surprised to find Lucy sitting alone on the couch, a cup of coffee in her hand. She looked up at me and smiled, that familiar smile that always made my heart skip a beat. But something about it felt different this time—lighter, maybe, or more content.

I raised an eyebrow as I set the donuts down. "Is Jordan not up yet?"

She set her coffee on the end table and gave me a small, casual shrug. "Oh, he woke up early. Got dressed and left. Said he had some things to do today."

I nodded slowly, unsure of how to respond. I sat down next to her, the need to talk suddenly overwhelming me. I wanted to ask her about last night—about what she and Jordan had done, about how she felt, about how we were now. I needed to know if things between us were okay, if the connection we had was still strong. My heart raced as I tried to find the right words, but before I could say anything, Lucy turned to me, her eyes soft with understanding.

"Are you okay?" she asked, her voice gentle. "Was last night fun for you?"

The question hung in the air, and I realized she had seen right through me. Of course she had. She always knew when something was weighing on me, and now was no different. She could probably sense the anxiety bubbling under the surface, the uncertainty I hadn't yet voiced.

I hesitated, my mind a swirl of emotions. The night had been... everything I'd fantasized about and more. But it had also been so much more intense than I had expected. The sight of Jordan fucking her, the sounds of her moans, the way she had responded to him—it had all left me shaken, aroused, and conflicted.

I blurted out, "Yes," perhaps a bit too quickly, and the word hung in the air between us. I felt my face flush as I tried to gather my thoughts. "Well... most of it," I continued, stumbling over my words. "Uh... some of it made me feel... um... weird, I guess."

Lucy's smile was soft, understanding. She slid closer to me, wrapping an arm around my shoulders and kissing my cheek. The warmth of her touch helped ease some of the tension in my chest. "I love you," she said gently, her voice full of sincerity.

I turned and kissed her back, my lips brushing against her cheek as I rested my head on her shoulder. "I know," I said, my voice quiet. "It's not about that. I know we're in love... and married... and together, or whatever... it's just..." I trailed off, trying to find the right words to explain the knot of emotions twisting inside me. "It's just an awkward feeling, you know?"

Lucy sat up straight, her expression softening into one of curiosity and concern. She leaned back into the cushions, lifting her bare feet and resting them across my lap. "Are you jealous of Jordan?" she asked, her tone light but probing.

I hesitated for a moment, feeling the weight of the question. My hands instinctively went to her feet, rubbing them gently as I spoke. "Well, yeah," I admitted, forcing a small laugh. "He's... well, he's pretty hunky... and... well, hung." I laughed again, more nervously this time, but Lucy chuckled too, her eyes gleaming with amusement.

The moment lightened a little, and I relaxed as I began to tell her about the guy I saw at the store that morning. Lucy listened intently, her smile never fading as I talked about how I'd caught myself wondering if she'd find him attractive, if she'd want to fuck him. As the words tumbled out, I realized how ridiculous it sounded, but Lucy's smile remained warm, her gaze fixed on me.

"Have I created a monster?" she teased, her laugh soft and playful. But then her tone shifted, a subtle seriousness entering her voice. "You have questions, don't you?"

I looked up from her feet, caught off guard by how well she read me. "What?" I asked, feigning innocence, but I could see in her eyes that she wasn't fooled.

"OK... OK..." I relented, shifting a little under her gaze. "Maybe... a few." I grinned sheepishly, feeling like I'd been caught in a lie. Lucy's smile widened, and she turned her body to face me more fully, her curiosity piqued. She wasn't going to let me off the hook.

I gently pushed her feet off my lap and turned to face her, my heart beating a little faster. "I don't know... it's just random details," I began, trying to put my thoughts into words. "Not about the sex," I added quickly, though that was only half true.

Lucy's smile softened as she leaned in, her eyes meeting mine. "So ask, babe," she said gently, her voice full of reassurance. "I don't ever want things to get weird between us. You know you can be yourself with me. I don't judge you."

Her words hit me harder than I expected. There was no hesitation, no hint of discomfort in her voice—just love, openness. "I know that," I said, feeling a bit sheepish now. "Why would you judge me?" I added, laughing awkwardly, trying to ease the tension that had built up in my chest. "Yes, I really liked seeing the way he fucked you... and how much you seemed to enjoy all of him," I said with a teasing wink, trying to keep the mood light.

Lucy chuckled softly, but I could see that she was waiting, sensing there was more. I hesitated for a moment, feeling the weight of my own thoughts. "But I find myself having all these questions, about what you two said to each other. More personal stuff... like when I wasn't around."

Her smile grew wider, her eyes twinkling with amusement. "Aw... are you worried I'd leave you for him?" she asked, her voice teasing but gentle. She took my hands in hers, patting them softly. "You know, there isn't a man alive, a cock big enough, or sex great enough to ever make me leave you."

Her words sent a rush of warmth through me, but there was still that knot in my chest, that lingering insecurity that I couldn't quite shake. I smiled back at her, grateful for her reassurance. "I know," I said, though my voice betrayed the small seed of doubt that remained. "Maybe it's just morning-after jitters."

"I guess so. I'm not really sure how all this works," Lucy said, following me into the kitchen. Her voice was light, but there was a trace of curiosity in it, as if she was still processing everything. "I mean, there aren't really any rules for this kind of thing, and if there are—fuck it! We'll figure it out and do it the way we want to."

Her words hung in the air for a moment, and I felt the weight of her approach as she came up behind me, wrapping her arms around my waist. The warmth of her body pressed against mine, and I felt her lips brush softly against the back of my neck, sending a familiar shiver down my spine. She kissed me again, slower this time, and I turned to face her, feeling the need for reassurance.

"So... we're good?" I asked, my voice quieter than I expected. "As good as we were a few months ago?"

Lucy's lips parted into a wide, confident smile, her eyes glinting with amusement. "Read my lips," she said softly, leaning in closer, her breath warm against my skin. "We will always be good."

She sealed her words with a kiss, her lips soft but firm against mine. "No matter how many guys I fuck, or how many you watch... I married you," she continued, her voice unwavering. "Even though this was all your idea, I'm enjoying the game. But if you ever want me to stop... I'll stop. You know that, right?"

I smiled, feeling the weight of her promise settle over me like a blanket. I kissed her deeply, letting the moment speak for itself. Her words, though playful, carried a serious undercurrent that reassured me. The connection between us hadn't faded—it had only evolved, shifting into something more complex, but still grounded in the trust we had built together.

As we pulled apart, I took a deep breath and asked the question that had been nagging at me. "Did you make any plans with Jordan before he left?"

Lucy tilted her head, thinking for a moment as we moved back toward the couch. "Not exactly," she said, sitting down next to me. "He said he really enjoyed the sex... but he had some reservations about you being there."

I raised an eyebrow, surprised by the admission. "Yeah, tell me about it," I replied with a half-laugh, feeling a bit awkward about it myself. I sank into the couch as Lucy slid onto my lap, her legs draped casually over the armrest.

"Maybe I'm not really a 'cuckold,' per se," I mused, more to myself than to her. "Maybe I'm just... more of a voyeur?"

Lucy's eyes sparkled with curiosity as she gazed out the bay window for a moment, considering my words. "Hmm... that could be," she said thoughtfully. "You like hearing about it, and I guess you enjoyed watching it... but some of the things I've read about the cuckold dynamic seem a little... far, I guess."

I nodded, grateful for her insight. There was a fine line between voyeurism and cuckolding, and while we had explored both, I wasn't sure where I stood on the spectrum. I leaned in, kissing her cheek softly. "So... no more 'bitch boy'?" I teased, half-joking but curious about her thoughts.

Lucy giggled, her smile lighting up her face. "Well," she said playfully, turning to face me with a mischievous glint in her eye.

"I kind of liked that one."

She leaned in closer, her lips brushing against mine before pulling back just enough to speak. "How about you still let me call you that," she suggested with a sly smile, "but we just won't tell the other men that you're my 'bitch boy.'"

I couldn't help but laugh, shaking my head in amusement. Her playful attitude was infectious, and as much as I had mixed feelings about it, the dynamic had added a new layer of excitement to our relationship. I knew it wasn't something I'd want all the time, but the occasional teasing? That I could handle.

"Deal," I said with a grin, leaning in to kiss her again. I knew it wouldn't become a regular thing, but there was something thrilling about the way she wielded that power over me. Watching her in the bedroom, seeing her in control... I had enjoyed it more than I'd expected. More than I'd enjoyed being right in front of her during the act.

The rest of the day passed lazily, the tension from the morning easing into something more comfortable as we lounged around the house, watching TV and savoring the quiet moments together. It was a lazy Sunday, the kind of day we both needed after the intensity of the night before. But as we lay there, my thoughts drifted back to Jordan, and I wondered what Lucy would say to him when they inevitably talked again.

Would she tell him about what we had discussed? About my questions? My insecurities? The thought gnawed at the back of my mind, but I pushed it aside for the time being. There was no point in overthinking it now. Lucy had been honest with me, and for now, that was enough.

As the afternoon sun dipped lower in the sky, I found myself glancing at Lucy, who was curled up on the couch beside me, lost in the movie we were half-watching. The image of her with Jordan, the sounds of her pleasure, the way she had responded to him... it was still fresh in my mind. But the knot in my chest had loosened, replaced by something more settled. This was our life now—our game. And as long as we played by our rules, I knew we'd be okay.

THE DAY AFTER

T he next day at work, I found myself checking the time more often than usual, waiting impatiently for Lucy's daily lunch call. It was a routine we'd had for years, but today felt different. I was on edge, eager to hear what she had to say about her conversation with Jordan, wondering what she might reveal. When my phone finally buzzed right on time, I quickly picked it up, my heart racing.

"Did you talk to Jordan?" I blurted out, the words spilling from my mouth before I could even think to greet her.

There was a pause on the other end, then Lucy's light, teasing laughter. "Whoa... hello to you too," she said, clearly amused by my eagerness.

I immediately felt a little sheepish. "I'm sorry, babe," I said, laughing awkwardly at myself. "I didn't mean to jump right into it."

She chuckled again, the sound soothing some of the tension in my chest. "It's alright. I get it. You're curious." There was a brief pause, and I could feel her thinking, weighing her words before she continued. "Yeah, I talked to him. A little bit, anyway. I didn't go into a lot of detail, but he seemed understanding. Agreed it was a little wild, even for him."

That was a relief. A small part of me had worried that Jordan might have found the whole thing too much and backed away from it all. Hearing that he was on the same page eased some of the uncertainty swirling in my head. "Good," I said, exhaling slowly. "I just wanted to make sure he was alright with everything."

There was a brief silence on the other end before Lucy spoke again, her tone shifting slightly. "I've been reading about this new club that opened up downtown," she began, a note of excitement creeping into her voice. "I think we should check it out."

Her words caught me off guard. Lucy wasn't usually the one to suggest going out to clubs—at least, not in years. "A club?" I asked, my surprise clear. "You want to go to a club? Really?"

Lucy laughed, clearly sensing my surprise. "Yeah," she said, her tone light but serious. "I've been doing my usual slacking at work, and, well, after what we talked about yesterday, it got me thinking. Maybe we're better suited for something different—like swinging—rather than the whole cuckold thing."

Swinging. The word hung in the air for a moment, and I let it sink in. The idea of it had crossed my mind before, but I hadn't seriously considered it. The whole dynamic we'd been exploring with Jordan was more focused on Lucy being with other men while I watched or heard about it after. But swinging —that was different. It involved us both participating, sharing the experience together. Maybe she was right. Maybe this was a better fit for us.

"Swinging, huh?" I mused, letting the thought settle. "I guess it's something to talk about."

Lucy seemed to sense my hesitation, but she pressed on, her enthusiasm bubbling up. "OK, but we need to decide before Wednesday," she said. "That's when the party is, and they only do it once a month."

"Party?" I asked, raising an eyebrow. The idea of going to a club for a party seemed odd to me, especially since we hadn't done anything like that in years. "We're going to a club... for a party?"

"That's what they call it," Lucy explained, her voice bright with excitement. "It's a private party. They shut the club down for the night, and only people on the list can get in."

I chuckled, shaking my head. "A list? Babe, we're not in L.A. They don't have clubs like that around here."

"No, silly," she laughed. "It's not like that. You have to pay to go, and then you pay for drinks if you want them. But you have to pay for entry before you even get there... they accept payment on their website." There was a brief pause, and then she added, "It's $25 for couples, $50 for single men, and women get in free."

Lucy laughed a little at that last part, and I couldn't help but smile. The idea was starting to grow on me, but it was still unexpected. Lucy, of all people, suggesting we go to a club like that? It was a far cry from the quiet nights at home or our more intimate fantasies.

"Okay... we'll talk more about it tonight when we get home," I said as we wrapped up the phone call. The rest of the day, I couldn't stop thinking about it—about the party, the idea of swinging, and more than anything, why Lucy had suddenly become so interested in this new dynamic. There was a nagging feeling in the back of my mind that I couldn't shake.

That evening, when I walked in the door, as usual, Lucy was already home. She was sitting on the couch, her laptop balanced on her knees, typing away with an excited expression. I watched her for a moment, noting the focus in her eyes and the slight smile playing on her lips.

"Hey babe, what's up?" I asked as I set my things down and walked over to her.

She looked up with a grin. "Just looking more into this party I told you about," she said, her excitement evident.

I hesitated for a moment, something in my chest tightening. I couldn't help but wonder why she was suddenly so enthusiastic about this whole swinging idea. It felt... sudden. Almost as if she was trying to shift the focus. Maybe it was just my own insecurity, but I had to ask. "Can I ask why you're so interested in this all of a sudden?"

Lucy paused, her fingers freezing on the keyboard. She sat up a little straighter, her brow furrowing as she looked at me with mild confusion. "I'm not," she said slowly. "It just looks fun."

I gave her a look, raising my eyebrows, letting her know I wasn't entirely convinced. She stared back at me for a moment, her expression softening as she read the doubt on my face. "Fine," she said with a little laugh. "You caught me. I do have ulterior motives."

I waited, my curiosity piqued.

Lucy snickered to herself, shutting the laptop and setting it aside. "I guess I just feel a little bad about being the only one having sex with other people," she admitted, her voice laced with amusement but also a hint of guilt. "Now, don't get me wrong, I think it's fucking amazing," she added quickly, her eyes gleaming, "but you're only getting me... and not any, what do you call it? 'Strange.'"

She laughed as she finished the sentence, closing the laptop and swinging her feet to the floor, her playful tone hanging in the air. I sat down next to her, trying to process what she was saying.

"Oh, baby doll, it's cool..." I began, trying to reassure her, but before I could finish, she cut me off, her tone growing a little more serious.

"I get that," she said, shifting slightly to face me, "but you really don't have any desire to fuck some hot chick?" Her eyes widened a little, her eyebrows lifting in a playful challenge. "I mean, you're a very attractive man, and I know for a fact that there are a few gals who wouldn't mind taking a ride!"

I blinked, surprised by her bluntness. "Wait, really? What do you mean 'for a fact'?" I asked, suddenly intrigued. My mind raced, wondering who she might be talking about.

Lucy smiled, her lips curving into a mischievous grin as she slid closer, straddling my lap. "Well, Beth for one," she said with a teasing glint in her eye.

"Beth?" I repeated, the name catching me off guard. "I could never with her." I shook my head, stunned by the suggestion. "I've known her as long as I've known you!" I exclaimed. Beth had been a lifelong friend of Lucy's—they'd gone to school together, grew up together, and had stayed close ever since. She was there the day Lucy and I met, and over time, she had become a good friend to me as well. But I had never looked at her 'that way.' Beth was like family, a constant presence in our lives. The idea of anything sexual with her had never crossed my mind.

Lucy tilted her head, watching me with a smirk as I tried to wrap my head around her suggestion. "And why her?" I asked, more out of curiosity than anything.

She laughed, her eyes bright with amusement. "What are you talking about? She's always thought you were hot, ever since the first time we met." Lucy's grin widened as she saw the disbelief on my face. "You're the only 'white boy' she'd ever date, she told me once."

I blinked, my surprise deepening. "Beth said that?" I asked, still trying to process it.

Lucy nodded, laughing again. "Yep. She's always had a thing for you, babe. And let's just say, if you're ever interested, I don't think she'd mind."

I stared at her, a mixture of shock and intrigue swirling in my mind. The idea of being with someone else—someone like Beth —had never seemed real before. But hearing Lucy talk about it so casually, with such certainty, was both confusing and strangely exciting.

After Lucy climbed off me, she settled back into the seat beside me, picking up her laptop again. "Well, I was just saying. If you're fine with our current arrangement, then I guess never mind," she said casually, though there was a hint of something unspoken in her voice as she resumed typing.

I smiled at her, leaning back on the couch, the conversation still playing in my mind. "If I get the urge or meet someone I want to sleep with, I'll let you know, okay?" I said, my tone light but teasing.

She flashed me a smile, her eyes twinkling for a moment before she turned her attention back to 'surfing' the net. We let the topic drop for now, but the possibilities lingered between us, unspoken but present.

The next day, she called at her usual time. I picked up the phone, trying to sound casual, but I could feel the lingering curiosity from our conversation yesterday gnawing at me.

"Hey, guess what?" Lucy's voice was laced with excitement, a hint of something new.

"What?" I asked, though the mockery in my voice was clear.

"Jordan is moving..." she said, her voice lighter than I expected. "He found a new job in Midtown."

"Wait, and... you're happy about this?" I asked, genuinely surprised. I had expected something different—maybe disappointment, maybe sadness—but her tone didn't match the "amazing" nights she'd shared with him.

"Well... sort of," she replied, her tone shifting as she considered it. "Things have been getting weird around here, with him, I mean."

I could sense there was more, and I waited for her to continue.

"And," she added after a moment, "the talk we had at lunch...

whoa."

That got my attention. "You two went to lunch?" I asked, a bit thrown off by that detail.

"Really?" Lucy shot back, her tone laced with playful exasperation. "That's what you got from what I just said?"

I smiled to myself but stayed quiet, waiting for her to explain.

"Anyway, yes..." she continued, her voice softening. "We went to lunch together. I'm guessing he wanted to tell me about his new job."

There was a pause, and I could almost hear the gears turning in her head as she sorted through her emotions.

"But, honestly," she went on, her tone more thoughtful, "it just made me realize things between us had gotten... complicated."

I stayed quiet, giving her space to share what she was feeling. The fact that she seemed almost relieved made me wonder what else had been going on beneath the surface.

Lucy sighed softly before continuing. "Well... yeah, the sex was fun," she admitted, a small chuckle escaping her lips. "It was incredible, really, but..."

She paused again, and I could feel the shift in her mood, something more serious creeping in.

"But after the other night, I've been thinking." She hesitated, her voice growing softer, as if she was weighing each word carefully. "Him and I... we probably shouldn't see each other anymore."

That surprised me, but before I could respond, Lucy added, "Because of how weird it got for you."

I felt the knot in my chest tighten, but I knew she wasn't wrong. The night had been intense—hot, thrilling—but the aftermath left me feeling a little off-balance. "Weird for me?" I echoed, my voice thoughtful.

"Yeah," she said gently. "It was hot in the moment, but afterward..."

Another pause, this one longer. I could tell she was trying to find the right way to explain it.

"I started to wonder if this was what we really wanted long-term," she admitted. "I don't know. Maybe it's good that Jordan is moving. It feels like a natural end to this, you know?"

Her words hit me harder than I expected. She was right. The heat of the moment had been exhilarating, but the idea of making this a regular thing? That was where it got murky.

"Yeah," I agreed after a moment, exhaling slowly. "Maybe this is for the best."

It was strange, the idea of Jordan being out of the picture. He had been such a major part of our dynamic recently, and yet, the thought of moving forward without him didn't feel as daunting as I'd expected. Maybe this was what we needed—a chance to reset, to take a step back and figure out what worked best for us without the complications that had started to creep in.

"So, what now?" I asked, curious to hear her thoughts.

Lucy laughed softly, her voice lighter now. "Now? Well, we take it one step at a time," she said. "We've still got that party to think about, remember?"

I chuckled, the tension between us easing as the conversation shifted back to the possibilities ahead. The dynamic was still evolving, but for now, it felt like we were on the same page

"Yeah," I said with a grin. "We'll see where that takes us."

"Well, besides the point... back to my story," Lucy said, her tone shifting back to something more focused. "When Jordan told me he'd be moving, he sort of... teared up a little bit." She paused, her voice carrying a note of disbelief, as if she still couldn't quite believe it herself. "That really started to freak me out. I mean, I'm married, he knows I love you and would never, ever leave you. We had great sex together, but it was just that—sex."

Her words hung in the air, and I could hear the slight edge in her voice. This wasn't just a casual revelation; it had clearly unsettled her.

"I see," I said, my voice soft but unsure. I didn't really know how to respond to that. What could I say? The situation was more complicated than I'd anticipated.

Lucy sighed, as if sensing my uncertainty. "I let him know I was completely okay with him moving. It was fun, but it's over now... I guess. And that's okay with me." She said it with a finality, like she was trying to put the whole situation to rest.

"Okay," I replied, still feeling a bit at a loss. I didn't have much of an opinion on whether Jordan left or stayed, and I wasn't sure what she expected from me.

Lucy let out a frustrated sigh, her voice tinged with exasperation. "Ugh... never mind," she said, clearly flustered. "I'm going back to work. I'll see you when I get home."

When I got home that evening, I saw her standing in the kitchen, looking lost in thought. Without hesitation, I walked over to her and wrapped my arms around her, pulling her into a hug.

"I'm sorry, baby," I said, my voice soft against her ear. "If I acted... uh... wrong, or whatever, I just don't know how to react to all of this." It was the truth. The situation had thrown me off, and I hadn't been sure how to handle it

She hugged me back, her arms tightening around me. "It's okay, not your fault," she murmured, her voice more relaxed but still carrying traces of frustration. "It just really freaked me out, his reactions to everything. You know, he actually said he loved me today. Do you fucking believe that?"

I pulled back slightly, looking at her face, and I could see the anger flickering in her eyes. "He said he loved you?" I repeated, surprised.

"Yeah," she said, shaking her head, her tone sharp with disbelief. "Can you fucking believe that? It wasn't supposed to be like that. It was supposed to be fun, just sex, nothing more."

I could feel the tension radiating from her, the frustration bubbling just beneath the surface. Jordan's unexpected emotional attachment had clearly crossed a line for her, turning what had been a playful, open dynamic into something more complicated—and uncomfortable.

"That's... wow," I muttered, not knowing what else to say.

Lucy let out a sigh, her fingers playing with the edge of the kitchen counter as she tried to calm herself. "Yeah, exactly. I didn't sign up for that. It's over, and honestly... I'm relieved."

I hesitated for a moment, knowing the question I was about to ask might not be entirely appropriate, especially given how frustrated Lucy seemed. But I couldn't help it—my curiosity was burning a hole in my chest, and I had to know. With a small, mischievous grin, I finally spoke.

"This may not be the right time to ask, but... I'm going to anyway, because... well, because it's all I'm thinking about now. Does this mean you're done having sex with other men?"

Lucy's shoulders sank, and for a second, I thought I had crossed a line. Her eyes widened in disbelief, but then, to my relief, her expression softened, quickly turning into a smile. "No," she said, shaking her head slightly. "It does not mean that."

I felt a wave of relief wash over me, but I stayed quiet, waiting for her to explain further.

"I guess the next one will just need to be... different," she continued, her voice thoughtful but carrying that same determined energy I'd come to love. "Someone who understands the boundaries, who's not working with me, and—most importantly—who doesn't already have a crush or end up falling in love." She smiled, though there was a hint of steel behind it. "I'll just be more upfront next time, letting them know love is off the table."

Her ambition and confidence shone through, and I couldn't help but feel reassured by her attitude. This wasn't something that was going to derail us or change our dynamic—it was just a bump in the road, a lesson learned.

I pulled her closer, hugging her tightly as I felt the tension between us ease. "Well, like you said... there aren't any rules for this," I murmured into her ear. "We'll just count this as a practice run."

Lucy laughed softly, the sound warm and familiar. "Yeah," she agreed, her voice lightening. "Practice makes perfect, right?

With that, the heaviness of the conversation lifted. Jordan's confession, though uncomfortable and unexpected, hadn't ruined anything for us. If anything, it had strengthened our resolve, showing us both what we wanted—and what we didn't —in this new chapter of our relationship.

Over the next couple of weeks, life settled into its usual rhythm. Jordan had stopped coming into the office as he prepared for his move, and Lucy and I hadn't really talked about him since. Things felt... normal. Uneventful, even, as we fell back into the routine of work, dinners, and quiet nights together.

But one evening, as we were sitting at the dinner table, Lucy broke the silence with a sudden, unexpected announcement.

"I made a profile on this website," she blurted out, her eyes gleaming with excitement.

I looked up from my plate, caught off guard. "Wait... what?"

Lucy grinned, clearly enjoying my surprise. "I made a profile," she repeated, her voice teasing. "You know... to find someone new."

"Oh, you did?" I asked, my curiosity instantly piqued.

"Yeah," Lucy said with a grin. "I was going to go for that 'Ashley Madison' thing, but you have to pay for that shit, so I went ahead and found a free, regular dating site."

Her smile widened, and I could see the excitement in her eyes. She seemed eager—almost too eager—to find a replacement for Jordan. It was clear she wasn't letting her experience with him deter her from continuing this exploration. My thoughts drifted for a moment. I wondered if she was just enjoying the newfound freedom of being able to sleep with whomever she wanted, whenever she wanted. Part of me couldn't help but feel a twinge of jealousy, but it was also... exciting.

"What did you put in the profile?" I asked, half-joking. "Not that you're single and looking for love, right?"

Lucy laughed, shaking her head. "Oh god, no," she said quickly, a trace of seriousness slipping into her voice. "No miscommunication this time. I just put that I'm married, and my husband doesn't mind what I do... and that I'm looking for a 'hook up.'"

I raised an eyebrow, impressed by how direct she was being. "To the point, huh?" I said, trying to keep my tone light. A part of me might've gone a little softer in her approach, but then again, after everything with Jordan, it made sense she'd want to be clear from the get-go.

"Yup," she replied, leaning back in her chair, her smile returning. "No more room for confusion. I'm making it clear what I want."

There was something about the way she was handling it—her confidence, her ambition—that both reassured and intrigued me. She wasn't letting the Jordan situation shake her; instead, she was moving forward, taking control.

"I've already gotten a few replies," Lucy added with a touch of pride in her voice, though she quickly followed up with a laugh. "But they were just creepy guys who were way too ugly for me to have sex with randomly."

I couldn't help but laugh along with her, imagining the kind of messages she must've received. "Well, that's the internet for you," I said, shaking my head.

The conversation about the dating site drifted off after that as we finished our dinner, the subject dropping as naturally as it had come up. But even after the dishes were cleared and the night wound down, the thought of Lucy actively looking for someone new lingered in the back of my mind. It was a strange feeling—equal parts excitement and uncertainty.

The next day at work, her call came in right on time, as usual. Lucy had always been punctual with her lunch calls, but this time, there was something different in her tone. I could sense it as soon as I answered.

"Hey, honey," she said, her voice softer than usual.

"Hey, babe. What's up?" I replied, leaning back in my chair.

There was a brief pause before she spoke again, her voice a little more tentative. "So, where do we stand on... who I choose to have sex with?"

Her question caught me off guard, and I felt a flicker of confusion. "What do you mean?" I asked, trying to keep my tone casual even though her question had thrown me. "Whoever you want, I guess. I don't know."

I laughed a little, trying to lighten the moment, but her tone had me curious.

"I mean, do you want a say in it?" she asked, her voice shy, almost hesitant, as if she was worried about stepping on a line we hadn't fully defined yet.

It took me a moment to process her question. I hadn't even considered that aspect—having a say in who she slept with. Up until now, it had felt more like her exploration, and I was there for the ride. But now, with her looking for someone new, it felt different, more real. Should I be involved in that choice?

"I don't know," I said again, more thoughtful this time. "I guess I haven't really thought about it like that."

Lucy's pause on the other end was telling. She was waiting for me to work through it, to give her an answer that felt right for both of us. But honestly, I wasn't sure where we stood on this either.

A BLAST FROM
THE PAST

L ater that day, I returned home and found Lucy standing in the kitchen, her back to me as she worked on something at the counter. She looked up when she heard me come in, a warm smile on her face.

"Hey, babe. How was your day?" she asked, her voice light and casual.

"Not too bad," I replied, though there was an edge of anticipation in my voice. "But I'd rather finish our conversation from this afternoon."

Lucy turned around, her eyebrows lifting slightly as she leaned back against the counter. "Oh... you mean what I asked you?" she said, playing coy, though we both knew she was well aware of what I meant. She didn't wait for me to respond before continuing. "I recently got a call from someone I haven't talked to in quite a while."

Her words made me pause, a flicker of worry creeping in. I hoped it wasn't her ex-boyfriend Eric. I'd never liked him much, especially after meeting him a few times back when they stayed friends after their breakup. He wasn't exactly trustworthy, and he'd cheated on her several times before they finally ended things for good. But surely, it couldn't be him. Why would it be?

My mind raced through the possibilities as I tried to hide my unease.

Lucy glanced at me and must've sensed my concern. She backed up against the sink, leaning on the counter with a small grin tugging at her lips. "Lewis," she said, her tone colored with a hint of surprise, as if even she hadn't expected his name to come up.

My stomach twisted slightly at the mention of him. Lewis. He wasn't a serious ex—more of an old fling. They'd never officially dated, just had rebound sex in between relationships. But the way she always talked about him, it was clear he'd left an impression on her, even though she'd often told me the sex wasn't all that great. He was smaller than what she preferred, she'd said, almost dismissively. Still, there was always this... connection between them, and I'd never quite understood it.

I tried to keep my expression neutral. "Lewis," I repeated, nodding slowly. "And what did he want?"

Lucy pushed herself off the counter and crossed her arms, a thoughtful look crossing her face. "Honestly, I think he just needs a friend," she said, her tone softening slightly. "He and his wife are going through a divorce, and they've been fighting over the kids. He sounded... pretty lost."

I could hear a note of sympathy in her voice, which only made me more uneasy. She'd always had a soft spot for Lewis, and that concerned me more than the physical history they shared. He had this way with her, this charm that always seemed to draw her back in, even when she claimed the sex wasn't anything to write home about.

I walked over to the table and sat down, my thoughts racing as she continued.

"And get this," she added, her voice picking up a little, as if she was still processing the shock of it. "His wife was selling herself for pills."

That caught me off guard. "Oh my god, really?" I asked, genuinely surprised. I leaned forward, trying to wrap my head around it. "And he had no idea?"

Lucy shook her head, her expression serious. "Nope. Complete surprise to him."

I sat back in my chair, trying to absorb the information. I could see why Lewis might be reaching out to her—he was going through a tough time, and Lucy had always been someone who people felt they could turn to. But still, there was something about this that didn't sit right with me.

As much as I tried to focus on the drama of Lewis's life, my mind went where it always seemed to go when Lucy had an opportunity to be with another man. It wasn't the sex itself that bothered me. She'd been with others before, and it had turned me on more than I'd ever expected. But with Lewis, it felt... different. She'd always had a weak spot for him, and no matter how many times she told me the sex wasn't that good or that he was too small for her, there was something about the way she talked about him that made me uneasy.

He had this... charm, this way of talking her out of her panties, as I used to tease her. It wasn't just physical attraction—there was something more to it, something emotional, and that's what made me nervous. It was one thing for her to sleep with someone new, someone we didn't have history with, but Lewis? That felt like familiar territory, and familiar territory was dangerous.

"So, other than that..." I said, trying to shift the conversation and move past the whole Lewis situation.

"What?" Lucy asked, looking at me with a bit of confusion.

"Well, that just didn't seem like something that big to 'wait until we got home,'" I said with a slight laugh. "I was expecting something more... intense."

Lucy smirked and walked over to the table, sitting down next to me. "Oh no, that was just letting you know I talked to him. What I really wanted to talk about was Steve," she said, her tone shifting slightly. "He texted me today, right before lunch."

I raised an eyebrow, curious now. "And what did he want? More than just a blow job from a married woman?" I teased, laughing at my own joke.

She giggled, her eyes lighting up with amusement. "We didn't really talk in detail. He just told me he was thinking about me, that he really had fun that night, and that he's sorry he hasn't called." She paused for a second before adding, "Oh, and he started school!"

"School?" I asked, raising my voice in surprise.

"Yes, college!" she said with a giggle, shaking her head. "Not high school! Jeepers, I'm not a pedophile!" she added, laughing at the absurdity of it.

"Okay, okay," I laughed, holding up my hands in mock surrender. "I kind of figured. So... what's the big deal about all this?" I asked, still curious about where she was going with the conversation.

"Well," she said, her tone softening a bit as she looked at me, "I thought it would be fun if we had a fire this Friday, and Steve could come over and hang out with us."

I raised an eyebrow, feeling a little nervous at the suggestion. "Not like the last guy you had over, right?" I asked, half-joking, but there was a serious undertone to my words.

"Oh, no way!" she said quickly, shaking her head. "Nothing like that. I just figured we could hang out by the fire, drink some beers, and get to know each other a little better."

She paused for a second, watching me for my reaction before adding, "I really think he could be a good friend, you know? He's taking computer classes in school." She said it in a way that was clearly meant to be a selling point, something that might spark my interest.

I couldn't help but laugh a little. "Uh... are you going to want me to get this kid a job?" I asked, only half-joking.

Lucy laughed, shaking her head. "Not at all," she said with a smile. "I just figured, since he's into all that tech stuff, and that's what you do for a living, you two would have something in common to talk about. You know, break the ice."

The idea of hanging out with Steve still felt... strange. There was a part of me that was wary of the whole situation, but Lucy's excitement about it was hard to ignore. I nodded, though I couldn't shake the feeling that there was more to this than just a casual hangout.

The next day, Lucy called during her usual time. "What's up, babe?" she asked as I answered the phone.

"Not much," I replied with a chuckle. "Just another day at the salt factory."

"So, I texted with Steve today," she said, her voice sounding cheerful. "And he said it's cool if we do the fire tonight."

"Sounds good," I said, though I still felt a little unsure about the whole thing. We wrapped up the call, and as I hung up, I had to laugh to myself about the entire situation. The fact that Steve was taking computer classes was amusing to me, especially knowing how these conversations usually went. I hated talking to people who thought they knew more than they did about my field—like that cocky kid at work who constantly threw around tech jargon that didn't fit into what we were actually doing.

I filled up my coffee and headed to a brainstorming meeting, still thinking about how the night might unfold. Would Steve be like one of those guys? Eager to show off his limited knowledge of my world? I hoped not, but the thought lingered as I walked into the conference room, preparing myself for the day ahead.

"It was 'brainstorming' day at the office," I started, already feeling the frustration bubbling up.

Lucy's eyes met mine, curious but amused. She knew how I felt about these meetings.

"I still don't understand why we waste our time with those meetings," I continued, shaking my head. "We never come up with anything new."

Lucy raised an eyebrow, but her smile hinted that she was entertained by my little rant. "Uh-huh," she prompted, leaning back in her chair.

"Seriously," I added, throwing my hands up. "Nothing gets done, and we just waste an entire day. Time that could've been better spent... you know, actually churning out code."

She laughed softly, shaking her head. "Sounds like someone had a rough day."

"Rough doesn't even begin to cover it," I muttered, though her laughter eased some of my frustration.

A little later in the conversation, I leaned back in my chair, smirking as the topic turned to Steve's visit.

"Fair enough," I said, my lips twitching into a teasing smile. "But, honestly... what are we all going to talk about?"

Lucy tilted her head, giving me a knowing look. "What do you mean?"

"I mean, considering his age..." I trailed off, raising an eyebrow playfully, "and the fact that I have absolutely no interest in sleeping with him."

Lucy burst out laughing, swatting at me playfully. "You're terrible!" she exclaimed, still giggling.

I shrugged, my smirk widening. "Just saying."

This version breaks up the dialogue with added reactions, making the interaction more natural and reflective of the couple's playful dynamic. Let me know if this works or if you'd like any further tweaks!

When I got home, Lucy was already sitting at the kitchen table, her nose buried in one of her usual paranormal romance novels. The cover caught my eye—a dark, brooding vampire holding a half-naked woman. She had a thing for those kinds of stories, the ones where women were having intense love affairs with vampires or demons. I didn't quite get it, but I knew she enjoyed it. She always liked the more... intense stuff than I did.

"Hey, babe," she said, looking up from her book with a warm smile as I set my briefcase down.

"How was the rest of your day?" she asked, closing the book but keeping her finger between the pages.

"Oh, you know," I started, feeling the familiar frustration bubbling up. "It was 'brainstorming' day at the office." I sighed, rolling my eyes.

Lucy raised an eyebrow, sensing where this was going. "Brainstorming, huh?"

"Yeah," I replied, leaning against the counter, my frustration spilling out. "I still don't understand why we waste our time with those meetings. We never come up with anything new. Nothing gets done."

She nodded, a knowing smile playing on her lips. "Uh-huh."

"Seriously, it's such a waste of an entire day," I continued, throwing my hands up. "Time that could've been better spent... you know, actually churning out code."

Lucy laughed softly, shaking her head as she watched me rant. "Sounds like someone had a rough day," she teased, her eyes sparkling with amusement.

"Rough doesn't even begin to cover it," I muttered, but her laughter managed to ease some of my annoyance.

I shifted gears, changing the subject. "Chinese," I blurted out.

Lucy blinked, confused. "What?"

"For dinner. Do you feel like Chinese?" I clarified with a chuckle.

"Oh," she giggled, shaking her head. "Sure, that sounds good."

After placing the order, I sat down at the table with her. She was back to reading, flipping through her 'girl porn'—as I liked to call it.

"So, what time is Steve supposed to get here?" I asked, leaning back in my chair.

"Not until seven," Lucy replied, closing the book and looking up at me. "It wouldn't be any fun to have a fire when it's still light out."

I nodded, thinking it over. "Fair enough," I said with a smirk. "Though, I'm not sure what we all have to talk about, considering his age..." I paused for a moment before adding, "and the fact that I have absolutely no interest in sleeping with him."

Lucy burst out laughing, swatting at me playfully. "You're terrible!" she exclaimed, shaking her head.

I shrugged, my smirk widening. "Just saying," I teased, watching her still giggling at the joke.

"Ha ha... not funny," she said, rolling her eyes but clearly amused by the banter.

The Chinese food came, and we ate, alternating between comfortable silence and light conversation about our day. After we finished, Lucy stood up and made her way over to the fridge. I saw her pause for a moment before she turned to me, a mischievous glint in her eye.

"Oh, shit," she said with a dramatic sigh. "Baby, can you run to the store and pick up some beer? Steve will be here soon, and you don't want to leave me alone in the house with him, do you?" Her voice carried that teasing edge I knew too well.

I raised an eyebrow, recognizing her playful manipulation. This was her way of getting me to do something I didn't particularly feel like doing. But still, I agreed, figuring I might need plenty of beer to deal with this kid tonight.

"Alright, alright," I said, grabbing my keys. "I'll be back."

The store run was quick, and I grabbed a case of beer as requested. As I pulled into the driveway, I spotted a familiar car parked there—Steve's. He was already here.

I grabbed the beer from the car and noticed the crisp evening air. It was late fall, and though the chill wasn't unbearable, it was enough to make me want a fire to keep warm. I figured I'd grab the cooler from the garage before heading inside.

When I walked into the house, Lucy and Steve were already sitting at the kitchen table, laughing softly about something.

"Hey, you two," I called out, setting the cooler down on the floor.

Lucy turned to me with a smile, leaning over to give me a quick kiss. "Hey, honey," she said. I noticed she was wearing my favorite pair of jeans—the ones that hugged her ass perfectly—and a snug turtleneck sweater that made her look effortlessly sexy.

I forced a smile, doing my best to ignore the mild annoyance bubbling up. "I'm just going to change into something more comfortable. Be right back," I said, starting to undo my tie as I walked toward the stairs.

"Okay," Lucy replied casually. "We'll go out and start the fire."

I nodded, undoing my tie as I headed upstairs, but a small part of me couldn't shake the feeling that I'd just walked into something I wasn't entirely prepared for. After changing into a pair of sweats and an old hoodie, I headed back downstairs. The house was quiet now—too quiet.

I stepped out onto the deck, noticing that Lucy and Steve had already taken the cooler outside with them. The fire pit was crackling, its warm glow lighting up the surrounding trees. The backyard stretched out in front of me, a wide expanse of lawn leading to the wooded area beyond. The deck spanned the entire length of the house, and in the far corner, just below our bedroom window, sat our hot tub, steam occasionally rising from it into the cool night air.

As I walked closer to the fire, I noticed three chairs set around the pit, with Lucy in the middle. Steve was sitting to her right, his chair noticeably closer to hers than mine. I wasn't sure if she'd arranged it that way or if he had scooted in.

"Where's the beer at?" I asked with a smile as I sat down in the empty chair on her left.

Lucy leaned over the side of her chair, reaching down into the cooler. I could hear the clink of bottles as she fumbled around before handing me one. "Here you go," she said with a grin.

"Thanks," I muttered, twisting off the cap and taking a long sip. The fire's warmth seeped into me as I stretched out, propping my feet on the brick rim of the pit.

The tension in the air was subtle but palpable. Steve was sitting just a little too close to Lucy, and I couldn't help but feel like a third wheel despite this being my own backyard.

"So, Steve," I said, breaking the silence and trying to find a neutral topic. "What are you taking in school?"

Steve glanced over at me, his boyish smile lighting up his face. "Computer classes," he replied, almost too casually. "Just starting my first semester, but I'm really into it. Figured it was a good field to get into."

I nodded, sipping my beer as I tried to gauge his enthusiasm. There was always something about talking to people just starting in my field—they tended to either underestimate how difficult it could be or overestimate their current knowledge.

"Good field," I said, keeping my tone neutral. "Definitely a lot of opportunity there."

Lucy chimed in, smiling as she looked between us. "I told him you work in tech, too. Thought you guys might have something to talk about."

"Yeah," I replied, eyeing Steve. "Maybe."

I leaned back in my chair, watching the fire dance in front of me, but the flicker of tension in the air was hard to ignore. Something about tonight felt off—different from the usual playful dynamic Lucy and I shared. Steve was just a kid, really, but there was something about his easy confidence, the way he seemed so comfortable around Lucy, that made me more than a little wary.

I took another sip of beer, forcing myself to relax. It was going to be a long night.

"Oh, computer science," Steve replied, casually throwing one leg over his knee and poking the fire with a stick as he spoke. His movements were relaxed, confident, as if he was completely at ease in our space.

"Yeah," he continued. "I was actually going to go for bartending at first, but figured I could make a lot more money with a corporate job."

I smiled at him, though there was a part of me that couldn't help but feel a little skeptical of his plan. "Yeah, sure... as long as the economy doesn't take another dive," I said with a chuckle, trying to keep the conversation light.

Steve grinned back, but before he could respond, Lucy cut in, clearly bored by our work talk.

"Okay, that's boring," she said with a laugh, shaking her head. "Change of topic."

Steve looked over at her, his smile widening. "Fair enough."

"So," Lucy said, leaning forward slightly. "What have you been up to, Steve?"

He shrugged, looking thoughtful for a moment. "Not much. Just working and going to school," he said, glancing between us. "Glad I get a day off from life to come hang out with you two."

Lucy nodded, pulling her sweater tighter around her as a cool breeze drifted through the yard. "It's nice out here, don't you think?"

"Yeah," Steve agreed. "Really peaceful."

I got up and threw another log onto the fire, watching the flames flare up again as they caught the wood. "I guess we should've stocked the wood pile before we started," I said with a laugh. The pile was getting low, with only two logs left, and it wasn't long before we'd need more.

Lucy glanced at me and smiled, that mischievous glint back in her eyes. "Well," she said, standing up and stretching, "I could always have Steve help me find some more in the woods."

She held out her hand toward him, and without hesitation, Steve took it, standing up to join her. I watched as they walked away from the fire, their figures disappearing into the dark woods beyond the yard.

I stayed behind, settling back into my chair and watching the fire crackle. The sound of the leaves rustling as they walked away quickly faded, leaving only the crackling of the fire and the quiet sounds of the night. The flames danced in front of me, casting shadows across the yard, and I tried to shake off the unease creeping into my mind.

Fifteen minutes passed, and I started to wonder if they were having trouble finding wood. I glanced toward the woods, squinting to see if I could catch any movement, but the firelight was too bright, making it impossible to see anything beyond its glow.

After a while, curiosity—and maybe a touch of concern—got the better of me. I stood up, making my way toward the tree line, peering into the darkness as I walked. The cold air felt sharper as I left the warmth of the fire behind.

At the edge of the woods, I stopped, listening for any sounds —footsteps, voices—but there was nothing. Just the soft rustle of the trees swaying in the breeze. I frowned, staring into the inky blackness, but still saw no sign of them. After a moment, I turned back toward the fire, figuring Lucy knew her way around. They'd be back soon enough.

Another fifteen minutes passed before I finally heard the sound of leaves rustling behind me. I turned around, and sure enough, Lucy appeared from the darkness, Steve trailing a little behind her.

They were both carrying a few logs, but not much. It didn't look like their search had been all that successful.

"That all you found?" I asked, raising an eyebrow as I watched them approach.

Lucy gave me a sheepish grin, shrugging as she dropped the logs by the fire. "Slim pickings out there," she said.

Steve just chuckled, adding his few logs to the pile before sitting back down in his chair, closer to Lucy than before.

I took a swig from my beer, glancing between them, my mind swirling with questions I wasn't ready to ask.

We sat around the fire for what felt like hours, the warmth from the flames steadily fading as the night stretched on. It was around two in the morning when Steve finally stretched, letting out a small yawn.

"I think I should get going," he said, standing up and brushing off his jeans. "Got class in the morning."

Lucy nodded, standing up to walk him out. "Thanks for hanging out with us," she said, giving him a warm smile. "It was fun."

I stayed behind, still sitting by the fire, watching as they disappeared toward the front of the house. The air had grown colder, and I rubbed my hands together, thinking about how the night had gone. It was better than I'd expected—Steve wasn't as much of a kid as I'd thought. But there was something lingering in my mind, an odd feeling I couldn't quite shake.

After a few minutes, Lucy returned, a small smile on her lips as she made her way back to the fire. She didn't say anything, just walked over and sat down on my lap, her body settling into mine like it always did. I wrapped my arms around her, pulling her close to keep her warm as the fire slowly died out.

"That was nice," I said, breaking the silence. "He's a pretty cool kid."

"Yeah," Lucy agreed, leaning her head against my shoulder. "I think so too. At least he's smart... not that all young guys are stupid, but come on, a lot of them are." She laughed softly, the sound light and easy in the quiet night.

I chuckled, tightening my hold on her as we sat there, watching the fire fade into embers. The night had been simple, but there was something comforting about the stillness now, just the two of us in the cool night air.

We sat like that for another half an hour, sipping the last of our beers as the warmth from the fire faded completely. The embers glowed dimly, casting soft, flickering shadows across the yard. I felt Lucy shift slightly in my lap, her body starting to relax, and I knew she was getting sleepy.

She tilted her head up to look at me, her eyes soft. "Well, it's getting colder out here, and I'm getting sleepy," she murmured. "Care if we call it a night and go to bed?"

"Yeah, I'm pretty tired too," I said, standing up and helping her to her feet.

The next morning, I woke up and noticed Lucy already dressed, sitting at her vanity, carefully applying her makeup. The light from the window caught the edges of her hair, making her look ethereal, as if she were glowing. I glanced at the clock—the alarm still had another ten minutes before going off.

"You're up early, babe," I said, my voice raspy with sleep as I sat up on the edge of the bed.

"Yeah," she replied, her focus still on her eyeliner. "I wanted to get an early start. It's Saturday, and if I can finish up the pile of work on my desk, I'll have the rest of the weekend free."

I grinned, catching her eyes in the mirror. "Ah... one of those showers?" I teased, unable to resist.

She turned, her expression playful but sharp. "No, nothing like that," she said with a smirk. "You've got such a dirty mind."

I laughed, standing up to start my morning routine. As she finished with her eyeliner, I crept behind her, wrapping one arm around her waist and leaning down to kiss her neck softly. The familiar warmth of her skin sent a spark through me.

She set down the eyeliner, tilting her head slightly to give me better access. "You know what?" she murmured.

"What?" I whispered back, feeling the heat of her body so close.

"Steve fucked me in the woods last night," she said, her voice casual but with a wicked smile playing on her lips.

I froze for a moment, my breath catching. My eyes locked onto hers in the mirror, my heart pounding in my chest. "I thought you two took an awfully long time for such a small haul of wood," I said, half-laughing but needing to know more.

Lucy turned, her eyes glinting with mischief. "It was more than just a walk in the woods," she whispered. "It was... intense."

I raised an eyebrow, curiosity and arousal battling inside me.

"Tell me," I demanded, my voice thick with anticipation.

She leaned in closer, her breath warm against my ear. "He came up behind me while we were looking for wood. Out of nowhere, he slid his arms around me, pulled me back against him, and started kissing my neck. His hands were so firm, so sure." Her eyes flicked up to meet mine as she continued, her voice low and teasing.

"He reached down, slid his hand into my jeans, and started rubbing my pussy. I was already wet from the cold air, and the way he touched me..." She trailed off for a second, clearly enjoying my reaction. I could feel the blood rushing south as I imagined the scene.

"And then?" I urged, my hand already drifting toward my boxers.

"Then he unbuttoned my jeans, pulled them down to my knees, and bent me over against a tree," she said, her voice a mixture of breathy excitement and nostalgia. "His cock was so thick... not longer than yours, but the width of it. When he pushed inside me, I felt so... stretched."

I felt my cock twitch at her words. "Thicker than mine?" I asked, a pang of jealousy and arousal flooding through me.

Lucy nodded, her lips curling into a smile as she watched my reaction. "So much thicker," she whispered. "It felt incredible. He filled me up completely. My pussy stretched around him... tighter than it ever felt with you."

I swallowed hard, my hand finding its way down to my boxer shorts, stroking myself through the fabric as I listened to her.

"He grabbed my hips," she continued, her voice soft but filled with heat. "And started fucking me from behind, hard. Each thrust pushed me up against the tree, the bark rough against my skin, but I didn't care. The cold air hit my face while his thick cock filled me up from behind." She paused, watching me, savoring the effect her words had on me.

I groaned, picturing the scene vividly in my mind, imagining Steve's thicker cock stretching her in ways I couldn't. "Did you cum?" I asked, my voice husky.

"Of course," she said, her smile widening. "I came pretty quickly, actually. Not sure if it was him or just the excitement of being outside, exposed like that. It was intense... raw." She leaned closer, her eyes burning with mischief. "And then, after I came, he kept going. His thick cock pounded into me, deeper and harder."

I could feel myself pulsing in my hand, growing harder with every word she said. "And him?" I asked, needing to know.

"Oh, he came too," Lucy said with a wicked grin. "He pulled my hair back, whispered in my ear, asking me if I wanted him to cum inside me. I told him yes. I told him that you liked it when I let other men fill me up." She chuckled softly, watching the effect her words had on me.

My cock throbbed in my hand, my grip tightening. "Fuck," I muttered, stroking faster now. "I wish I'd seen it."

Lucy smiled and took a step closer, her hand brushing against my shoulder. "Want to hear more?" she whispered, her eyes locked onto mine.

I nodded, unable to speak.

She leaned down and took hold of my cock, her fingers wrapping around me as she gave it a slow, deliberate stroke. "You know..." she said, her tone shifting slightly, "Steve's cock was a lot thicker than this." She gave me a mock-pensive look, her hand squeezing my shaft gently. "Not that you're small... but... it was just so thick, you know?" Her voice carried a hint of pretend disappointment—or at least, I hoped she was pretending.

My chest tightened at her words, and I could feel the familiar surge of jealousy and arousal flood through me. "Really?" I asked, my voice barely a whisper.

"Mmm-hmm," she purred, her hand twisting around my cock as she stroked. "He stretched me out in ways you just... can't." Her words were casual, but the sting of them cut deep, fueling my need.

She leaned in closer, her breath hot against my ear. "Can you cum for me in the next ten seconds?" she whispered, her voice laced with seduction. "I've got work to do, and I'll leave whether you're done or not."

Her teasing grin flashed before my eyes, and with her hand twisting and stroking me, I felt the pressure build quickly. My body tensed, and with a low groan, I felt the first pulse as my cock erupted. Cum spurted from me, thick streams coating her hand and splattering across the room. Lucy didn't stop, her grip firm as she milked every last drop from me.

As the last spurt dripped from me, she gave me a satisfied smile, wiping her hand casually. She kissed me on the cheek and whispered, "Good boy."

OLD FRIENDS

The next day passed slower than usual. By noon, I realized I hadn't received our usual lunchtime call from Lucy. At first, I shrugged it off, thinking she was probably busy, or maybe she had called Lewis to catch up. With everything going on with his divorce, it wouldn't surprise me if they were figuring out where they'd meet. Still, it nagged at the back of my mind.

On my drive home, just as I was debating whether to call her, my phone rang. It was Lucy.

"Honey, I'm going straight to Lewis's after work," she said, her voice casual but quick, like she didn't want to make a big deal of it.

"To Lewis's? Like... his house?" I asked, feeling a small knot form in my stomach.

"Yeah," she replied. "He's not handling the whole divorce thing very well, so he asked me to come over and chat with him. Besides," she added with a slight hesitation, "it'd be nice to catch up. I haven't seen him in years."

My fingers tightened slightly around the steering wheel. "So, you're telling me you're going to see an ex of yours for a strictly platonic 'talk'?"

She let out a soft laugh, but I could sense the tension

underneath. "I guess you could say that. Look, I'm at his house now. I'll call you when I'm done, okay?" she said quickly before hanging up the phone.

I stared at my phone for a moment, the empty line echoing louder than it should. The rational part of me wanted to believe her, but I couldn't shake the thought of Lucy sitting in Lewis's house, with all their history.

Trying to distract myself, I entered the house and slumped down on the couch. A thought popped into my head—Dennis. I hadn't seen him in ages, and it might be good to catch up with him, especially tonight when I was feeling so restless. I pulled out my phone and dialed his number.

"Hey, Dennis, it's Ray," I said when he picked up.

"Oh, hey! What's up with you, man?" His voice was warm, familiar. It had been a while since we'd talked.

"Not much," I replied. "You want to hang out tonight?"

"Sure," Dennis said, sounding pleased. "I don't have any plans. What do you have in mind?"

I leaned back on the couch, already feeling a little lighter. "I don't care. Bar... bowling... whatever, I just need to get out of the house."

Dennis chuckled. "Alright, bar it is then. Come over in ten?"

"Yeah, I'll be there. Later, man," I said, hanging up the phone.

It felt good to know I'd be hanging out with Dennis again. We used to spend a lot of time together before Lucy and I got married. Even though we didn't see each other as much anymore, there was something about our friendship that never changed. No matter how much time passed, we could always pick up right where we left off. Dennis had been through three wives since Lucy and I got together, and he still hadn't found one that stuck. Maybe that's why he was always open to hang out—

no one else pulling him in different directions.

I stood up and started getting ready, my thoughts drifting back to Lucy and Lewis. I trusted Lucy, but it was impossible not to feel that nagging sense of unease. I pushed the thoughts aside. Tonight wasn't about that. Tonight was about catching up with an old friend.

On the drive to the bar, my mind wandered back to Lucy and Lewis. I couldn't help but wonder if they would end up having sex. It seemed almost inevitable, given their history and the way Lucy had embraced what she called her "newfound license to cheat." That phrase had stuck with me ever since she first said it, and the more I thought about it, the more I realized how much Lucy enjoyed this new freedom.

Lewis and Lucy had been together years ago, but they were always... complicated. The guy clearly had something—some way of getting her to do whatever he wanted. It wasn't his looks or his skill in bed, as Lucy had often mentioned the sex was nothing special. No, it was something else. He must've had a hell of a 'mouthpiece,' as Dennis used to call it. The guy knew how to talk her into things, and even after all these years, it seemed like that charm hadn't faded.

I shook my head, trying to clear the thoughts as I pulled into the parking lot. This wasn't the time to overthink it. Lucy knew what she was doing... right?

Inside, the bar was exactly as I remembered it. The dim lights, the low hum of conversations, and the familiar smell of stale beer and wood. Dennis was already there, sitting on a stool with a beer in hand. As soon as I walked in, he spotted me and grinned.

"About time, man!" he called out as I approached. "Lucy finally let you out tonight?" he added with a smirk.

"Ha ha," I muttered, rolling my eyes as I sat down next to him.

"Yeah, well, she's out with an old friend."

Dennis raised an eyebrow. "Oh yeah? That's what made you call me up for a hangout?"

"Something like that," I said, leaning against the bar. The bartender, George, nodded in my direction, already remembering my usual order. "Scotch on the rocks, as usual," I added.

Dennis waved over the bartender with a casual motion. "You heard the man. Hook it up, George."

As George got my drink, I looked around the place. This bar held so many memories for me and Dennis. It was the first place I drank legally after turning twenty-one, but Dennis, being five years older, used to sneak me drinks here long before I was of age. He had always been like a big brother, watching out for me, leading the way when I needed guidance—or trouble.

The scotch arrived, and I took a slow sip, letting the familiar burn settle in. I slouched over the bar, the weight of my thoughts pressing down on me. Finally, I blurted out, "So, Lucy's fucking some guy."

Dennis paused mid-sip, his eyebrows raised in surprise. "Oh yeah?" he asked, leaning back a bit. "And she told you this?"

I smirked, shaking my head. "Well... I was kind of there when it happened."

Dennis's laughter erupted from deep in his chest. He set his beer down, his eyes gleaming with amusement. "You're serious? You were there?"

I nodded, feeling the heat rise in my face. "Yeah, man. It's this whole thing we've gotten into. It's... weird, but it's fucking hot, you know?"

Dennis chuckled, clearly enjoying this revelation more than I expected. He knew me better than anyone else, and he knew about my fantasy—one I had never acted on before Lucy. "Damn, so it's really happening, huh?" he said, leaning in with interest.

I couldn't help but grin awkwardly. "Yeah... it's happening. With Lucy, of all people."

"Lucy?" Dennis's eyes lit up with something close to admiration, maybe even a little envy. "I mean, come on. That's wild."

I couldn't deny the strangeness of it all. I'd always trusted Lucy, but the idea of her having sex with another man, and me being okay with it—or even turned on by it—was something I never imagined fully embracing. Yet, here I was, talking about it openly with Dennis.

"It's really hot, though," I added, my voice lowering. "I never thought I'd be into it this much, but... I don't know, man. It's like this mix of jealousy and excitement, all rolled into one."

Dennis took another sip of his beer, his gaze thoughtful now. "Well, you've always had a thing for this kind of stuff. And Lucy... man, I don't blame you. She's sexy as hell."

He wasn't wrong. Dennis had always had a bit of a thing for Lucy himself. She had this habit of squatting down instead of bending over when she picked things up, and when she did, her jeans would ride down just enough to reveal a hint of her ass crack. Dennis used to mess with her, sliding his finger down the exposed part of her back just to get a rise out of her. It used to piss Lucy off, but it was all in good fun.

"You remember that time at your old place," Dennis said, grinning at the memory. "She was picking something up in the kitchen, and I got her right as she squatted down. She nearly smacked me, but I swear I saw her smile for a second."

I laughed, shaking my head. "Yeah, she was always good at pretending to be mad."

We both took a long drink, the easy camaraderie flowing back between us. Dennis's teasing was nothing new, and it helped lighten the weird tension I'd been feeling all day about Lucy and Lewis. Still, in the back of my mind, I couldn't help but wonder what was happening between them at that very moment.

"So, do I get a chance at her too?" Dennis asked, his smile wide and mischievous, clearly emboldened by the alcohol.

I laughed, finishing off my drink. "You're more than welcome to try," I replied, smirking. The whole idea seemed absurd, though the alcohol made it easier to joke about. The thought of Dennis, my best friend, trying to have sex with Lucy felt strange, even a bit surreal. He was overweight, not exactly Lucy's type, and definitely not someone she'd ever shown interest in. That was part of the reason his finger-down-the-crack-of-her-jeans routine used to piss her off so much. Still, it was all in good fun.

Dennis raised his glass and grinned, clearly entertained by the conversation. We continued talking, the beers flowing as we delved into old memories and banter. Hours passed, the drinks stacking up, and the bar's usual buzz growing louder around us.

It wasn't until my phone vibrated in my pocket that I realized how long we'd been there. I pulled it out and saw a text from Lucy. Downing the last of my drink, I glanced over at Dennis, who was starting to show the signs of his intoxication. His eyes were a little glassier, his posture more relaxed.

"Hey, I gotta run," I said, slipping my phone back into my pocket as I stood. "Are you going to be okay to drive?" I grinned at him, knowing how much he'd had.

Dennis waved me off, patting me on the back with a sloppy grin. "Yeah, you know me," he said, his voice thick with the effects of the night.

I nodded, though I wasn't entirely convinced. "Alright, man. Take care," I said, heading for the door. The cold air hit me as I stepped outside, waking me up a bit as I walked to my car.

Once inside, I started the engine and pulled out my phone again. The text from Lucy flashed on the screen: "On my way home... See you in a few."

I quickly replied, "You're just now leaving Lewis's?" The question lingered in my mind as I hit send, wondering what had kept her there for so long.

A few minutes passed as I sat there, pondering the implications. Finally, her reply came: "Yeah."

The response didn't give me much to go on, so I pressed a little more. "Why so long?" I typed, sending the message before I could second-guess myself.

Another minute passed, and then her reply: "We'll talk when I get home, driving right now."

I let out a quiet sigh, still unsure what to make of it. There was an odd mix of jealousy and curiosity stirring inside me, the kind I'd gotten used to ever since Lucy had started seeing other men. I couldn't help but wonder what had really happened with Lewis, but I pushed the thoughts aside as I drove home.

We didn't live far from the bar, so I beat Lucy back to the house. After kicking off my shoes and tossing my coat aside, I settled on the couch, flicking through channels to kill time. The hum of the TV filled the otherwise quiet house, but my mind was elsewhere —caught between the conversation with Dennis and the cryptic texts from Lucy.

A few minutes later, I heard the familiar sound of her car pulling into the driveway, followed by the soft clink of keys as she unlocked the front door.

"Hey," I called out as she walked in, pulling off her coat. "I hung out with Dennis tonight. We went to The Breeze."

"Oh, really?" she replied, sounding casual as she hung up her coat and walked over. "What's he up to these days?"

"Same old," I said, watching her settle into the living room. Then, without missing a beat, I dropped the bomb. "I told him about what we've been doing."

Lucy's eyes widened in surprise, her hand freezing mid-motion. "You did?" she exclaimed. "And what did he say to that?"

I smirked, enjoying her reaction. "He just laughed. Said he figured I'd convince you sooner or later." I paused for dramatic effect, then added with a mischievous grin, "Oh, and he also asked if he could get in on it."

Her eyes narrowed, lips curling into a half-smile. "He did, huh?" she said, clearly amused. "Dennis always had a thing for me, didn't he?"

I laughed, shaking my head. "Yeah, I'm pretty sure he's been eyeing you since day one."

Lucy chuckled softly, moving closer as she sat beside me. "Well, tell him to keep dreaming."

"I'm sure you don't have anything to worry about," I said, laying my hand gently on her thigh as she sat down next to me on the couch. "He'd never even try anything, even if he knew I was okay with it and thought he had a shot." I squeezed her leg lightly, reassuring her. "It's not his style."

Lucy shook her head with a small, knowing smile, acknowledging what I said. But there was a mischievous glint in her eyes as she shifted, getting on her knees in front of me. She reached out, coupling my hands in hers, her face lighting up with excitement.

"Well, guess what I did tonight?" she asked, her voice playful, the smile widening across her lips.

I tilted my head, playing along. "Uh... let me guess, something sexual with Lewis?" I replied with a grin, already sensing where this was headed.

Lucy made a mock-annoyed face, sticking out her tongue at me. "Don't take the fun out of it," she pouted, but quickly her expression turned sultry. "But yes," she added, her voice dropping into a teasing tone, "we fucked."

I couldn't help but smile at her confession. "Aren't we a dirty slut," I teased, my hand drifting higher on her thigh as I spoke. The thrill of her words, combined with her playful attitude, was enough to stir something deep inside me.

She shot me a wicked grin in return, rising gracefully to her feet as she began unzipping the back of her dress. "Don't you know it," she quipped, pulling the top of the dress down and exposing her naked breasts, her nipples hardening in the cool air. There was no bra, and as she let the dress fall further, I realized she wasn't wearing any panties either. The sight of her completely bare beneath the dress sent a jolt of arousal through me.

She stepped closer, her eyes locked onto mine as she climbed onto my lap, straddling me. Her voice softened but stayed playful. "You want to fuck?" she asked, her lips curling into a seductive smile.

I raised an eyebrow, chuckling softly. "Didn't you just do that?" I teased, leaning back slightly as my hands rested on her hips.

Lucy laughed, her breasts brushing against my chest as she leaned in closer. "Well... some things never change," she purred. "It was more like he did, sort of, and I just laid there while he fumbled around." She rolled her eyes with a playful smirk, clearly unimpressed by the encounter. "But I'm really horny because..." Her voice dropped to a conspiratorial whisper. "...he's still really good with his tongue."

Her naughty laugh filled the room as she reached down, her fingers deftly working at the buckle of my belt. She pulled the leather strap loose with ease, her hands moving to the button of my pants.

"So... other than the failed sex," I said, my voice teasing as she tugged my pants down over my hips. "I'm guessing he went down on you, right?"

"Um..." Lucy began, her eyes flicking to mine as her fingers wrapped around my soft cock. "I sucked his cock for a while, and yeah, he did go down on me... for a long time, actually." Her voice trailed off as she gently stroked me, her touch slow and deliberate. "I mean, it felt good," she admitted, a small smirk playing on her lips, "but I didn't cum."

As she continued to stroke me, her grip tightened just enough to make me harder with each passing second. "He's still as small as I remember though," she added with a soft chuckle, her eyes gleaming with amusement. "Which, to be honest, made the sex a little boring."

Her chuckle vibrated in the air as she bent down, her lips parting as she took me into her mouth. The warmth of her mouth engulfed my cock, and I couldn't help but let out a low groan. I watched as she slowly pushed her mouth all the way down my shaft, taking me deep with little effort, her lips brushing against the base of my cock.

"Wow," I managed to breathe out, my fingers brushing through her hair. "You're getting pretty good at this whole deep-throat thing, aren't you?"

"Mm hmm," she murmured, the vibration of her voice sending ripples of pleasure through me. Her hand wrapped around the base of my cock, guiding her mouth as she started to bob her head faster. Each time she moved down, her tongue slid teasingly along my balls, and every time she came up, the tip of her tongue flicked against the sensitive head of my cock.

The sensation was intoxicating, and I felt myself getting lost in the rhythm of her mouth. She pulled away for a moment, a strand of saliva still connecting her lips to the head of my cock, her breath warm against my skin. Her hands took over, stroking me with practiced ease as she looked up at me, her eyes gleaming.

"Okay..." she said with a smirk, standing up from her knees and wiping her lips. "Trade me."

I smiled as she stepped aside, my body already aching with anticipation. I stood up and turned, watching as she plopped down onto the couch, her legs spreading wide in front of me. Her naked pussy was already glistening with arousal, and her smile was wicked and full of promise.

"Hmmm... okay," she purred, her voice low and sultry as she leaned back into the cushions. "I'm ready for this."

Her grin was persuasive, drawing me in as I kneeled between her legs. The heat radiating from her body made me throb in response, and as I positioned myself between her thighs, I could feel the pull of desire tightening between us.

I hadn't been down on my knees for long when Lucy suddenly stopped me, her hands grabbing hold of my ears, pulling me back up to face her. Her eyes were bright with desire, but her voice was firm.

"No," she said, her breath quickening. "I want to feel your dick."

Without hesitation, I rose from my knees, moving myself closer to her as she spread her legs wider, allowing me to position myself between her thighs. She was already dripping wet, and the moment I pushed forward, my cock slid into her with ease. Lucy let out a sharp gasp, her hands gripping my arms as I fell into her, the heat between us building immediately.

I started with slow, deliberate thrusts, my hips rocking in a steady rhythm as I leaned closer, my lips hovering just above hers. "Tell me about Lewis," I whispered, the words barely audible, but the tension clear.

Lucy's eyes flickered with a mix of surprise and excitement. "What do you want me to tell you?" she asked, her voice soft and breathy, her chest rising and falling with each shallow breath.

"How did he fuck you?" I murmured, my thrusts deepening as I spoke. "Where were you?"

Her legs tightened around my waist, and she shifted, repositioning her feet above her head, allowing me to thrust deeper. "Mmm... he started to lick my pussy," she said with a radiant smile, her hips rising to meet each of my movements. "Kind of sitting just like we are now."

"Oh yeah?" I whispered, my lips brushing against hers as I continued to pump into her, the steady rhythm quickening slightly at the thought of her with Lewis.

"Yeah..." she moaned, her hands roaming over my back, fingers digging into my skin. "He licked me for a while," she continued, her voice faltering as small whimpers escaped her lips. "Then he sat up... and fucked me like this."

Her words were punctuated by soft moans as I began to thrust faster, spurred on by the mental image of them together. "Go on," I urged, my grip on her hips tightening as I pulled her closer to me, one of her legs now resting on my forearm.

Lucy's breathing hitched as she spoke. "Not long after..." she gasped, "I went down... and sucked his cock." Her hands slid up to cup my face as she locked her gaze on mine, her lips curling into a wicked smile. "It didn't take him long to shoot on my face," she added, her voice dropping to a sultry whisper.

I groaned at her words, my hips moving with more urgency as I pressed her deeper into the couch, the heat between us intensifying. "Was that all?" I asked, my voice strained with desire as I shifted, lifting her right leg higher, angling myself for deeper thrusts.

Lucy let out a soft cry, her fingers tangling in my hair as she brought her face closer to mine, her tongue flicking playfully against my lips before she kissed me deeply. "Oh no," she murmured between breaths, her voice laced with pleasure. "After a rest... I told him I needed to take a shower."

Her eyes gleamed as she paused, letting the moment hang in the air.

"And?" I pressed, my body moving faster, the anticipation driving me wild.

"And when I got in," she whispered, her lips brushing against mine, "he decided to join me." A sly smile spread across her face as she playfully darted her tongue out, teasing my mouth. "He couldn't keep his hands off me... we fucked again, under the water."

"He didn't last long though," Lucy continued, her voice heavy with arousal, "and pulled out... came all over my ass." Her breath hitched as she spoke, her words coming faster now, driven by the growing intensity between us.

Her moans became more urgent, her breathing heavier with every thrust. "Oh... fuck me, Ray!" she gasped, her legs wrapping tightly around my waist. Her hands found the back of my head, pulling me closer as her hips rocked in time with mine, each movement more deliberate, more demanding.

I could feel her taking control of the rhythm, the pace quickening as she gripped my head tighter, her breath hot against my skin. "Oh... bite my nipples, baby," she urged, her voice filled with both command and need.

Without hesitation, I lowered my head to her breasts, my lips brushing against her soft skin before I took one of her nipples into my mouth. I licked it gently, teasing at first, before biting down just hard enough to elicit a sharp gasp from her. The heat of her skin and the salty taste made my heart race as I moved to the other nipple, biting a little harder this time.

Lucy's body responded immediately, her moans filling the room as her hips bucked against mine, her movements becoming more frantic. I tried to keep up with her increasing speed, my hands gripping her hips to match her harder, faster thrusts. The feeling of her tight, wet pussy squeezing around me sent shivers through my body.

"Oh fuck!" she screamed, her voice raw with pleasure. "I'm cumming!"

Her body tensed beneath me, her legs tightening around my sides as she reached the peak of her orgasm, her hips grinding against me. I felt her pulsing around me, her whole body shuddering as she let out a long, desperate moan.

As her movements slowed, I took the opportunity to quicken my thrusts, chasing my own release. But before I could reach it, Lucy pushed me back, her hands firm on my chest. She was panting, her eyes wide with a mischievous gleam.

Without a word, she stood up quickly, shoving me onto the couch where she had been lying moments before. The switch in positions left me breathless as she dropped to her knees between my legs, her eyes locked onto mine with a sultry grin.

Without hesitation, she took my still-throbbing cock into her mouth, resuming the deep, rhythmic sucking she'd perfected earlier. Her hands worked my shaft in sync with her mouth, her tongue swirling over the head with every upward motion. I groaned, my hands gripping the couch, my body alive with sensation as she pushed me closer and closer to the edge.

"Oh..." I gasped, my voice ragged. "I want to cum on your tits."

Lucy continued to work her mouth over my cock, her tongue swirling expertly around the head, sending jolts of pleasure through me. I was so close, my body tense with anticipation, every muscle wound tight as I approached the edge of release.

My breath was ragged, and I could feel the pressure building in my core.

But then, just as I was about to let go, Lucy slowed down. Her hand, which had been stroking me steadily, suddenly loosened its grip, and she began to move at an agonizingly slow pace. I groaned in frustration, my hips instinctively trying to thrust up into her hand, but she held me firmly in place.

"Not so fast," she teased, her lips curling into a wicked smile as she looked up at me, her hand still lazily stroking my cock. "I'm not done playing with you yet."

I groaned again, my body aching for release, but she didn't speed up. Instead, she took me right to the edge once more, her hand moving faster, my body tensing as I braced for the orgasm that was just seconds away. But again, she slowed down, pulling me back from the brink with a teasing grin.

"Lucy... please..." I gasped, barely able to speak through the haze of frustration and desire. My cock twitched in her hand, desperate for some kind of release, but she just kept me teetering on the edge.

She chuckled softly, clearly enjoying every second of my torment. "You're so easy to tease," she whispered, her hand picking up speed again, her fingers wrapping tightly around me, stroking me faster, bringing me closer and closer to the breaking point.

This time, I was sure it would happen—sure she was going to let me cum. But just as I felt that familiar surge, she slowed down again, her hand barely moving now, my cock throbbing in her grip.

I couldn't take it anymore. My body was on fire, every nerve buzzing with need. I needed to cum, and I needed it now.

Finally, after what felt like an eternity, Lucy lowered her mouth onto my cock again. I gasped in relief as her warm lips slid over me, her tongue flicking against the sensitive tip. Her mouth moved down, taking me deep, her hand working in perfect rhythm with her mouth.

I was sure—certain—this was it. I was going to cum in her mouth, and the relief would be blissful. My body tensed, my hips lifting slightly off the bed as I felt the orgasm surging forward, my breath catching in my throat.

But then, just as the sensation was about to explode, Lucy suddenly pulled her mouth away. Her hand released me completely, and she sat up straight, a playful grin on her lips as she watched me with amusement.

I stared at her in disbelief. "Lucy, no... please..." I groaned, but she just laughed softly, clearly relishing in my torment.

I could feel my cock twitching, spasming, desperate for some kind of stimulation, but there was nothing. No hand, no mouth —just the empty air and my body's need for release.

And then, it happened.

I watched helplessly as my cock spasmed again, the built-up tension finally too much for my body to hold back. I came without any touch, thick ropes of cum spurting from my cock and landing all over the bed. My body shuddered as I watched, still barely able to believe what had just happened.

Lucy laughed, a low, teasing sound that made my stomach flip. "You came without me even touching you," she said, her voice full of amusement. "I guess I teased you pretty badly, huh?"

I let out a long, frustrated breath, my body still aching from the denial of proper release. The orgasm had been strong, sure, but something about it felt... incomplete. Unfinished.

Lucy curled up next to me, still giggling softly as she pulled the covers over us. I lay there, my cock still twitching slightly as the last remnants of my orgasm faded away, my mind racing.

As we settled into bed, Lucy pressed a soft kiss to my cheek. "Goodnight," she whispered, her tone still playful.

But as I drifted off to sleep, a lingering sense of frustration remained. Even though I had cum, it didn't feel satisfying. I still felt on edge, as though I hadn't really been allowed to finish properly.

A DRIVE INTO
THE KNOWN

I t was Friday night, and Lucy and I were curled up on the couch, watching one of our usual rom-coms. I'd always had a soft spot for them, not that I was embarrassed to admit it. They had a certain charm, even if they were a little too neat and tidy for real life. But tonight, with Lucy snuggled into my side, the movie was just background noise to the comfort of her warmth.

As we lay there, Lucy began absentmindedly tracing her fingers along my arm, the gentle strokes sending shivers down my skin. "You know," she started, her voice soft and thoughtful, "I've been thinking..." She paused, letting her words hang for a moment. "I don't think I'm going to sleep with Lewis again."

I shifted slightly, surprised by the sudden mention of Lewis, though I kept my expression neutral. "Yeah?" I asked, curious but letting her continue at her own pace.

"Yeah," she said, glancing up at me. "He's kind of a hot mess with everything going on with his wife, and honestly... I don't need the drama."

I looked down at her, catching the slight furrow of her brow, and bent down to kiss her forehead. "Whatever you want, babe," I murmured, my lips brushing softly against her skin.

She smiled back at me, the kind of smile that always made my chest feel warm, then snuggled closer, her attention turning back to the movie. I squeezed her gently, content to stay like this for as long as she wanted.

The movie was nearing its predictable end when her phone, which had been sitting quietly on the coffee table, buzzed with a notification. She leaned forward to grab it, her fingers sliding across the screen as she unlocked it. From where I sat, I had a clear view of the message, though I wasn't exactly trying to sneak a peek.

It was a text from Steve.

"At the bar, you feel like coming down?"

I watched her read it, my heart picking up pace just slightly. There was something about seeing that message from Steve, knowing she was on his mind. Lucy glanced up at me, catching my eye, clearly aware that I had seen the text. Her lips curled into a half-smile.

"What do you think?" she asked, her tone casual but laced with a hint of excitement. "It's still pretty early, and it is Friday night."

I glanced at the clock. She was right. It was only half-past nine, and the movie was wrapping up. There wasn't any reason she shouldn't go, and part of me was already intrigued by what might unfold.

"I don't see a problem with that," I said, leaning in to kiss her forehead again. The familiar scent of her shampoo filled my senses, and I felt the usual stirring of anticipation deep in my stomach.

She grinned, a glint of excitement flashing in her eyes as she quickly typed out a reply to Steve. The sound of her nails tapping against the screen filled the room for a brief second before she set the phone down and stood up from the couch.

Just as she was about to head upstairs, she paused, turning back to me with a playful smile. "You don't care if I don't finish the movie, do you?" she asked, her voice teasing but sincere.

I chuckled softly. "Nah," I said, waving her off. "Go have fun."

Her smile widened, and she leaned down to give me a quick kiss on the lips before heading toward the stairs to get ready. I watched her go, my mind already swirling with thoughts about what the night might bring.

It had been a few weeks since she'd last seen Steve, that night when they had sex in our woods. But she talked about him often. She mentioned they'd been texting a lot, and even talking on the phone when she was at work. It was clear she was enjoying his company—or at least the idea of many more outings together. The age difference, which had initially been a point of hesitation, no longer seemed to bother her. And honestly, I liked the guy. He was easy to talk to, and he fit right in when we hung out around the fire.

As I sat there, finishing the movie by myself, my thoughts kept drifting back to Lucy and Steve. What was it about him that excited her so much? Was it his youth, the novelty? Whatever it was, it seemed to keep pulling her back toward him.

About half an hour later, I heard her footsteps on the stairs. When she appeared, I turned to see her standing in front of me, clearly ready for the night. She paraded across the living room in an all-black cotton dress that ended just above her knees, her strappy black open-toed shoes clicking softly on the floor. I noticed immediately that she wasn't wearing a bra—her nipples were slightly visible, pressing against the thin fabric. The sight sent a small surge of excitement through me, and I couldn't help but wonder if she had decided to forgo panties as well.

Since they'd only had sex the one time, the thought of her going out like that made me curious. If she wasn't wearing any panties tonight, did that mean she was hoping for another round with Steve? The possibility sent my mind racing.

"So," she asked, spinning around playfully, her dress swirling around her legs. "How do I look?"

Her blonde hair was pinned up in a loose, elegant updo, with her bangs falling just slightly over her eyes. She wore long, dangling earrings with emeralds at the ends—her birthstone, and a subtle touch of elegance that made her look even more striking. I took a moment to appreciate how put-together she looked, from her confident posture to the glint of excitement in her eyes.

"Very sexy," I replied, my voice a bit lower than I intended, my eyes tracing the curve of her body.

She smiled as she turned toward the closet, her hand reaching for her coat. "I'd like to say I'll be back around two-thirty, when the bar closes..." She pulled the coat from its hanger and paused, glancing back at me with a playful glint in her eye. "But, you know..." She cracked a smile. "If I get lucky, it may take a bit more time."

My eyebrows shot up at her comment. That certainly answered my unspoken question about the panties. "So, you're hoping to get lucky, are you?" I asked, grinning with a mix of curiosity and eagerness.

She walked over to the front door, pulling it open as she zipped up her black fuzzy coat, which hung just below her ass. She turned back one last time, her hand on the doorknob, her eyes dancing with excitement. "Well, hell yeah. I want to see if the sex with him is just as good inside as it was outside," she teased with a smile, before opening the storm door.

I couldn't help but chuckle at her playful response. "Alright, love you, babe," I called after her.

"See you later," she said over her shoulder as she stepped out, pulling the door closed behind her.

The click of the door echoed in the now-quiet house, and with it, that familiar feeling settled into my chest—a strange blend of excitement, curiosity, and something deeper, harder to name. She had already had sex with three different men in the last few months, and most of it played out exactly as I had imagined when I first coaxed her into exploring this part of her desires.

Except for Jordan. He had thrown a wrench into things, making me feel... well, more conflicted than I'd expected. But with Steve, it was different. I liked him, and the thought of her with him didn't stir that same unease. If anything, I was more curious—wondering how the night might unfold for her, and maybe for us.

The jealousy that had once been sharp and biting was becoming less severe. In fact, it was starting to feel... normal. Strange, really—how quickly things had shifted. Now, every time Lucy left the house, part of me assumed she might be hooking up with someone, and I'd be left waiting to hear about it after the fact. But even that had changed. She no longer felt the need to ask for my approval or coax me into it. She was taking the reins more often, steering the ship of our marriage with a confidence that was both unsettling and thrilling. She had grown comfortable in this new dynamic—her freedom expanding with each encounter.

And oddly enough, I was beginning to enjoy it, too. There was something liberating about letting go, about allowing her to explore this part of herself. It was like stepping into a new reality, where the rules we once followed had shifted into something far more flexible.

We had picked out two movies for the night on Netflix, but it appeared I'd be watching the second one alone. I loaded it up, hoping it would be engaging enough to distract me from the gnawing thought that Lucy might be getting fucked tonight. That familiar tension stirred in my chest as I started the movie, heading to the kitchen to grab a beer.

About twenty minutes into the film, my phone buzzed in my pocket, pulling my attention away from the screen. I fished it out and saw Lucy's picture flashing on the screen, her avatar lighting up with a new message. I swiped it open and read her text:

"OK, so we're not hanging out at the bar. We're leaving."

A quick pang of excitement mixed with curiosity hit me. My fingers tapped quickly on the screen as I sent a reply: "Where to?"

Her response came almost immediately: "Not sure. If I don't get too busy, I'll update you."

If I don't get too busy.

Those words hung in the air, playing on a loop in my mind. My head swirled with images, trying to piece together what could be happening. Were they going to check into a hotel? Was she heading back to his place? My mind painted vivid pictures of Lucy with Steve, and though I tried to keep myself grounded, it was hard not to wonder. Not to imagine the possibilities—the scenarios that could be playing out tonight.

I shifted on the couch, taking a long swig of my beer, trying to focus on the movie, but it was no use. My thoughts kept drifting back to Lucy, to what she might be doing, to whether Steve had his hands on her now, the way I imagined he did. I shook my head, forcing myself to turn back to the screen, but the film was just background noise at this point.

The movie ended a little after midnight, and still, I hadn't heard anything more from Lucy. A flicker of disappointment ran through me—part of me had been hoping for more updates, maybe even a play-by-play. But I reminded myself that this was what I'd wanted—her freedom, her control.

I decided I'd sleep in our bed tonight. The couch was too rough on my back, and I didn't feel like waiting up any longer. Heading upstairs, I opened the bedroom door and was hit with the quiet stillness of the room. I slid into bed, pulling the covers over me, my mind still racing with the images of Lucy's night. What would she tell me when she got back? Would she be flushed, still glowing from whatever happened? Or would it be like any other night—casual, as though nothing extraordinary had taken place?

I closed my eyes, but the anticipation still buzzed under my skin.

I was awoken by the softest kiss on my forehead, stirring me from a light sleep. Groggily, I opened my eyes to find Lucy standing over me, her silhouette faintly illuminated by the dim light of the room. I sat up slowly, rubbing the sleep from my eyes as I watched her reach down and peel off her black dress, letting it slip to the floor in a quiet heap. My suspicions had been right—she had been out all night without panties. As the dress pooled at her feet, she stood before me completely naked, her skin glowing faintly in the soft light.

Without a word, she climbed into bed beside me, gently pushing me to slide over as she made room for herself under the covers. Her bare feet pressed against mine, sending a subtle thrill through me. I felt her fingers trace over my chest hair, moving in slow, lazy circles. Her touch was light, teasing, and it made the anticipation inside me grow stronger.

"So... how was everything?" I asked, my voice still thick with sleep but filled with curiosity.

She giggled softly, her hand moving down to rest on my stomach as she continued to swirl her fingers across my skin. "Oh... pretty good," she said, her tone casual, but there was a playful gleam in her eyes.

I waited, hoping she would elaborate on her outing, but she didn't say anything more. Instead, she kept rubbing her feet against mine, her touch soft and warm, while her fingers traced idle patterns across my skin. The silence stretched between us, and I could feel my erection growing in my pants, the anticipation of hearing about her night turning into a physical ache.

"Well..." I prompted, my voice edged with impatience

"Well, what?" she replied, her expression blank, though I could sense the teasing in her voice. Her hand drifted lower, grazing the waistband of my boxers.

"Are you going to give me any details?" I asked, my hand instinctively moving over my growing bulge, rubbing myself through the fabric of my shorts.

Lucy looked at me with a playful, almost puzzled look on her face. "Who says there's anything much to tell?" she teased, her fingers now lightly brushing my stomach, sending sparks of excitement through me.

I couldn't help but chuckle at her coyness. "Because I know you," I said, my voice low and eager. "And you just spent the night out with a 25-year-old... the same one you've already sucked off and had sex with," I added, hoping my joke would coax a story out of her.

She smirked, her hand lingering at the waistband of my boxers as if considering whether to continue teasing me or give in to my curiosity. The room felt charged with the unspoken tension between us, and I could feel my pulse quicken as I waited for her to reveal what had happened.

She snickered softly, her foot gliding up and down my leg in a slow, teasing rhythm. "Oh..." she began, her voice light with amusement. "Are you asking if I had sex with Steve tonight?"

I nodded, my heart picking up pace as my erection grew even harder beneath the covers. The anticipation was almost unbearable. My stomach felt hollow, a knot of tension twisting inside me as I waited for her next words.

"Well..." she said, drawing it out, clearly enjoying the control she had over the situation. "We were only at the bar for a few minutes before he suggested we go for a drive." Her voice was soft, teasing, as she flashed me a faint smile. Her hand slid lower, gently moving mine aside as she took over. "We didn't drive far, just stopped in that empty field not far from the bar."

I could feel her fingers rubbing my cock through my boxer shorts, her touch light but firm, sending waves of pleasure coursing through me. Her other hand propped her head up, her eyes locked on mine, watching my reaction. Every movement of her hand, every word, only heightened my arousal.

"Did you park in the field?" I asked, my voice shaky with excitement as her hand expertly fondled me, moving from my balls to the head of my cock in slow, deliberate strokes.

"Yes," she whispered, her tone dropping lower, more intimate. "We started kissing... and necking." As she spoke, she slid my boxers down, freeing my cock. Her hand wrapped around me, jerking me slowly, teasingly. "He slid my dress up... and began to rub my clit, gently," she added, her voice barely above a whisper as she continued stroking me, her touch sending jolts of pleasure through my body.

My heart pounded in my chest, my breath coming faster now. The thought of her with Steve, sitting in a parked car, her dress hiked up while he kissed her and rubbed her, made my pulse race. The jealousy and excitement tangled together, filling me with an almost unbearable arousal. I could feel my palms start to sweat, my body reacting to the vivid imagery she painted with her words.

Just knowing that another man had been sitting there, touching her like that—her clit under his fingers, her body responding to him—made my cock throb in her hand. And as Lucy continued her slow, rhythmic stroking, I found myself completely lost in the story, the tension building with each passing second.

"As I began to get wet, he could easily slide a finger into me..." she murmured, her hand still slowly fondling my cock. Her words were soft, tantalizing, pulling me deeper into the story. "He started slow, teasing me... but it didn't take long until he was shoving it deeper as we kissed harder. Then he went for two fingers after I slid my hand into his jeans to feel his hard cock." Her voice lowered, and she tightened her grip around my shaft, increasing the pressure as she spoke.

The vivid image of her hand wrapped around Steve's cock, sliding into his jeans, only fueled the arousal already boiling inside me. I could barely contain myself.

"I moved so he could pull his pants down, hiked my dress up, and climbed on top of him," she continued, her hand moving faster now, her words spilling out in a rhythm that matched the jerking of my cock. "I started grinding my bare, wet pussy on his dick, just rubbing it against him, teasing him, feeling how hard he was. I did that a few times... until he just slipped right inside me."

Her words hit me like a wave, and my heart pounded in my chest. I could almost picture it—her grinding on top of him, feeling the slick heat of her body against his cock, the tension between them before he finally entered her. The way she told it, her voice filled with casual excitement, made me even harder.

"I started riding him," she whispered, "slowly at first, but I couldn't help myself. I began to speed up, grinding harder, and it wasn't long before I came, my body shaking on top of him. He pulled my tits out of my dress and sucked on them while I came."

I couldn't take it anymore. I took over, stroking myself faster now as she continued to recount every detail. The vividness of her description sent shivers through me. I was hanging on her every word, lost in the story of her night.

"He kept fucking me," she added, a smile playing at the corners of her lips as she licked her bottom lip. "And I wound up cumming again."

"Yeah?" I asked, breathless, my hand still working at my cock as I urged her to keep going.

"Yes," she purred, her voice thick with satisfaction. "It was really hot. I hadn't fucked in a car since high school, and it thrilled me. He tried to bend me over the console, but his car was too small... sports car, you know. So we stepped outside." She gave me that grin again, the one that sent heat rushing through me. "He bent me over the hood and began pounding me from behind."

I let out a low groan, unable to hide how much her words turned me on. "Oh... I love how much of a slut you are," I said, the words spilling from my lips as I stroked myself even harder.

"I know," she replied, her grin widening. "I'm starting to enjoy it too." There was a gleam in her eyes, a thrill in her voice that only drove me wilder. That look—knowing I was okay with her slutty behavior—seemed to make it easier for her to act on her desires. "Then he lifted me up onto the hood," she continued, her hand now drifting lazily through my chest hair again, "and I opened my legs, inviting his cock inside me... but he had other plans."

Lucy snickered softly, her foot still gliding up and down my leg. "He went down on me," she began, her voice low and teasing. Her fingers lazily traced circles on my chest, almost as if she was casually talking about any other part of her night.

I swallowed, my heart quickening, my cock throbbing in anticipation. "And?" I asked, trying to keep my voice steady, but the question came out more eager than I intended.

She grinned, sensing the effect her words had on me. "He licked my pussy... and I actually came again," she said, her tone carrying that unmistakable excitement.

I felt a jolt run through me, the image of it flashing in my mind. She came for him again. My stomach twisted, the jealousy biting at me, but right alongside it was something else—something darker, hotter.

"I don't know if it was the thrill of being out in the open... or maybe just the feeling of my youth again," she continued, her voice soft but filled with a casual kind of thrill. Her hand slid lower, brushing over my stomach now, sending jolts of anticipation through me. "But I was so turned on. It was almost too easy for me to cum tonight."

I could barely respond. My breath came in shallow gasps, my cock now painfully hard as her words fueled the swirling storm of emotions inside me. "And after you came?" I managed to ask, my voice catching in my throat.

"He heard me climax," she said with a soft giggle, "and that's when he slid himself inside me... right there on the hood of his car." Her eyes sparkled as she added, "He grabbed my hips, pulled me closer, and started fucking me hard."

My mouth went dry, the tension between us thickening with every word she spoke. My mind spun, trying to process the rush of conflicting emotions—the jealousy, the arousal, the need to know every brutal detail.

"And then?" I pressed, my heart hammering in my chest, my whole body tense, waiting for the next part.

She looked down at me, her lips curling into a mischievous smile. "Then... he reached in to feel my ass while he fucked me harder."

I could feel my heart racing as she spoke, my cock now painfully hard as I imagined her being taken like that, the vivid imagery sending waves of excitement and jealousy through me.

She paused, her lips curling into a playful pout as she looked down at me. "He came in me... so, I want to know if you mind if I ride your face now."

I swallowed hard, the words hitting me like a jolt. I shifted to the side, making room for her as she straddled my face, lowering herself down. As soon as my lips made contact with her soaked pussy, I was hit by the overwhelming taste of salt and dampness. It was more cum than I had ever tasted before—so much so that it was almost unbearable. It filled my mouth, coating my tongue with Steve's thick, sticky seed, mixed with her own juices. My stomach twisted in disgust for a moment, but then her moans broke through, pulling me back into the moment.

I wanted to make her feel good. That was all that mattered now.

I shoved my tongue deeper inside her, my hands gripping her hips as she began to rock against my face. The intensity of the taste, the sheer volume of cum dripping from her pussy, almost made me gag. But I forced myself to push through it, determined to please her, to give her the best oral sex I could. Her moans grew louder, her movements more urgent as she ground her pussy against my nose, riding my face harder and faster.

The more she moaned, the more I wanted her to cum. I twisted my tongue, licking her clit in rapid strokes, ignoring the thick, salty cum that continued to flood my mouth. My jaw ached, and my stomach churned from the taste, but I refused to stop. I could feel her body tensing above me, her breathing quickening, and then, suddenly, she let out a sharp cry of pleasure.

"Oh... yes... yes..." she gasped, her whole body trembling as she came hard, her juices spilling onto my face. I could barely breathe, but the sound of her climax was everything. I sucked in her juices, swallowing what I could, even as the sensation of another man's cum inside her continued to gnaw at me.

Finally, she pulled away, climbing off my face with a satisfied sigh. She rolled onto her side next to me, her hand trailing across my chest as she kissed my cheek. "That was nice," she murmured, her voice soft, content.

But I wasn't finished. My cock was painfully hard, throbbing with the need for release. I shifted, hoping she would notice, but instead, she nuzzled into the pillow, her eyes heavy with sleep. I gently reached for her, trying to coax her into taking care of me, but she brushed my hand away with a lazy smile.

"Mmm... I'm too tired now," she said with a soft giggle. "I've had all the cock I can handle tonight... but you can take care of yourself, babe."

Her words stung. I lay there, watching as she rolled over, pulling the blanket up around her naked body. The heat of the moment faded slightly, but my cock was still rock-hard, desperate for release. She lay next to me, fully satisfied, while I was left with nothing but my own hand to finish the job.

I hesitated for a moment, conflicted and confused. But the aching need in my body outweighed the frustration in my mind. Slowly, I began to stroke myself, my eyes flicking to Lucy's still form beside me. She didn't move, didn't offer to help. Instead, she reached over to the nightstand, grabbed her vape, and took a long drag as I continued jerking off, the glow from the vape illuminating her face in the dim room.

Her indifference only fueled my desire, and soon I was close. My hand moved faster, my breath ragged as I felt the orgasm building, so close, but still out of reach. Then, just as I was about to cum, she glanced over at me, her expression calm, almost amused.

I groaned as the orgasm hit me hard, my cock twitching in my hand as I came everywhere—hot spurts of cum spilling over my chest, onto the bed, even hitting the blanket. Lucy watched, silent, as I finished. The satisfaction I craved didn't come. Instead, there was only that same hollow feeling, that same lingering conflict.

She smiled faintly, leaned over, and kissed me on the cheek. "Goodnight, babe," she whispered, her lips brushing my skin before she rolled over, turning her back to me.

I lay there, my body spent but my mind racing, unsure of what to feel. The release had come, but it felt empty. Even as sleep crept in, the confusion and conflict lingered, gnawing at me like an unanswered question.

NEXT STEPS

Saturday afternoon, as we sat together on the couch, Lucy casually mentioned that Steve had texted her earlier. "He asked if he could come over today," she said, her eyes gleaming with that playful spark I'd come to recognize whenever Steve was involved. "I thought it might be fun if he played Canasta with us."

I smiled, though the game was not my strong suit. Lucy adored Canasta, and no matter how many hours I spent practicing online, I could never come close to beating her. "Sure, why not?" I replied. "I could use another shot at trying to beat you." I chuckled, already knowing my fate. She was practically a master, and I was always the amateur, no matter how much I tried.

She grinned, clearly pleased with the idea. "Great. I'll set it up," she said, grabbing her phone to text Steve back. "I'm sure he'll love it. Plus, it'll be fun to see how he does his first time."

Steve had been becoming more than just a friend to her—he was what she teasingly called a 'special' friend. I didn't mind, though. Honestly, I liked Steve. He was a cool kid, and despite the jealousy that sometimes crept in, there was something undeniably thrilling about the sexual adventures he took my wife on. Ever since the night in the abandoned field, I found myself eagerly anticipating their next encounter. What would happen this time? Where would their fun take them next?

When Steve arrived later that afternoon, we gathered around the table, and Lucy laid out the cards. The tension between the three of us was casual but thick with unspoken possibility. I suggested that Steve and I play the first game, seeing as he had never played before. "I'll take it easy on you," I joked, though in reality, I was grateful to avoid the inevitable thrashing Lucy would've handed him on his first try.

Steve laughed, giving me that easygoing smile of his. "Thanks, man. I appreciate it."

As we played, Lucy watched with a mischievous grin, her eyes flicking between us. It was clear she was enjoying having both of us there, and I couldn't help but wonder where her mind was drifting. When our game finally ended, Lucy stretched her arms overhead, glancing at the empty fridge.

"You know what?" she said. "We're out of beer. Why don't we go grab some?"

"Good idea," I replied. I could feel a flicker of anticipation building in my chest. Lucy stood up, already grabbing her keys from the counter, but before I could offer to go, she turned to Steve with that smile again.

"Steve, why don't you drive me to the store?" she asked, her tone casual but hinting at more.

I raised my eyebrows slightly but didn't object. The way she said it made me wonder. It wasn't just about beer; it was never just about beer. "Sure," Steve said, getting up from his chair. He didn't hesitate.

"Alright," I said, leaning back in my chair, pretending not to care but feeling the knot of excitement tighten in my chest. "Bring back something good." I smiled, but inside, I couldn't help but wonder what would happen while they were out. Would something happen? Would they find another secluded spot, another adventure? I could feel the eagerness rising, and I tried to distract myself as they left the house together, the door closing softly behind them.

They were gone for about half an hour, and when they returned, both of them were all smiles. I could tell something had happened—after all, the store wasn't that far from our house. My mind immediately raced, wondering where they could have stopped, imagining the places they might have pulled over so Steve could enter my wife. I was almost certain they had fucked tonight. Still, I pushed those thoughts aside and tried to focus on the card game ahead.

Steve came in first, sitting across from me at the table. Lucy followed, heading to the fridge to put the beer inside. As she did, Steve pulled out a vape pen and took a long drag, blowing a cloud of vapor into the air. Without missing a beat, Lucy walked over, took the vape from his hand, and inhaled deeply as she slid onto his lap.

I noticed her movements but pretended not to, focusing on the cards instead. She draped one arm around his neck, the other hand holding the vape as she blew the vapor softly into the room. I dealt the cards, but it was hard to ignore how she acted —her lips brushing his neck, occasionally nibbling on his ear, all while she sat there, completely at ease with the situation. Every now and then, she'd look at me with a smile, almost checking in, making sure I was okay with what was happening.

Her actions didn't bother me; in fact, I found them kind of hot. Watching her flirt so openly, right in front of me, gave me a strange sense of excitement. The worst part of her stepping out to fuck other men was not knowing what she was doing or how it looked. I preferred this. I liked watching—seeing her in action made the whole thing more real, more thrilling. In many ways, I was a voyeur, and this felt like a perfect display of that.

The constant flirting between them—the light touches, the glances, and the way Lucy kept finding excuses to brush against him—was starting to get to me. My excitement was growing steadily, and by the time she bent over to French kiss him, I had a full hard-on. She made sure I could see it too, her tongue slipping into his mouth with deliberate slowness, her eyes flicking toward me for just a second as if to gauge my reaction. The entire scene felt like a slow burn, every little gesture stoking the fire inside me.

I excused myself, needing a moment to gather my thoughts. "Be right back," I mumbled, heading to the restroom. As I closed the door, I heard the distinct sound of the sliding glass door to the back deck. I took my time, flushing and washing my hands, but when I came back out, I noticed they hadn't returned from outside.

A surge of curiosity hit me. Do I go out there? Or do I wait for them to come back? The question buzzed in my mind, and without fully realizing it, I moved to the kitchen and peered out through the glass door.

They were standing by the steps, close—very close. Her arms were wrapped around his neck, pulling him toward her as his hands roamed over her ass, squeezing her through the tight denim of her jeans. The way her body pressed against his, the soft moans I could just barely hear from my hidden spot—it all made the situation feel that much more intense. She was wearing her favorite pair of jeans, the ones that hugged her curves perfectly, making her ass look even more incredible. Her black tank top, braless of course, clung to her in a way that made her breasts stand out every time she moved, her nipples brushing against the fabric.

I stood there, watching, my heart pounding. My cock was throbbing again, but I couldn't pull my eyes away. Just then, she tilted her head back, giving him access to her neck, her soft moans drifting through the quiet air. As he kissed down her neck, I saw her glance toward the doorway—toward me. Our eyes locked for a moment, and she didn't stop. Instead, she moved her body, sliding slightly to the side, deliberately positioning herself so I could see exactly what she was doing. Her hand slid down the front of Steve's pants, and I caught a glimpse of her fingers stroking him through the fabric.

I froze, watching, my body tense with the strange mix of jealousy and arousal. It was like I had been pulled into their private moment, witnessing something I both dreaded and craved. They were so lost in each other, but Lucy knew I was there, watching. She wanted me to see this.

Eventually, I could tell they were winding down, so I slipped away from the door and quickly returned to the table, my heart still racing, my mind reeling with what I'd just witnessed. By the time they came back inside, I was trying to act normal, though the lingering tension in the air was impossible to ignore.

Steve sat down first, his face a little flushed, and I could sense his nervousness. Was he on edge because he knew I might have seen them? Or was it something else? I couldn't be sure, but I had a strong suspicion that the sight of my wife's hand down his pants was the reason.

Lucy, still looking satisfied, announced she was going to change and headed upstairs. I dealt the cards again, my mind racing with everything I'd just seen. There was no denying it now—I was more than a little excited by the whole thing.

When my wife returned downstairs, she had changed into something a little more relaxed. Her new outfit consisted of loose-fitting grey shorts and a tighter blue tank top. This one hugged her figure in all the right ways, and the material was so snug that her nipples were clearly visible through the fabric. She made her way back over to Steve, smiling as she slipped onto his lap again, like it was the most natural thing in the world.

We played a few more hands, but my focus was elsewhere. I couldn't stop glancing at them—how her body fit against his, how comfortable she seemed sitting there, draped across him. The flirting between them hadn't let up, and every little touch made the air feel thicker with tension.

Lucy caught my eye and gave me a subtle nod toward the stairs. I took the cue, stifling a fake yawn. "Well, it looks like you're getting the hang of this, Steve," I said, trying to keep my voice casual. "I think I'm going to hit the hay and let Lucy take over."

Steve laughed softly, shuffling the cards for the next round. "Alright, man. Thanks for showing me the ropes."

I stood up, stretching. "Watch out, though," I joked, "she's sneaky." I started to head toward the stairs, feeling Lucy's eyes on me as I went.

"I'll walk you over, dear," she said, standing up with that same playful smile. I knew what was coming next, and it sent a thrill through me.

When we reached the stairs, she leaned in and kissed me, her lips soft against mine. "I'm horny as hell and want to fuck," she whispered, her voice low and sultry. "You can watch if you want to, but don't get caught. Is the couch a good place for you?"

The heat in my body surged at her words. "Wait..." I whispered back, grinning. "Why were you two gone so long at the store? It's not that far, so don't tell me nothing happened." My grin grew wider as I asked, already guessing the answer.

She smiled wickedly, her eyes gleaming. "Well," she began, "he stayed in the car while I ran inside to grab the beer. But when I got in there, I grabbed the bathroom key too." She paused, licking her lips. "I told Steve to come with me, unlocked the door, and then... I turned around, bent over the sink, and undid my pants."

My heart raced as she spoke, the vivid image forming in my mind. "And?" I pressed, eager for the rest.

She leaned closer, her breath warm against my ear. "He fucked me from behind, right there. We didn't take long, just a few minutes. He didn't cum, but I did." Her smile was broad, clearly proud of how turned on she had made me.

I couldn't help but chuckle softly, shaking my head. "That's so hot. You're turning into such a slut," I teased, my own excitement barely contained.

She kissed me quickly, her eyes shining. "I know, right?" she whispered with a grin. "Now make sure you stay out of sight—he's a little nervous about you watching."

I nodded, letting her head back into the living room while I slipped upstairs. Once I reached the landing, I waited, giving her enough time to coax Steve away from the card game and over to the couch. It felt like forever, though it was probably only about ten minutes before I heard the muffled sound of their voices, followed by the TV turning on.

Quietly, I crept down the stairs, moving as slowly as possible. When I reached the first few steps, I peeked my head through the banister, just enough to see the scene unfolding before me.

Lucy had positioned them perfectly, with Steve's back to me. She was lying across his legs, her head resting on his thigh, and I could see the way her body moved slightly as they whispered to each other. I couldn't make out their words, but the intimacy between them was palpable. I watched, waiting, my pulse quickening as I anticipated what might happen next.

As I settled into my spot on the stairs, I strained to catch more of the action. From my vantage point, I could tell that something had already been happening between them. Lucy's body was comfortably draped across Steve's lap, her head resting on his thigh, while his arms were lazily stretched behind his head. They were talking about random, mundane things—what was on TV, maybe a movie they wanted to watch—but there was something else underneath, something electric.

I watched Lucy shift her gaze toward me for a brief second, as if checking to see if I had a good view. Then she leaned in and kissed him deeply, her hands moving toward his waist. Her fingers fumbled with his pants, though I couldn't see clearly what was happening yet. Then her head lowered, and her body started moving rhythmically. It wasn't hard to guess what was happening—Lucy was giving him a blowjob.

I couldn't see it clearly from where I sat, but the unmistakable motion of her head bobbing up and down told me everything I needed to know. My cock stirred as I reached down to undo my pants, pulling myself out and starting to stroke. Her head kept moving in that deliberate way, and soon enough, Steve's hands went to her hair, guiding her as she worked his cock with her mouth. The sight of them together, right there on our couch, sent a surge of excitement through me.

Then, they shifted positions. Steve gently pulled her head up, their lips meeting in a messy, heated kiss before he moved her onto the cushion beside him. As they changed positions, my eyes caught it—a flash of his cock as he pulled his pants down. That's when I saw it clearly for the first time.

Lucy had told me Steve was thicker, but seeing it now was a whole different experience. It wasn't just thick; it was massive. The girth of it stunned me, taking me completely by surprise. I knew that, technically, I had him beat in length, but somehow that didn't matter in the moment. All I could focus on was how much larger his cock looked in every other way. It filled the space between them as Lucy shifted to give him access, and for the first time, the reality of it hit me hard.

I should've felt some kind of relief knowing that I was longer, but there was none. Instead, all I could feel was jealousy—and a strange, overwhelming arousal. Steve moved to the floor in front of her, sliding Lucy's shorts to the side. My hand tightened around my cock as I watched him dive into her pussy, his face buried between her thighs. Her body responded immediately, her hands gripping his head as her hips rocked against his tongue.

Lucy's moans filled the room, growing louder as Steve licked her with slow, deliberate strokes. She arched her back, her breasts pressing against the fabric of her tight tank top. Without a second thought, she pulled the shirt up, exposing her tits and teasing her nipples between her fingers. Her legs wrapped around Steve's head, her heels digging into his back as he devoured her. I watched as she gasped and panted, completely lost in the pleasure he was giving her.

"Oh, Steve... yes, just like that..." she moaned, her voice thick with desire. "You're so good with your tongue... fuck..."

My jealousy deepened with every word, but so did the arousal. I couldn't stop staring at his cock, hanging thick and heavy between his legs as he worked Lucy to the edge. She moaned louder, her hands tangling in his hair as she pressed herself harder against his mouth. My hand was moving faster now, stroking in time with their movements. The sound of her climax building was intoxicating, a mix of envy and desire swirling inside me.

Then it happened—Lucy's entire body tensed, her back arching off the couch as she came hard. She gasped and moaned his name, her body shaking as the orgasm took over. "Oh god, yes!" she cried, her voice echoing through the room. Steve didn't stop, his tongue working her through the final waves of pleasure, leaving her trembling beneath him.

I sat there, stunned and breathless, my cock aching in my hand as I tried to keep myself quiet. Watching him lick her like that, watching her cum for him—it filled me with so many conflicting emotions, but there was no denying the heat between my legs.

As Lucy finally relaxed, her chest rising and falling with deep breaths, Steve leaned back, wiping his mouth with a satisfied grin. I watched as she leaned forward to kiss him again, her legs still trembling slightly from the aftershocks of her orgasm.

I hadn't expected it to feel like this—to be caught between jealousy and arousal in such an intense way—but there I was, stroking my cock harder as I watched them together, the reality of it all sinking deeper into my chest.

As Steve positioned himself between Lucy's legs, I couldn't help but feel a wave of emotions—jealousy, arousal, and something darker, a humiliation that gnawed at my chest. I'd known Steve's cock was thicker than mine, but seeing it in this moment, as he guided it toward my wife's waiting pussy, made the reality hit harder than I expected. It filled the space between them in a way that made my own cock seem insignificant, and even though I was still technically longer, I couldn't shake the feeling that size didn't matter when she was so eager for him.

Steve slid into her slowly, his thick cock parting her slick folds with ease. Lucy's head fell back, a loud moan escaping her lips as he stretched her open. I swallowed hard, my hand frozen mid-stroke for a moment as I watched, completely mesmerized by the sight. There was no denying it now—he filled her in ways I never could. That realization burned, even as it aroused me.

"Oh, Steve... yes," Lucy moaned, her voice dripping with pleasure. She bit her lip and looked directly toward where I was hidden, her eyes sparkling with mischief. She knew I was watching, and I could see that she was reveling in it, pushing the boundaries. "You feel so good, so much better than... oh god... so much better than him."

My heart pounded in my chest. Her words were like a knife, twisting inside me, but instead of turning me off, they only made me harder. I couldn't stop stroking, couldn't tear my eyes away from the sight of Steve's cock moving in and out of her, each thrust making her moan louder.

She lifted her legs higher, wrapping them around his waist as he picked up the pace, thrusting deeper into her. "Mmm... I love how thick you are, Steve. So much thicker than my husband," she groaned, her hips meeting his with every thrust. "I wish he had a cock like this... god, I wish he could fuck me like this."

Her voice was heavy with lust, each word hitting me with a

mix of shame and arousal. My stomach churned, but my hand only moved faster as I watched her give herself completely to him, praising him in ways she never had with me. I wanted to look away, wanted to stop, but I couldn't. The humiliation was overwhelming, but it fueled the desire coursing through me.

Steve grunted as he drove into her harder, his hands gripping her thighs tightly as her legs shook in the air. "Fuck, Lucy... you're so tight," he groaned, his voice strained with the effort of holding back.

Lucy's moans became more desperate, her fingers clawing at the couch as she rocked her hips, meeting each of his powerful thrusts. "Oh god, Steve... faster... just like that," she panted, her head tilting back as she lost herself in the pleasure. Her eyes found mine again, and this time, she smirked, her lips curling into a knowing smile.

"See that, baby?" she teased, her voice breathless but dripping with seduction. "Look how much I need this... look how much I need a real cock like Steve's."

My cock throbbed painfully in my hand, the heat of her words combined with the sight of them fucking just feet away from me pushing me to the edge. I was torn—part of me wanted to be the one giving her that kind of pleasure, the other part of me was addicted to the humiliation of watching someone else do it. Lucy knew exactly what she was doing, and she was taking full advantage of it.

Steve shifted, lifting her legs onto his shoulders, and began pounding into her harder, deeper. Lucy's moans became screams of pleasure, her hands gripping the back of the couch as she bucked her hips wildly. "Oh god, yes! Fuck, I'm going to cum!" she cried, her voice echoing through the room.

I could feel myself on the verge of cumming too, the tension building in my cock as I stroked faster, trying to match the rhythm of Steve's thrusts. Lucy's body arched, her moans reaching a fever pitch as her orgasm overtook her, her legs trembling around his shoulders.

"Yes, yes, Steve... just like that... don't stop," she moaned, her body shaking as waves of pleasure coursed through her.

I could barely hold back anymore. Watching my wife cum so hard on another man's cock, hearing her beg for more, tore me apart inside, but the arousal was undeniable. I was right on the edge, my cock twitching in my hand as I watched them, completely lost in their own world of pleasure.

Steve's thrusting began to slow, matching Lucy's rocking hips, but he didn't stop. He kept driving into her, his thick cock disappearing into her soaked pussy with each push. The slow, deliberate pace felt intimate—like he was savoring every moment inside her—and I couldn't tear my eyes away. As Lucy's legs slid down from his shoulders, Steve leaned in, bringing his lips to hers. Their kiss was deep, slow, and full of passion. It was the kind of kiss we hadn't shared in a long time. The connection between them was raw, undeniable, and it hit me harder than I expected.

I watched, my breath shallow, as Lucy melted into the kiss, her body arching to meet his. There was something primal about the way they moved together, like they couldn't get enough of each other. My hand on my cock stilled for a moment, overcome with the strange mix of jealousy and desire swirling inside me. My wife was giving herself completely to him, and though it hurt, the thrill of it was undeniable.

The kiss broke, and in one smooth motion, Lucy flipped onto her knees. Her feet dangled off the edge of the couch, her ass high in the air, perfectly presented for Steve. My pulse quickened as I watched him position himself behind her, his thick cock hovering just at the entrance of her pussy. Lucy looked over her shoulder at me, her face flushed with pleasure, and her lips curved into a teasing smile. She knew exactly what she was doing, pushing me further, testing my limits.

Steve wasted no time. He grabbed her voluptuous ass with both hands, squeezing and kneading her soft cheeks as he guided himself back inside her. His cock slid into her with ease, her wetness coating him, and her moan filled the room. His focus shifted to her ass, spreading it with his strong hands, and I could see his eyes fixate on her puckered asshole. I could tell by the way his fingers twitched, how desperately he wanted to explore every inch of her.

I repositioned myself on the steps, trying to get a better view as I continued to stroke my cock. Every thrust of Steve's hips sent shockwaves through Lucy's body, her ass jiggling with each impact. I could hear the wet slap of their bodies colliding, and it drove me wild.

Then, I saw it—her mouth forming a perfect 'O' shape as Steve slid a finger between her ass cheeks. He circled her rim, teasing her, before finally pressing it inside. Lucy's reaction was instant, her body arching, her moan turning into something deeper, more guttural. "Oh, fuck..." she breathed, her voice laced with pleasure as he buried his finger deeper into her ass with every thrust of his cock.

Steve's rhythm quickened. He was fucking her harder now, his hips slamming against her ass with every thrust. His hand continued to work her asshole, pushing his finger in and out in perfect sync with his cock. Lucy's gasps turned to cries of pleasure, her body shaking with the intensity of it all. She reached forward, grabbing the edge of the couch, her knuckles turning white as she struggled to hold on.

"Oh my god, yes... just like that, Steve," she moaned, her voice filled with lust. "Your cock feels so fucking good. I love it when you fuck me like this."

Her words cut through me, a mix of humiliation and arousal flooding my system. My cock throbbed painfully in my hand as I stroked faster, unable to tear my eyes away from the scene unfolding in front of me. Steve's thick cock was filling her, stretching her in ways I never could, and watching her enjoy it so much... it was intoxicating.

With each thrust, Steve's grip on her ass tightened, his focus never wavering from the way her body responded to him. He was completely absorbed in her, his eyes drinking in every detail —the way her ass bounced, the way her pussy clung to his cock, the way she moaned his name with abandon.

Lucy's face twisted with pleasure, her lips parting as another wave of ecstasy rolled through her. "Yes, fuck me harder... fill me up," she begged, her voice cracking with need. She was so lost in the moment, so consumed by the pleasure Steve was giving her, that it made my chest ache with jealousy and longing. I wanted to be the one making her feel that way, but at the same time, I couldn't stop watching.

I pumped my cock faster, trying to keep pace with Steve's thrusts. Every time he buried himself inside her, I felt a sharp pang of jealousy, but it was mixed with a deep, twisted sense of satisfaction. Lucy's body was his now, at least for this moment, and it was both torturous and exhilarating to watch.

As Steve leaned in, kissing the nape of her neck while still thrusting into her, I knew they were close. Lucy's moans became frantic, her body trembling beneath him. "Oh god, I'm going to cum," she cried out, her voice breaking as the orgasm built inside her.

The sight of her, the way her body surrendered to him, pushed me to the edge. My cock twitched violently in my hand as I watched, ready to explode. I was so close, so fucking close.

Steve's free hand slid around Lucy's body, snaking up to her throat as his thrusts grew more intense. The sight of his large hand wrapping around her delicate neck sent a shock of arousal through me, but also a pang of jealousy. That was something I never dared to do to her, something she never asked me to. As

Steve tightened his grip, her lips parted in a guttural moan that echoed through the room, deeper and more erotic than I'd ever heard from her.

He pulled his finger out of her ass, focusing all his attention on her throat now, squeezing harder, making her arch into him. Her body trembled as the pleasure took over, and the control he had over her only seemed to make her more desperate, more vocal. My hand moved faster on my cock, but my mind was a whirl of emotions—lust, envy, and a strange satisfaction knowing that this scene was unfolding just for me to witness.

Lucy's moans became louder, more frantic, and I could tell she was close to cumming again. Her breathing quickened, each gasp more desperate than the last. "Oh fuck, oh fuck," she cried, her voice raspy from the pressure on her throat. Steve's thrusting matched the intensity of her voice, his cock plunging into her pussy with forceful, rhythmic strokes, his hips slamming against her ass.

I could feel my pulse racing, my hand tightening around my own cock as I watched her unravel beneath him. Her face twisted with ecstasy, her eyes wild with pleasure, and then she looked directly at me. It was a moment of pure connection, even in her most vulnerable state—she knew I was there, she knew I was watching, and she wanted me to see this. Her lips parted, and she let out a scream of pleasure. "I'm fucking cumming again!"

The words hit me like a blow. She wasn't just having an orgasm —she was telling me, reminding me of how fully she was giving herself to Steve, how he was making her feel in ways I never could. The jealousy twisted in my gut, but my cock throbbed in my hand, betraying me.

Steve grunted, his grip tightening on her ass as he pounded into her harder, using her body to push deeper with every thrust. Her back arched more, her ass lifting as he gripped her cheeks, spreading them apart with both hands. The slapping sound of their bodies meeting was deafening in the otherwise quiet room, and I could only imagine how wet her pussy must be now, dripping for him, taking every inch of his thick cock.

"Do you like that, Lucy?" Steve growled, his voice strained with effort as he continued to fuck her, each word punctuated by a hard thrust. His hands squeezed her ass harder, his fingers digging into her flesh as if he was claiming every inch of her.

Lucy's breath came in ragged gasps, and she nodded, her face still flushed from the force of her orgasm. "Oh god, yes... I love it," she moaned, her voice trembling with lingering pleasure. She shot another glance at me, a wicked smile curling at her lips. "I wish my husband had a cock like his," she added, her words dripping with tease and lust.

The humiliation was like fire in my chest, burning deep, but the arousal only grew stronger. I stroked my cock faster, desperate to release the tension building inside me, but her words made it impossible to ignore how much I was being pushed. She was enjoying herself completely, giving herself fully to Steve, and the worst part was—I loved it.

"Oh god, yes, Steve... yes, I fucking love your cock," Lucy moaned, her voice growing breathless as she neared another orgasm. I couldn't believe what I was seeing—surely there was no way he could make her cum for a third time in a row, but as Steve's pace quickened, her body reacted instantly. Her eyes fluttered shut, her lips parted, and she bit down on her bottom lip, a familiar sign that she was right on the edge.

Her voice rose with each thrust, her words barely forming as her moans filled the room. "Oh fuuuuuck," she screamed, her voice trembling with each powerful stroke Steve drove into her. I watched in disbelief as her body shuddered once more, the unmistakable signs of yet another orgasm taking over.

My own climax was close—I could feel the pressure building, my hand working my cock feverishly as I watched them, unable to hold back any longer. But just as I was about to lose myself in my own release, Steve suddenly pulled out of her. I paused, expecting him to finish on her ass like before. But Lucy had something else in mind this time.

She shifted, her body moving gracefully as she knelt in front of him, positioning herself directly in the center of my view. She looked up at Steve with that same teasing smile, her hands sliding down his body as she guided his cock toward her face. Her eyes flicked toward me, making sure I was watching. "I want to taste it... I want it all over me," she whispered seductively to him, her voice loud enough for me to hear, though clearly meant as a show for both of us.

I swallowed hard, my hand pausing on my cock as I realized what was happening. Lucy never let me cum on her face, no matter how much I begged. But now, with Steve standing over her, his thick cock twitching in her hand, she was offering herself to him, letting him do what I only fantasized about.

Steve's hand moved to her hair, pulling it back gently as he stroked his cock, aiming it at her face. Lucy closed her eyes, tilting her head up, her lips parted slightly as she whispered, "Give it to me... I want it all over my face."

The visual was overwhelming. My hand moved again, jerking my cock in time with Steve's strokes as he grunted, his breathing heavy and uneven. Then, with a guttural moan, he exploded. His cum shot out in thick streams, splattering across Lucy's face and tits. She gasped in pleasure as the warm liquid coated her skin, her hands running over her breasts to smear it across her body, making sure every inch was covered.

I watched in awe, my own cock throbbing in my hand, as Steve's cum dripped down her face, landing on her lips, her chin, and her heaving chest. Her nipples, already hard, glistened with his cum, and she let out a soft, satisfied moan as she wiped her finger across her lips, tasting him.

"Oh god, Lucy," Steve groaned, watching as his cum dripped down her body. His cock twitched again, and another smaller spurt hit her cheek, adding to the mess.

Lucy didn't wipe it away—she just knelt there, covered in his cum, basking in the afterglow of her orgasms. She glanced at me, a wicked smile on her face, knowing exactly what she was doing. "Mmm, I wish my husband could give me this much," she teased, her voice low and sultry, her words cutting deep.

My heart raced, torn between humiliation and arousal. I stroked my cock faster, the sight of her, drenched in another man's cum, pushing me closer to the edge. She looked so satisfied, so content in her role, and I couldn't help but feel both turned on and devastated by it.

"Thank you, Steve," she whispered, leaning in to kiss the tip of his cock, still wet with his release. "That was amazing."

I came then, unable to hold back any longer. My own orgasm was sharp, almost painful, as I shot my load into my hand, the release feeling strangely inadequate compared to the intense display I had just witnessed. My cum dribbled out weakly in comparison, and I couldn't help but feel the sharp contrast between what I could give her and what Steve had just done.

As I wiped my hand, trying to clean up the mess I made, Lucy stood, her body still glistening with Steve's cum. She didn't rush to wipe it off, didn't even seem to care. Instead, she leaned into Steve, pressing her body against his as she kissed him deeply. "Mmm... I love how you taste on me," she purred, her voice dripping with satisfaction.

"No problem, baby... it was just as good for me," Steve murmured, pulling Lucy into a tight embrace. Their lips met again in a slow, lingering kiss, and as they lost themselves in each other, I quietly began to creep up the stairs. I didn't want to interrupt, didn't want to break the spell they were in, and honestly, I needed some time to process everything.

As I reached the top of the stairs, I paused for a moment, listening to the faint sounds of their hushed conversation below. Their words were muffled now, intimate whispers exchanged between two lovers. I felt a mixture of pride and confusion— pride in how Lucy had embraced this new dynamic between us, how effortlessly she could let herself go and indulge in these experiences, but also confusion over my role in it all. My head was still buzzing with the intensity of what I had just witnessed, my body still humming with the aftershocks of my own release.

I made my way to our bedroom, the cool air of the room a stark contrast to the heated scene I'd just left behind. I slipped into bed, pulling the covers over me, but sleep felt a long way off. My mind kept replaying everything—how she knelt before him, how his thick cock sprayed across her face and tits, and how she looked at me with that wicked, knowing smile. It was all so vivid, so raw.

I thought about Lucy, my incredible wife, and how she had not only embraced my fantasy but exceeded every expectation I ever had. When I first broached the subject, I wasn't sure how far we would go, how much she would be willing to indulge me. But now, seeing her like this—so free, so completely herself—it was almost overwhelming.

"Damn," I whispered under my breath, a smile tugging at the corners of my lips. I loved this woman. I loved how she could be this wild, uninhibited version of herself, yet still come home to me, still hold me close, still love me in ways that went beyond the physical. Watching her with Steve, watching how effortlessly she could switch between roles—wife, lover, friend —it only made me appreciate her more.

There was a part of me that reveled in her sluttiness, in the way she owned her sexuality now. She wasn't afraid to be exactly who she was, and it was one of the things that turned me on the most. I thought about how good she was at playing this role, how natural it all seemed to her once she let herself go. She wasn't just doing this for me anymore—it was for her, too. And that's what made it so powerful.

But even as the thoughts swirled, there was that familiar pang of insecurity, a gnawing sense of inadequacy that tugged at the edges of my mind. Steve had given her something I couldn't. There was no denying that. I'd seen it in her eyes, in the way her body responded to him. It wasn't just the size of his cock—it was the whole experience, the thrill, the danger of it all.

I shifted under the covers, the sheets cool against my skin as I tried to calm my racing thoughts. I couldn't help but wonder what she was thinking now. Did she still feel the same way about me? Or had this changed something between us?

But then I reminded myself—this was my fantasy, one I had coaxed her into. And Lucy, being the incredible woman she was, had embraced it fully. She had given me exactly what I wanted, maybe more than I even knew I wanted. And despite everything, I knew she loved me. There was no question about that.

As I closed my eyes, trying to settle into sleep, I could still hear faint movements downstairs, the quiet murmur of voices. I smiled to myself, letting go of the lingering doubts. I had the most amazing wife, a woman who could be wild and free, yet still come home to me at the end of the night.

"Damn," I whispered again, sinking deeper into the pillow. "I really fucking love this woman."

PRESENTING LIAM

She chuckled, rolling onto her back and pulling the blanket up slightly, her eyes drifting toward the ceiling as she thought. "I don't know, honestly. Steve didn't really say, but he's hinted before that his roommate is aware of... some things," she said with a sly grin, tracing her finger along the edge of the blanket. "But who knows how much. Could just be a guess."

I turned to face her, watching her expression closely. There was a certain casualness in the way she spoke about it that intrigued me, like this whole thing had started to feel normal to her. I was still adjusting, but the more I watched her embrace it, the more I found myself sinking into it too, fully wrapped up in the thrill of it all.

"So, are you thinking of going over there, playing some cards?" I asked, the curiosity thick in my voice. "I mean, just cards?"

She gave me a smirk, raising an eyebrow. "Cards, baby?" she teased, her voice dripping with sarcasm. "Do you really think we'll just be playing cards?"

I laughed, shaking my head. "Probably not," I admitted, feeling that familiar stir in my stomach. The jealousy was still there, simmering just beneath the surface, but it was twisted with something else—excitement, curiosity, maybe even pride. Lucy had come into her own, more confident and liberated than I had ever seen her. It was intoxicating.

"I don't know, though," she continued, her voice softer now as she rolled back onto her side, facing me again. "Like I said... the sex is fine, but... it's not about the actual act with him. It's more about... how he makes me feel." Her gaze locked onto mine, searching. "It's weird, I know. It's like I get to be this younger, more daring version of myself, and I feel free. It's not something I ever thought I'd be into."

I nodded, taking it in. "It makes sense, though," I said after a moment. "I think that's what makes this so hot for me too. Watching you like that, knowing you're enjoying this... knowing you're doing things you'd never thought you'd do." I paused, stroking her arm lightly. "I don't think it's just about the sex for me either."

She smiled at that, leaning into my touch. "Yeah," she whispered. "I guess we're both getting something out of this we didn't expect."

For a while, we just lay there in silence, the morning light filtering softly through the curtains. I couldn't help but think about everything—the twists our relationship had taken, the unexpected turns that had somehow deepened our connection, made us more open with each other than we had ever been.

Eventually, she broke the silence. "So, do you think you'd be okay with me going over there? Meeting his roommate?" Her tone was casual, but there was something in her eyes, a flicker of curiosity, maybe even a test.

"Does his roommate know the situation?" I asked, my voice steady, though a mix of curiosity and something darker churned beneath the surface.

Lucy looked up at me, a playful smirk curling on her lips. "Of course, Steve told him everything. He really likes the fact that he's sleeping with a married woman... and that her husband knows all about it." She let out a soft, almost teasing laugh, the sound laced with an erotic confidence that sent a surge of conflicting emotions through me.

I chuckled, though a part of me squirmed at the thought of being the subject of their conversations. The idea of everyone knowing —knowing that I let my wife fuck other men—was a strange blend of thrilling and unsettling. Still, the heat in my chest told me what part of me craved. "That's... cool," I managed, the words feeling lighter than what I really felt. "Any plans yet?"

"Maybe tonight," she replied, her tone casual as she slid off the bed, her movements fluid and unbothered, as though our conversation was perfectly normal. My eyes fell to the shorts crumpled on the floor beside the bed, the ones she'd worn last night. Her naked legs moved gracefully as she crossed the room, and I couldn't help but track the sway of her hips as she grabbed her robe from the hook on the door. "I'm jumping in the shower," she said, not looking back as she disappeared into the hallway.

I lingered there for a moment, my gaze drifting back to the discarded shorts. The room felt heavy, filled with her scent and the faint echoes of last night. I bent down, slowly picking them up. The fabric felt soft in my hands, and as I turned them over, I spotted it—the telltale white streaks that had dried overnight, faded but unmistakable. My heart quickened.

Without thinking, I brought the shorts closer, inhaling deeply. The scent was overpowering—her scent. The pungent mix of sex and sweat hit me hard, making my pulse race. I could smell her on the fabric, the musky sweetness of her pussy lingering in the material. A shiver ran through me as I exhaled slowly, feeling both aroused and slightly ashamed. I took one more deep breath, savoring it, before guilt caught up with me. Feeling perverted, I tossed the shorts into the hamper, my heart still thudding in my chest.

I stood there for a moment, trying to collect myself, before grabbing my robe and following her down the hall. The sound of running water grew louder as I approached the bathroom, and when I reached the door, I paused, peeking inside.

Through the misted glass of the shower, I could just make out Lucy's body—naked, wet, and moving languidly under the spray. Her skin glistened under the water as she ran the loofah over her tits, her nipples hard and inviting. She dragged the sponge lower, over her stomach, down between her legs, slow and deliberate. I could feel myself getting harder, my breath catching as I watched her wash herself with such sensual ease. She raised her arm behind her, cleaning between the curve of her ass, the movement unhurried, as if she knew I was there.

Lucy glanced over her shoulder, her eyes catching mine through the foggy glass. A sly smile tugged at the corner of her mouth, and she didn't stop, her gaze holding mine as she continued to wash herself, teasing, daring me to come closer.

I leaned against the doorframe, transfixed, my heart pounding in my ears. This was the woman I shared my life with, but somehow, in moments like these, she felt like someone entirely new—bold, untamed, and unapologetic. The kind of woman who could take control of a situation with a younger man like Steve and make it sound so easy, so thrilling.

And here I was, standing in the doorway, silently watching, wondering what tonight might bring.

"Whatcha doing'?" she asked with a snigger, her voice light and teasing, the sound carrying over the steady rush of the water. I could just make out her silhouette through the steamed glass, her body moving under the spray.

I leaned against the doorframe, caught between being playful and honest. "Oh, just savoring the show," I answered, my voice casual, though there was an undeniable edge of arousal behind it.

She gave a little chuckle, her laugh echoing off the tiled walls. "You seem really happy this morning. Happier than me, and I'm the one that got laid," she teased, her words dripping with a kind of carefree amusement that only deepened the heat between us. "Did you find my shorts? I left them by the bed."

I hesitated, feeling a sudden rush of awkwardness. How the hell did she always know? My eyes darted to the hamper where I had tossed them just minutes ago, guilt and arousal swirling in a messy cocktail inside me.

"What?" she pressed, the playful lilt in her voice becoming more curious.

I could hear the shower door slide open, the sound sharp in the steamy room. Her head popped out, wet strands of hair sticking to her neck as she looked at me, her expression half-amused, half-expectant. "C'mon... I know you, little pervert," she said, her lips curling into a knowing smirk. There was no accusation, only the comfortable teasing that came from years of knowing exactly how to push each other's buttons. She laughed softly, then slid the door closed again, disappearing behind the misted glass.

Damn, she really did know me. Even after all these years, she never ceased to surprise me. I stood there for a moment, my heart beating faster, the familiar warmth of excitement rising in my chest. The way she looked at me, called me out—it was part of what made her so intoxicating, always keeping me just a little bit off balance.

"Yeah... I did," I mumbled, feeling a strange mix of embarrassment and pride. My voice trailed off, almost too low to hear over the running water.

She didn't say anything at first, but I could hear her continue washing herself, the soft sound of the loofah dragging across her skin, making my pulse quicken.

"I can't help it," I added, louder this time, feeling the need to own up to it, to admit the truth in the open. "I think it's really hot."

There was a pause, then another laugh from behind the glass.

Her laughter was different now—deeper, more intimate, like she appreciated the honesty. "I know," she said simply, the words lingering in the air, sending a shiver down my spine.

I could feel the tension hanging between us, thick and electric, as if she could sense how much she affected me even without seeing my face. She was always in control, always knowing exactly what to say, how far to push.

I turned to leave, feeling the weight of my desire settling in my gut as I stepped out of the bathroom, the steam clinging to my skin like a reminder of her. The door clicked softly shut behind me, but my mind stayed in the room, replaying the image of her wet body through the glass, the teasing glint in her eyes as she called me out for what I was—her little pervert.

And damn if I didn't love it.

Later that afternoon, I was outside washing the car when I saw Lucy step out of the house, her bare feet padding across the driveway. The heat of the day clung to the air, and the sun glinted off the soapy water running down the side of the car. She moved with that familiar grace, the slight bounce in her step drawing my attention before she even said a word.

"Hey, babe," she called out, walking closer with a smile that I could already tell was up to something.

I turned off the hose, wiping the water from my hands on the edge of my shirt as I looked her over. "What's up?" I asked, already sensing there was more to her tone than a casual greeting.

Lucy stepped even closer, the scent of her skin mixing with the warm breeze. She handed me a beer she'd been sipping, her fingers brushing mine just slightly. I took a long gulp, the cold liquid sliding down my throat as she spoke.

"Steve texted me," she said, her grin widening, eyes sparkling with mischief. "He wants to pick me up around five."

I handed her back the bottle, feeling the stir of anticipation starting to build. "So, cards tonight, I take it?" I asked, trying to play it cool even though my mind was already racing.

"Yeah," she replied with a shrug, taking a swig from the bottle. "He wants me to teach his roommate to play. And I guess... stay and play with the two of them." Her voice was casual, but there was an underlying tease in her words, a suggestion hanging in the air between us.

I raised an eyebrow as I turned the hose back on, continuing to rinse the soap from the car, though my focus was no longer on the task. "Two guys tonight, huh?" I teased, the words slipping out with a smirk, though I couldn't shake the image from my head.

Lucy shrugged her shoulders, the movement playful and nonchalant as she chugged the last of her beer. "Maybe," she said with a laugh, a lightness in her voice that left me wondering just how serious she was.

I couldn't help but look at her a little more closely, my mind drifting to the latest book she'd been reading. It was about three brothers who shared a wife—a story that had sparked some wild conversations between us. She'd told me how the book ended, how all three of them had fucked the wife at the same time, and how she thought it was... hot. The casual way she'd mentioned it had surprised me, but I'd shrugged it off, thinking it was just a fantasy. I never pictured my wife taking more than one lover at a time. But then again, I'd been wrong before. Way off base when it came to Lucy.

She gave me one last glance, the kind that made my stomach flip, before heading back inside. I watched her go, her hips swaying slightly, and I finished rinsing the car, my thoughts drifting to what the night might hold. When I finally stepped inside the house, the air-conditioning hit me like a cool wave, but Lucy was nowhere to be seen.

"Lucy?" I called up the stairs, already guessing she was getting ready. It was almost four, after all.

"I'm almost done!" she shouted down, her voice light and full of anticipation.

I began to wonder what she was wearing for this outing. I knew Lucy well enough to know that her choice of clothes would tell me more than words ever could. If she was planning to wear something easy access, it meant sex was on the table. If she was more covered up, maybe it was just cards—no sex tonight. It was a habit I had, building everything up in my head before anything was even decided. I'd done it before, back when I was still trying to convince her to take other lovers, always analyzing every little detail.

A few minutes later, I heard her footsteps on the stairs. When I turned around, there she was—wearing a long, floral dress that flowed down to her ankles, the soft fabric swaying with each step. The dress tied around the back of her neck, and depending on how tight she tied it, it could either hide or showcase her tits perfectly. She had tied it snug this time, the neckline dipping low enough to tease just the right amount of cleavage. My eyes traced the line of the dress as it hugged her body, and the gold buckled straps of her brown sandals shimmered in the afternoon light. Her toes, painted a deep beige, peeked out from the sandals, matching her freshly manicured fingernails.

Her hair was pulled back into a ponytail, loose blonde bangs falling in front of her eyes. I loved her hair like that—it gave her a youthful, carefree look that I couldn't resist. She stood at the base of the stairs, turning slightly, giving me a view of her dress from all angles, her eyes full of that familiar sparkle.

"How's this?" she asked, her voice playful, but there was a hint of something more in the way she watched me, waiting for my reaction.

"You look very nice," I said with a smile, my voice soft but edged with anticipation. I couldn't take my eyes off her, the way her dress clung just right and the sunlight from the window caught in her hair.

Lucy slid her lips to the side, a teasing grin playing across her face. "Uh huh," she responded, clearly unimpressed with my attempt at subtlety. She twirled in place, the hem of her dress fluttering around her ankles as she posed in front of the stairs. "I'm going for laid back—not trying too hard to be too want-able."

"I think that'll do it," I said, a smirk tugging at my lips as I watched her, knowing full well how effortlessly want-able she really was.

She rolled her eyes, clearly catching on to my sarcasm, but before I could react, she spun back toward the door. "No panties, though," she said with a wicked smile, tossing the words over her shoulder as if it were a casual afterthought.

My jaw dropped. My mind instantly shifted gears. Change of plans, I thought to myself, my heart pounding harder now. Sex tonight it is.

Lucy crossed the room, grabbing a lighter coat from the closet. She slipped it on with ease, her movements graceful, every little detail of her outfit now radiating purpose. As she returned to the doorway, her eyes scanned outside, searching for her ride.

"Steve's on his way, I take it?" I asked, trying to keep my voice steady, though the thought of her heading out with no panties—and the possibilities that suggested—was making it harder.

"He said he was," she replied, turning slightly to glance back at me, her lips curved in that familiar, confident smile. "And I get to meet Liam tonight."

"His roommate?" I asked, feigning casual interest while my mind began swirling with images. The idea of her meeting someone new, someone who might be part of tonight's adventure, sent another wave of excitement coursing through me.

She nodded without turning back, her attention still on the world outside. I took a moment to really look her over. As my gaze wandered down her body, something caught my eye. A delicate gold anklet shimmered against her skin, something she rarely wore. Then I noticed the rings on her toes—two, one on each foot. That was new. Usually, Lucy only wore one. My mind, always prone to overanalyzing, started to spiral into thoughts about what that might mean. Was there a reason for the extra toe ring? Was it a signal, something subtle, or was I just getting caught up in the meaningless details again?

Before I could think too much on it, she turned back toward me, breaking my concentration. "Okay, that's him," she said, her voice light and full of excitement as she opened the door.

I stepped closer, my chest tightening as I watched her. She leaned in, giving me a quick kiss, her lips warm and soft against mine. "No idea what time I'll be back," she said with a playful glint in her eye. "But I'll text when I know the plans."

And just like that, she was out the door.

I stood there for a moment, the lingering taste of her kiss still on my lips, the soft scent of her perfume filling the space she had just left. The anticipation churned in my stomach as I watched her walk to the car, her dress swaying with each step, revealing flashes of bare legs as she moved.

No panties.

The thought echoed in my mind, sending a pulse of heat through me. I couldn't help but smile, knowing the night was bound to hold more than just cards.

Several hours had passed, and I found myself staring at the clock—10:00 p.m. Still nothing from Lucy. I unlocked my phone again, glancing at the screen as if somehow, in the few minutes since I'd last checked, there would be a new message. Of course, it's on, I thought to myself, the anxiety creeping in despite the logic. I turned the volume up, then down, toggling it back to vibrate, testing it for some reason, just to make sure everything was working. All right, relax. I needed a distraction.

She did say she'd text with the plans when she got them, so maybe they were just playing cards. But that nagging thought wouldn't leave me alone. The book. Her joking comment about having both of them. My mind kept circling back to it, replaying the possibilities over and over.

I sighed, shaking my head as I headed into the kitchen. I needed something to munch on while I waited. Maybe food would keep my hands busy, keep my mind from wandering. After rummaging around in the fridge, I found some nachos and cheese—nothing fancy, but enough to distract me. I nuked them, listening to the hum of the microwave as my thoughts drifted once again.

What was she doing right now? I could imagine her sitting at the table with Steve and Liam, dealing out cards, laughing, leaning forward just enough to tease them with the way her dress clung to her body. No panties. The thought sent a fresh pulse of heat through me, but I shoved it down. Stop it. Focus. I grabbed my plate and headed to the living room.

I flipped through channels, not really paying attention to what was on. Nothing caught my eye. After a few minutes of mindless browsing, I landed on something—a crime drama, I think—but I wasn't really watching. My thoughts kept drifting back to Lucy. She was with two young college guys, probably right now. What if she wasn't just playing cards? The image of her from earlier— the way she'd teased me before leaving, the way she'd laughed when I brought up the idea of two guys—played in my head, and I couldn't shake it.

I shifted in my seat, trying to focus on the TV. Okay, stop it. Focus on the show. But the thought wouldn't leave me alone. My stomach tightened. Was this what I wanted? Wasn't this what we'd talked about, fantasized about for months? Yet now that the moment was here, the uncertainty gnawed at me, twisting my insides into knots.

By midnight, my nerves were frayed. The TV show had come and gone in a blur, and I couldn't remember a single plot point. My phone buzzed on the coffee table, snapping me back to reality. I snatched it up, my heart racing as I saw Lucy's name pop up on the screen.

Finally.

I opened the message. My stomach dropped as I read her words: "Hey, remember that book I told you about?"

The book. My pulse quickened as I stared at the screen, the words taunting me. Of course, I remembered. How could I forget? The book had been all I could think about since she walked out the door earlier this evening.

I hesitated, fingers hovering over the keyboard. What should I say? Should I play dumb? Pretend like I had no idea where she was going with this? Or should I admit that I knew exactly what she was leading up to? If I played stupid, maybe she'd give me more details. Maybe she'd tease me, playfully leading me along with more descriptions of what had really happened tonight.

I opted for the former. Play dumb.

I typed out a quick reply: "What book?"

I hit send and stared at the phone, my heart hammering in my chest. The anticipation was unbearable. I could already imagine her smile on the other end of the phone, the way her lips would curl into that mischievous grin she always gave me when she knew she had me exactly where she wanted me. My mind raced with possibilities, wondering what she would tell me next.

Would she describe how they had played cards at first, maybe some light flirting? Or would she cut straight to the part where things escalated—the part where two guys, not just one, had her attention tonight?

I waited, my breath shallow, the silence in the room suddenly deafening as I stared at the screen, waiting for the next message.

I waited, staring at my phone, the anticipation clawing at me. My mind raced, heart pounding louder with each second of silence. The phone buzzed, and I immediately unlocked the screen.

"The one about the three brothers."

Her text was simple, but the implication hit me like a punch to the gut. My stomach tightened, and I let out a nervous laugh, though there was nothing funny about it. Oh shit. She wanted to have a threesome—with these young college guys. My mind raced, trying to figure out what to say, my fingers hovering over the keys. What to type back? I repeated to myself, heart thudding in my chest.

Fuck it.

I typed quickly: "Are you talking threesome now?"

I hit send before I could second-guess myself and immediately regretted it. My heart pounded even harder as I stared at the screen, waiting. My thoughts spiraled out of control. Was she hesitant to tell me because she was unsure? Or worse, was she already in the act and trying to fill me in between moments? The minutes ticked by, each one stretching into what felt like hours, the silence growing heavier and more unbearable with every passing second.

Finally, the phone buzzed again. One word.

"Yes."

Yes? That's all I got? Really? One word for something that, to me at least, felt monumental. This is a big deal! My fingers trembled as I typed again, feeling the rush of emotions swirl—excitement, jealousy, curiosity—all battling for dominance.

"Uh... more specific," I replied, my mind running wild with

images of what might already be happening. I hit send, and my heart raced again. I needed to know more.

Her next reply came more quickly this time, almost as if she had been waiting for me to ask.

"Yes, do you care?"

That simple question hit me square in the chest. The sensation intensified, my pulse quickening as I read and reread her words. Did I care? Wasn't this exactly what I'd wanted all along? The idea of her exploring, of me living vicariously through her? Yet, now that it was actually happening—or about to happen—the reality of it struck differently. Be careful, I told myself, my mind already spinning out of control.

But then, another thought crashed in. Who am I kidding? Of course, I wanted her to. The idea was as hot as anything I'd ever imagined, maybe even hotter. My throat was dry, and my fingers hovered over the screen. I had to tell her. What are you waiting for? My mind screamed. Just say "Hell yeah."

I typed: "No, I don't care..." but my thumb hesitated over the send button. No. It didn't feel right. I quickly erased it. I needed something more, something that would push her to give me more details.

Finally, I settled on: "What are you doing right now?"

I hit send and waited, the seconds stretching out again, my thoughts swirling wildly. What was she doing? Was she sitting there, undressed, teasing them both? Or had it already begun, the tension already boiling over into something more physical?

The reply came in almost immediately: "Just sitting at the table playing strip poker and I'm losing... badly."

Oh shit. My breath hitched. The image of Lucy sitting at the table naked, or at least mostly naked, with two other guys flashed vividly in my mind. My stomach flipped, my pulse racing faster as I imagined the scene unfolding. Her, laughing, playing coy, shedding clothes while they watched her, waiting for the game to turn into something more.

The idea filled me with a heady mix of jealousy and arousal. If I don't send the OK, I thought to myself, this could take even longer, and she'll be out even later. That meant I'd be left in the dark for hours, tortured by my own imagination.

I needed to know.

"Did they ask you to have a threesome?" I texted back, my fingers trembling as I pressed send.

Again, it took a while for her reply, and my mind ran wild with possibilities. Was it her turn to lose more clothes? Was she busy, her attention divided between me and them, her body the focus of their desires? The waiting was unbearable, and I could feel my heart thudding in my ears as the seconds dragged on.

Finally, my phone buzzed again.

"No. I want to bring it up."

Her words hit me like a jolt. Damn. She wasn't just playing around; she was enjoying this, savoring the control, the choices she was making. The way she threw around the word "slut" so casually, as if it was a badge of honor. And maybe, to her, it was.

I stared at the screen for a moment, processing her words. She really is leaning into this, isn't she? There was a part of me that reveled in it—her becoming the biggest slut she could be. She wasn't hesitating anymore; she was taking charge of her experiences. She wanted to be the one to bring it up.

"OK," I replied, keeping it simple, though the rush of thoughts in my head was anything but simple.

I set the phone down on the coffee table, exhaling a long, heavy breath. That's it, then. I probably wouldn't hear from her again until she came home, late into the night—or maybe not until morning. She was too busy, too wrapped up in the excitement of whatever was happening with those two guys. I tried to turn my attention back to the TV, but the anxious feeling in my chest wouldn't let me settle. My mind was buzzing, running wild with images of what she might be doing right now, the possibilities spinning out of control.

Damn it. I need a beer.

I pushed off the couch and made my way to the kitchen, hoping there was still some beer left in the fridge. But when I opened the door, there was nothing. Great. The empty shelves stared back at me, mocking my attempt at distraction. I sighed, running a hand through my hair. Alright, screw it. A drive to the store might help clear my head.

I grabbed my keys off the counter, deciding to go to the store in the next town over—anything to take up more time, to stretch out the night and keep my mind from spiraling further. The drive would give me space to think, to breathe. Or so I hoped.

As I got on the road, I cracked open a beer I'd stashed in the passenger seat, the cold bitterness sliding down my throat. The radio hummed in the background, but my mind wasn't on the music. It was on her. What was she doing right now? Was she laughing, flirting, letting them undress her piece by piece as they played strip poker? Or had things already progressed further? Were they all tangled up in each other by now?

The thought of her in the arms of those young college guys sent a rush of heat through me. Two guys, not one. The possibilities were endless, and I couldn't stop the images from flooding my mind. Would they take turns with her? Would she let them both have her at the same time? My stomach tightened, and my heart raced as I imagined her moaning, her body shared between them.

Focus. Focus on the drive.

I took another swig of beer and pushed those thoughts down, forcing myself to concentrate on the road. But no matter how hard I tried, the images kept coming back. The drive, though longer than usual, passed by in a blur, and before I knew it, I was pulling back into the driveway at home. It was about 1 a.m. now. I grabbed the remaining beers from the car and tossed them in the fridge, pulling my phone from my pocket as I did. Just in case.

I hadn't missed anything. Of course not. I'd been glued to the damn phone for hours, and still… nothing. I thumbed through the texts we'd exchanged earlier, reading and rereading them, feeling the anticipation build all over again. Each message was a tease, a reminder that she was out there, having an adventure that I could only imagine until she returned to tell me all the dirty details.

God, I hated the waiting. It was agonizing, torturous. But at the same time, I knew it would be worth it. When she came back and shared everything she'd done, I'd hang on every word, replaying it all in my mind while she spoke. That was the payoff—the stories, the images, the excitement in her voice as she described her slutty adventures in another man's—or, tonight, two men's —arms.

I cracked open another beer and headed back to the couch, hoping to distract myself with something on TV. I flipped through channel after channel, not really paying attention. My show had ended while I was out, and nothing else seemed worth watching. I settled on something—another mindless crime drama, maybe—and tried to lose myself in it. But it wasn't working.

My thoughts kept drifting back to Lucy. What if they really were fucking right now? Had she brought up the threesome yet, or were they waiting for the right moment? Maybe they were both undressing her, hands exploring her body as she moaned softly, enjoying the attention. The thought sent a rush of heat through me again.

By the time I glanced up at the clock, it was 3 a.m., and still no word. The silence weighed heavily on me, and my thoughts began to spiral again. What if she let them both take her at the same time? What if they were double penetrating her, one guy in her pussy, the other in her ass? Or maybe she was on her knees, sucking both of them off at the same time, letting them cum all over her, their bodies pressed up against hers.

Fuck! My body tensed with a mix of arousal and frustration. I couldn't handle the waiting anymore. I needed a new distraction, something to pull my mind away from the images flashing through my head. But no matter what I did, it always came back to her—Lucy, in that room, with those two guys.

I flipped through channels again, desperate for something—anything—that could pull me out of this mental loop. But nothing worked. The only thing that would bring relief was Lucy, walking through the door, telling me every filthy detail of what she'd done tonight.

I finally heard the unmistakable sound of her key sliding into the door around 6:00 a.m. My pulse quickened, and without a second thought, I jumped off the couch, crossing the room in seconds. I opened the door before she even had the chance to turn the knob.

"Hey," I greeted, trying to keep my voice casual despite the excitement bubbling up inside me.

Lucy stepped back in surprise, laughing as she looked up at me. "Wow," she said, raising an eyebrow. "Someone's excited." She slipped past me, setting her purse on the table and shrugging off her coat. The way she moved, so casual, so in control, only made the anticipation burn hotter.

She stepped closer, wrapping her arms around my neck, pulling me in for a deep kiss. Her lips were soft and inviting, and for a moment, I melted into her touch. But my mind was racing. I needed answers—details. Every minute she'd been gone had felt like torture.

"Have fun?" I asked, trying to keep it light, though the words came out too eager. Small talk. Play it cool. Don't interrogate her.

"It was an okay night," she replied, her tone infuriatingly calm as she turned away and headed toward the kitchen.

My heart skipped a beat. What the fuck was she doing? She was toying with me—she had to be. After everything, she was just going to brush it off like that? I felt the frustration rising in my chest, my thoughts running wild again. An 'okay' night? There was no way she'd just come home after a night with two guys and casually brush it off.

Without thinking, I reached out and grabbed her arm as she walked by, my grip gentle but firm. "Wait," I stammered, the urgency in my voice betraying my attempt at coolness.

She stopped and turned to face me, her eyes sparkling with amusement, a huge smile spreading across her face. She was enjoying this. She knew exactly what she was doing, and she was loving every second of it.

"Yes?" she asked, her voice dripping with playful innocence, as if she hadn't just spent the night with two college guys.

I let out an exasperated groan, stamping my foot in frustration. "Oh, come on!" I pleaded, feeling like I was about to burst.

Lucy's grin widened, and she extended her hand, gesturing for me to follow her back to the couch. I reluctantly sat down, my heart racing in my chest. She settled next to me, crossing her legs with deliberate ease, her posture relaxed as if she had all the time in the world. Meanwhile, I was on the verge of losing it, the suspense eating away at me.

She looked at me, her expression blank, as if nothing unusual had happened, as if the night had been as mundane as any other. It was killing me. She wasn't saying a word, wasn't offering up the details I craved, and it was driving me insane.

I stared at her, waiting for her to crack, to start spilling every bit of information. But she just smiled, her eyes twinkling with amusement. She's enjoying this way too much.

"Lucy..." I started, my voice thick with desperation. I couldn't take it anymore. I needed to know—everything. "You're killing me here. What happened?"

She leaned back, casually draping her arm over the back of the couch, her fingers playing with a loose strand of her hair. "What happened?" she repeated, drawing out the words as if savoring them. "Oh, you know... we played some cards. I lost a few rounds." She glanced at me, the corner of her mouth twitching as she tried to suppress a grin.

I narrowed my eyes at her, feeling the heat rising in my face. "That's it?" I asked, my voice rising with impatience. "You were gone all night, and all you have to say is that you lost a few rounds?"

She leaned in slightly, her eyes locking onto mine, and there was something wickedly playful in her gaze. "Well," she began slowly, "it wasn't just cards."

My heart pounded, and I leaned forward, hanging on her every word. Here we go.

She uncrossed her legs and leaned in closer, her voice dropping to a low, sultry tone. "Liam was a quick learner," she teased, her lips curling into a smile that made my stomach twist with anticipation. "And Steve? Well, let's just say... he wanted to try something new."

My breath caught in my throat as the images flashed through my mind. "Try what?" I asked, my voice barely above a whisper.

Lucy's smile widened as she watched me squirm. "I don't know... do you really want to know?"

I stared at her, my heart racing, my body tense with a mix of arousal and frustration. "Yes," I breathed, unable to hold back anymore. "Tell me everything."

She laughed softly, her eyes dancing with amusement. "Patience, baby," she whispered, her hand brushing against my thigh, sending a jolt of electricity through me. "I'll tell you... but only if you can handle it."

I swallowed hard, nodding. "I can handle it," I promised, though I wasn't entirely sure if that was true. But I needed to hear it, no matter what.

She leaned back again, her fingers tracing lazy circles on the fabric of the couch. "Alright," she said, her voice soft and teasing. "So, here's how it went..."

"Did you fuck them?" I asked, my voice trembling slightly, the anticipation coiling tighter in my chest. I couldn't hold the question back any longer; it had been gnawing at me from the moment she walked through the door.

Lucy's smile widened, a slow, sultry grin that sent a shiver through me. "Yes," she said simply, her voice smooth and confident. "Both of them. Mostly together, some one-on-one."

Her words hit me like a shockwave. I felt my erection begin to stir immediately, pressing hard against the fabric of my sweatpants—the ones I had changed into specifically, knowing I'd need the comfort when she returned home. The feeling in my chest intensified, my breath catching as my hands grew slick with sweat. This was a first. The most incredible, sluttiest thing my wife had ever done. She'd just fucked two guys—at the same time. And here she was, smiling as if it were the most natural thing in the world.

My mind spun with the images, my heart pounding in my ears. God, I wish I could have watched it. The thought sent a fresh surge of heat through me. She knew how much this turned me on, knew exactly how to tease me, to push my buttons. And yet, she was holding back.

"Why are you being stingy with the details?" I asked, my voice almost a plea now. I needed more. I needed every filthy detail of what had just happened.

Lucy, still smiling, casually reached for her purse, rummaging through it for a moment before pulling out a small flash drive. She held it out to me, her eyes twinkling with mischief.

"Liam is majoring in video editing," she explained, her voice teasingly casual. "So he had all the equipment. I suggested we film the whole thing for you, because I know how much you love jerking off to what I do with these other men."

I stared at the flash drive in her hand, my heart pounding in my chest, my mouth going dry. She filmed it. She filmed the whole thing for me. The realization made my cock throb painfully, straining against my sweatpants. I took the drive from her, my hand trembling slightly.

With a sudden burst of energy, I jumped off the couch and headed straight to the media player, practically tearing my sweatpants off in the process. My cock was rock hard now, aching for release. The anticipation, the excitement—it was almost too much to bear.

I slid the flash drive into the USB port, waiting for the file to load. As the screen blinked to life, I turned back to Lucy, expecting her to join me. But as I settled back onto the couch, I noticed she was getting up, preparing to leave the room.

"Aren't you going to watch it with me?" I asked, my voice tinged with desperation.

She paused, looking down at me with that same playful smirk. "Why?" she asked, her tone light and teasing. "I was there." She began to walk away, as if the thought of sitting through her own performance bored her.

I felt a pang of frustration. No. I didn't want her to leave. Not now. "Okay," I said quickly, my voice more measured this time. "Would you watch it with me?"

She stopped, turning slowly to look at me. Her eyes softened, a smile playing on her lips. "You really want me to?" she asked, her voice low and sultry.

I nodded, feeling the tension in the room thicken. "Yes," I whispered, the words barely audible. "I want to watch it with you."

"Baby, it's after six in the morning, and I've had a very tough night," Lucy said, her voice soft but firm, exhaustion lining every word. She leaned in, her lips meeting mine in a slow, tender kiss. "I'm seriously tired, and all I want to do is go to sleep."

I could hear the fatigue in her voice, and even though my mind was buzzing with questions and anticipation, I nodded. "Yeah, you're probably right," I said, disappointed but understanding. I let go of her hand as she turned and headed for the stairs. My eyes followed her, a knot of frustration tightening in my chest. She just spent the night fucking two guys, and she can't even sit down with me to watch the video?

As I sat back down on the couch, I stared at the blank screen, the remote heavy in my hand. I could still feel the lingering heat in the room, the charged energy between us before she disappeared. Why won't she watch it with me? The thought gnawed at me. She was there, living it, and now she didn't want to share that moment with me? I wanted this. I needed this. But she'd brushed me off so casually, leaving me alone with my thoughts and the damn video.

Frustrated, I pressed play, my heart pounding as the screen flickered to life.

It began with Liam, who I hadn't seen before, adjusting the camera. He was muscular, broad shoulders filling the frame, and his confident movements showed that he knew exactly what he was doing. So, this is the other guy, I thought, feeling a strange mix of curiosity and something darker as he set the camera to focus on the table.

And then there she was—Lucy—sitting on the table, completely naked, her skin glowing under the soft lighting. My breath caught in my throat. Steve stood beside her, his mouth already on her neck, his hands exploring her body as she casually stroked his cock. God, look at him. Steve's cock was thicker than mine, and seeing her hand wrapped around it, moving so easily, made my pulse race. His cock stood out, thick and solid, veins bulging as Lucy stroked him with a slow, deliberate motion.

Steve's cock was mesmerizing in a way that both excited me and made me feel that familiar pang of jealousy. He was younger, fitter, and there was no denying that his cock was impressive. The way it hung heavy in her hand, the way her fingers couldn't quite close around it—fuck, it was huge.

But then, Liam came back into the frame, stepping forward. Lucy extended her hand toward him, wrapping it around his cock as well. My eyes shifted to Liam. His cock wasn't as thick as Steve's—more like mine in terms of size—but there was one obvious difference. Liam wasn't circumcised. The foreskin slid back as Lucy stroked him, and I could see the way her eyes widened in curiosity. She's never been with an uncut guy before.

The camera captured the moment perfectly—her fingers exploring Liam's cock, her movements slower, more deliberate. I could see her fascination, the way she studied him. She leaned forward, and I watched her take him into her mouth, her tongue working over the head, sliding under the foreskin. Damn, she's really into this.

A surge of frustration and arousal hit me at once. She'd never been with an uncircumcised guy, and now she had this muscular, handsome man in her mouth. I felt my hand tighten around my cock, but it wasn't just about the size this time—it was the way she explored Liam's cock, her curiosity, her hunger for something new. Liam was muscular, his body glistening with a thin sheen of sweat, his hand resting on her head as she sucked him. God, she's loving this.

Steve, meanwhile, was still sucking on her tits, his thick cock now pressed against her thigh, waiting for attention. Lucy, ever the multitasker, switched back and forth between the two men, her hands and mouth working in perfect synchronization. One moment she was stroking Steve's thick shaft, the next she was leaning in to take Liam's cock back into her mouth, her eyes gleaming with interest as she explored the differences in each man.

The more I watched, the more I couldn't help but feel that mixture of jealousy and arousal growing. She's never been with a guy like Liam before, never experienced an uncut cock, and now here she is, fully immersed in it. I could see it in the way her mouth moved over his shaft, the way she savored every inch, every ridge of him. Her fingers played with the foreskin, pulling it back, and the way Liam's body responded told me how much he was enjoying the attention.

I slowed my strokes, knowing I wouldn't last long if I kept up this pace. Two guys fucking my wife. The thought sent a wave of heat through me. Steve's thick cock, dominating her hand, and Liam's uncut cock, filling her mouth as she explored him like something she'd never seen before—it was too much.

This is why she didn't want to watch it with me. She knew I'd be blown away, overwhelmed, and she didn't want to deal with my questions. God, I have so many questions. Was Liam's uncut cock better? Did she prefer it? Was she more into Steve because of how thick he was? Or was it the novelty of Liam's foreskin that made her so into it?

On screen, Lucy was now stroking both men, one in each hand. Steve's thick cock filled her hand completely, her fingers barely able to close around him as she stroked with a steady rhythm. Meanwhile, Liam's cock, though similar to mine in size, was different in the way she touched it—her fingers playing with his foreskin, her mouth moving over him with fascination.

She's never sucked a cock like that before. That realization hit me hard. It was something new for her, and she was fully engrossed in it. I could see the way her body reacted, the way her hips shifted as Liam's hands explored her, the way she moaned around Steve's cock.

I could barely contain myself. My hand moved faster, the tension in my body building as I watched them work over her, two men, each with their own unique qualities, each giving her something different. And she loved every second of it.

As Lucy took Liam's cock in her mouth, she shifted her hand over to Steve's stiff member, stroking him with a steady rhythm. Liam's eyes closed, his fingers tangling in her hair as she bobbed up and down, savoring every inch of his uncut cock. Then, Steve reached down and pulled her off the table. She dropped to her knees on the floor between them, her hands already reaching for both cocks again.

She looked like she belonged there—on her knees, in the middle of two men, moving effortlessly between them. Her head bobbed up and down, mouth switching from Liam to Steve, while her hands worked the shafts she wasn't sucking. The sight of her so completely lost in the act made my breath catch. Goddamn, this is hot! I couldn't believe what I was seeing, the way she moved, the way she handled both of them like she'd been doing it her whole life. I stroked myself harder, watching in complete awe, barely able to contain myself.

After a few minutes of watching Lucy skillfully take them both in her mouth, Steve pulled her to her feet. He wasted no time, bending her over slightly and entering her from behind, his thick cock pushing into her with ease. Liam stepped forward, positioning himself in front of her, sliding his cock back into her mouth.

What the fuck, I thought to myself, my mind racing. Lucy's really doing this. She was bent over, one man fucking her pussy while the other fucked her mouth. This wasn't just some casual fling—this was a new level of slut I hadn't imagined her embracing, and the realization both thrilled and shocked me.

I felt the pressure building inside me, the tightness in my chest intensifying. How much longer can I last? My cock throbbed painfully in my hand, and I had to stop stroking several times, trying to prolong the moment. Every time I slowed down, they switched positions, rearranging like it was the most natural thing in the world. Each man took his turn with her—both Steve and Liam fucked her from behind, their hands gripping her hips, her body rocking back and forth with every thrust.

Liam's cock, though not as thick as Steve's, seemed to intrigue Lucy even more. I could see the way her mouth moved eagerly over him, the way her body responded when he was behind her, thrusting deep into her. Was it the foreskin? Was it the way he felt compared to Steve? I had so many questions, but none that mattered in the heat of the moment.

Finally, Liam came closer to the camera, and with a flick of his hand, the screen went dark for a brief moment. Is that it? But no—the camera was clearly on a tripod, because the next scene opened with Lucy lying in a bed, her legs spread, one of them pounding into her in missionary.

I couldn't see his face—just his ass flexing with each thrust as his cock plunged into my wife, over and over. My mind raced again. Who is it this time? Is it Steve or Liam? Whoever it was, his cock was driving into Lucy relentlessly, her moans soft but steady as he fucked her.

A part of me felt like an outsider watching this—like I was witnessing something so intimate, so raw, and yet it was my own wife in the middle of it all. She was theirs now, at least for tonight.

Then, I realized it was Steve, his thick shaft sliding out of her pussy as he pulled back, standing up from the bed. Lucy groaned softly, her body quivering slightly from the loss of contact. But before she could catch her breath, Liam moved into the frame, taking Steve's place. His body was lean and muscular, his cock standing hard as he positioned himself between her legs.

As soon as Liam entered her, Lucy let out a sharp yelp, her body arching toward him. He wasted no time, lifting her legs into the air, exposing her feet as they flopped around while he fucked her. I could see the way his cock moved inside her, the foreskin sliding back as he thrust deep into her, her moans growing louder with each stroke.

There was something about this scene that hit different. She's moaning more with Liam. Was it because he felt different? Was it the way he lifted her legs, giving her that full feeling as he pumped into her? My mind wandered as I watched, wondering if she preferred him, if this experience would stick with her.

I began to contemplate something new, something that hadn't crossed my mind before. Would she do this again? Would she repeat this night, maybe even take Liam as a solo lover? I shook the thought away. Too far ahead, calm down and focus. But the idea lingered, teasing me, as I watched her moan louder under Liam's thrusts, her feet twitching in the air with each movement.

I stroked myself harder, trying to focus on the moment, on the way her body responded to each man, on how much she was clearly enjoying herself. But in the back of my mind, the thought wouldn't go away. What if she wants more? What if she wants Liam again?

It didn't look like either of them had cum yet. They seemed to be switching at random now, their movements more relaxed, more exploratory. Then, they pulled Lucy to the edge of the bed, just off to the side of the camera shot. Steve lay down in front of her, his thick cock still rock hard, and she immediately bent down to take him in her mouth, her lips sliding over him with a hungry determination.

Liam, standing behind her, watched for a moment before positioning himself. His cock, already slick from earlier, hovered behind her, but then he moved, switching places with Steve. I could see the unspoken coordination between them—the easy rhythm they had, moving around her like it was a practiced dance.

Lucy climbed back up to the center of the bed, her body glistening under the dim light. The camera stayed in the same angle, capturing every move as she straddled Liam's hips. She leaned down to kiss him, her mouth soft and slow against his as she began to grind on his dick, her body moving in perfect time. Liam's hands gripped her hips, his muscles tensing as she pumped up and down on him.

And then I saw it. Steve moved into the frame from behind, positioning himself with a focused intensity. He's going for her ass. My heart pounded in my chest as I watched him line up behind her. The anticipation built, and I could see the tension in Lucy's body as Steve pushed forward. Then, her groan—a mix of pain and pleasure—confirmed it. He's in.

Lucy was now taking both of them, at the same time. Jesus. My mind raced as I recalled the conversations we'd had, the teasing way she mentioned that book she'd read—the one about a woman taking two men. I remembered her laughing, saying how fun it sounded, but I never thought she'd actually go for it. Yet here she was, living out that fantasy, her body stretched and filled by two men.

Her groans turned to soft, desperate moans as Steve buried himself deeper in her ass, his thick cock testing her limits. I could see her body tremble with every thrust, and the way her hips moved, her back arched in a way that drove both men wild. Fuck. The image was overwhelming—Lucy, my wife, completely at their mercy, her body shared between them.

I gripped my cock harder, feeling the strain as I tried to hold back. I won't last much longer.

Then they began to switch again. Steve pulled out from behind, and Liam, still lying beneath Lucy, slid out of her pussy. Steve took over on the bed, assuming the lower position as Lucy slid down onto his thick shaft, her legs trembling as she adjusted to him. Liam moved behind, positioning himself at her ass this time, clearly eager to take her where Steve had been.

He pushed forward, but Lucy's body reacted instantly. Her head jerked back, and she let out a sharp gasp. Her voice cut through the room, strained. "Too fat... it's too fat for my ass. It hurts."

Liam hesitated, his body tensing at her words. I could see the frustration in his face—he wanted her, but she was clearly struggling with his size. His cock, though not as thick as Steve's overall, was enough to stretch her beyond what she could handle. The moment hung in the air, thick with tension.

After a brief pause, they switched again. Steve remained in her ass, his cock fitting her better, while Liam took her pussy once more. The rhythm between them returned, their bodies moving together with a practiced, almost instinctual ease.

Lucy moaned louder now, her body responding eagerly to the new balance between the two of them. Her hips rocked in time with their thrusts, her fingers digging into the sheets as the two men filled her completely. She was in control again, her earlier discomfort replaced by pure pleasure as the men continued to fuck her from both sides.

Watching her like this—seeing the way her body reacted, the way she moved with them—it was almost too much to bear. I could barely hold back the flood of sensations running through me, my cock throbbing in my hand as I watched her take everything they gave her.

When they each had their turn in my wife's ass, fulfilling her fantasy of being double-penetrated, the camera shifted again. It was still the same room, but from a new angle that focused on the floor where Lucy now lay. Steve and Liam stood over her, their cocks still hard, their bodies glistening with the sheen of sweat. The faint murmur of voices filled the room, and although

I couldn't make out every word, I caught enough to realize what was happening. Lucy was coaxing them, talking dirty, urging them to cum on her.

My heart pounded in my chest. Did she just beg them to cum on her face? The thought raced through my mind, almost too wild to comprehend. This wasn't Lucy's usual teasing. She'd always hated cum. Sure, she'd swallowed for other men recently, but it was never about enjoying it—it was always about turning them on, playing her part, or teasing me. But this... this looked different.

As if on cue, both men began jerking their cocks, standing over her. I watched, breathless, as Lucy lay there beneath them, her eyes half-lidded, her lips parted in anticipation. And then, they came—thick streams of cum shot across her face, splattering her cheeks, her lips, and her forehead. The sight was mesmerizing, overwhelming.

But what shocked me even more was her reaction. Lucy wasn't just enduring it. She looked like she was savoring it—actually enjoying the sensation of their cum coating her face. Her hands were still raised, one wrapped around each man's balls, squeezing gently as if coaxing every last drop out of them.

When the torrent of cum began to slow, instead of pulling away or wiping it off, Lucy did something that left me stunned. She pulled them closer, bringing their cocks toward her mouth. One by one, she took each cock into her mouth, licking them clean. I stared in disbelief, my mind racing. Lucy hates cum. She always has.

But here she was, her lips sliding over Steve's cock, cleaning the cum off with slow, deliberate movements. She swirled her tongue around the head, her fingers still between her legs, fingering herself as she worked on him. This wasn't just for them—she was into it.

My breath caught in my throat. What the hell is happening? It wasn't just about performing for them, or teasing me. I could see it in the way she moved, the way she moaned softly as she sucked them clean. She was enjoying every second of it—

relishing the taste, the feel of their cum on her skin.

Lucy switched to Liam next, her mouth wrapping around his uncut cock, her tongue sliding under the foreskin as she licked off the remaining cum. She was deliberate, slow, taking her time. She's loving this. I could see it in the way her body reacted, in the subtle way she shifted, her fingers still working between her legs. She wasn't just playing a role—she was enjoying it.

I felt a surge of arousal and shock at the same time, the intensity of the moment overwhelming me. Lucy had changed. This wasn't the same woman who used to cringe at the idea of cum touching her skin. She had fully embraced this, and it was the most erotic thing I had ever seen.

That's when I lost it. My body tensed, and I exploded, cum shooting everywhere. It was the largest load I'd ever remember releasing, the force of it catching me off guard as I gasped for breath. My cock throbbed in my hand, still twitching as it began to soften. But even as I came, my eyes were glued to the screen, unable to tear away from what I was seeing.

Lucy finally pulled back, her face still streaked with cum. But instead of wiping it off or showing any sign of discomfort, she smiled. She licked her lips slowly, savoring the taste, and then got up, walking toward the camera.

There was nothing familiar about what happened next. This wasn't the woman who normally recoiled from cum, who hated the mess it left behind. Lucy leaned in close to the camera, her face covered in cum, and she smiled—a deep, satisfied smile. She raised her fingers to her face, wiping a streak of cum off her cheek before slowly sucking it off her fingertips.

What the hell is going on? I thought, still in disbelief. She was enjoying this. She was loving it. And it wasn't just to turn them on—it was real. She was fully immersed in this, and that realization sent another jolt of arousal through me, even as my body trembled from the intensity of my own orgasm.

She looked directly into the camera, her eyes locking onto mine as if she knew I'd be watching.

"Did you like that, baby?" she asked, her voice sultry and full of satisfaction. "I did. Loved it, actually."

She twirled around, playfully kissing each guy on the cheek before turning back to the camera. Her eyes gleamed with mischief, and her lips curled into a teasing smile.

"Okay, babe, I'll be heading out of here soon... I hope you enjoyed the show and shot a big load for me." She winked, her voice teasing, a soft snicker escaping her lips as she leaned forward, her face still glistening with cum.

The camera cut off abruptly, leaving me sitting there in stunned silence. Wow. I could barely process what I'd just seen. My wife had made a porno—a full-on, hardcore threesome with two young college guys—and she had done more than just perform. She had enjoyed every filthy second of it. This was a new Lucy—a woman who embraced her desires without hesitation.

I grabbed my sweatpants off the floor, my body still shaking from the release as I turned off the Blu-Ray player and the TV. Lucy had truly transformed. And I couldn't help but wonder what she would be like the next time.

CARDS ON THE TABLE

T he next day was uneventful, but there was a tension hanging in the air that I couldn't quite shake. Lucy wouldn't talk about what had happened in the video she gave me last night. She didn't flat-out refuse to talk about it —there was no "I won't discuss this"—but every time I tried to bring it up, she'd change the subject, pivoting effortlessly as if she didn't even notice my questions. Why wouldn't she talk about it? The video had been so intense, so different from anything we'd ever done before, yet she seemed determined to avoid the topic altogether.

I decided to play it off, pretending not to notice her evasiveness. Maybe she needed time to process it herself. I'd wait a few days, let the dust settle, and bring it up again when the moment felt right.

She spent most of the day glued to her phone, her fingers tapping rapidly against the screen. She never offered to tell me who she was texting, and I didn't ask. It's probably Steve or Liam, I told myself, though the thought of it made my stomach churn a little. It wasn't jealousy, not exactly. It was something else—an unease that I couldn't quite place.

Later in the afternoon, Lucy casually mentioned that she and Beth were going to the mall to do some shopping, and they'd be gone all afternoon. She kissed me goodbye, her lips soft against mine, but there was a disconnect—something just didn't feel right.

As soon as Beth's car pulled into the driveway and Lucy waved me off with that usual smile, my mind started to wander. What was she hiding? Why wouldn't she answer my questions about last night? Was there something in those text messages that she didn't want me to know about? My thoughts spiraled into familiar territory, filling with paranoid possibilities. What if she's hiding something bigger?

I shook my head, trying to push the thoughts away, but they gnawed at me. And then, I did something I never thought I'd do —something that had always seemed unthinkable. I walked over to the kitchen table, and without even fully realizing what I was doing, I grabbed her laptop.

As I sat down on the couch, her laptop in my hands, a part of me screamed to stop, to put it back, to leave everything alone. Even if she's keeping something from me, she'd tell me eventually. Or maybe she was planning to make it a surprise for me—another erotic adventure. I hesitated, the weight of my actions settling in as I waited for the operating system to boot up. Should I really be doing this?

But the paranoia was eating at me, and I couldn't let it go. I had to know something. Anything.

The screen finally came to life, and I began to search. I started with the usual places—'My Documents,' a folder labeled 'Personal,' a folder named 'Notes,' and even dug through the 'Program Files' for anything that looked out of place. Nothing. My frustration grew with each passing minute. Was I just being paranoid? Was there nothing to find after all?

And then, by pure chance, I clicked on an unnamed disk that was in the drive. A folder appeared, filled with a ton of text files. The titles were obscure, nothing that gave any indication of what they contained. One file caught my eye—titled simply, 'One.' I clicked on it, my heart racing.

The screen filled with text. My eyes widened as I began to read. It was a detailed description of everything we had ever talked about—conversations we'd had late at night, things I'd said, every reason I'd given for wanting her to explore these sexual adventures. She wrote about how much I wanted it, how I'd convinced her to try it for me. This was a digital diary.

My heart sank as the realization hit me. I'd known for a while that she kept a diary, but I never thought I'd find it, let alone read it. And now that I was staring at the words she'd written—her inner thoughts, her reasons for doing what she did—it all felt too real. She was doing this for me.

I sat there, staring at the screen, my mind reeling. All this time, I'd thought she was just as excited about these new experiences as I was. But reading her words, it became clear that she'd been hesitant at first, unsure, but willing to do it because I wanted it so badly.

The weight of that realization settled heavily in my chest. Was I pushing her too far? Was this all too much for her? The paranoia that had driven me to open her laptop in the first place now gave way to guilt. She was doing all of this for me, and I hadn't even realized it.

I sat back, the laptop still open in front of me, my heart pounding. I wasn't sure what to do next. Should I close it, pretend I never saw any of this? Or should I confront her, ask her what she really felt about everything we'd been doing?

One thing was clear—this was more complicated than I had thought.

My hands shook as I clicked open the next file, my curiosity now fully overtaking any guilt or hesitation. The title didn't give much away, but as soon as the text filled the screen, I knew this one was different. It was all about Jordan.

My stomach twisted as I read the words, seeing my wife's inner thoughts laid bare in front of me. She described how sexy she found him, how she had thought about approaching him even before he ever made a move. I had no idea. She'd seemed so casual when she told me about him, so offhand about their encounters, but reading this now? There was nothing casual about it. She'd been drawn to him from the start, thinking about him, fantasizing about him. The sex, she wrote, had been amazing. Of course, she mentioned his cock—it was enormous, bigger than any man she'd ever been with before. That wasn't news to me, but seeing it written out in her words made it sting differently.

I scrolled through the file, feeling a strange mix of emotions —jealousy, excitement, and something else, something that felt like a punch to the gut. She wanted him. Not just physically.

Unable to stop myself, I started opening more files. They were all detailed accounts, meticulously recorded. There were more entries about Jordan, of course—about the times they'd been together, about her excitement and anticipation whenever she knew she'd see him. But there were other files too—ones about Steve, about their flirtation, about how she had been drawn to his youth and energy. One entry was about the time they had sex in his car after leaving the restaurant, another about a quick fuck at a gas station. I had no idea she was documenting all of this.

Each file was like a new revelation, giving me a more detailed view of everything Lucy had done since we started this arrangement. It wasn't just the physical act that intrigued her— it was the thrill, the feeling of power, the way she could control the situation. She was playing a role, but she loved it. My wife had fully embraced being the slut wife, and reading these entries confirmed it.

I paused, my fingers hovering over the cursor as I noticed one final file at the bottom of the list. The most recent one. I clicked it open, my heart racing. It was a detailed account of last night—

the threesome.

When the hell did she even have time to write this? I wondered, my mind spinning as I started to read. She had captured everything I saw on the video, but this time, I had her thoughts —her feelings. She described each moment in vivid detail, not just what happened, but how she felt about it, what parts she liked the most.

What surprised me even more was how methodical she had been about the entire thing. Lucy had planned the threesome before they'd even started playing strip poker. She purposely lost, gauging their reactions to her naked body as she sat before them, enjoying the way their eyes devoured her. She wrote that it was her idea to suggest playing poker and then strip poker as a way to test the waters. My wife had orchestrated the entire evening.

Wow. I sat back, dumbfounded. I'd known she had changed, that she had embraced this new side of herself, but reading her words made it real in a way that nothing else had. She wanted this as much as I did—maybe even more.

She also described how she'd overly fondled Steve in front of Liam, testing the boundaries and flirting with him throughout the night. There were little moments I hadn't noticed—how she sneaked kisses and fondled Steve during his bathroom breaks or when he went to get drinks. She was manipulating the situation perfectly, keeping them both on edge. Then came the part that threw me the most—when she wrote about confronting Liam about the threesome first, during one of Steve's absences. She'd been making out with him, and that's when she told him about me, about how I loved watching, how it turned me on.

She told him about me, just like that. That was when Liam had mentioned his major in video editing and offered to film the entire thing for us. The pieces started to come together in my mind as I read. Lucy had been the one to make the first move with Liam, and it had been her idea to set everything in motion.

Apparently, Steve didn't need much convincing, as Lucy didn't even mention having to bring up the idea with him. I could imagine that with the way she was flirting and touching them both, Steve probably didn't care as long as he got his turn.

At the end of that last diary entry, Lucy had mentioned something that sat sorely with me: the threesome was the second-best sex she'd ever had. It didn't take much guessing to figure out what the best was—Jordan. That stung, more than I wanted to admit. The thought of her putting him at the top, the best she'd ever experienced, gnawed at me. Why him? But I quickly pushed that feeling aside. She was exploring new experiences. Of course, she'd find them wonderful and exhilarating. It was part of what we'd agreed on.

But still, the sting lingered. Even as I tried to dismiss it, the comparison weighed on me.

Feeling a mix of emotions, I grew bolder. Maybe too bold. I decided to check her personal email. I needed to know more. Since this was her computer, the login was saved in the browser. No hacking required. My fingers hesitated over the keyboard, but then I hit enter, and her inbox popped up in front of me.

I scrolled through the usual clutter—random forwards from coworkers, messages from her mother, a few notes from Beth about their plans for the day. It was all mundane, ordinary stuff. But then, my heart skipped a beat as I saw it: recent emails from Jordan.

Why hadn't she mentioned that he was still contacting her? Regardless of what he was saying, why hide it? I clicked on the first one, my pulse quickening.

At first, it was harmless. Jordan talked about his new life in South Carolina, how he was enjoying his job and settling into his new apartment. But then, as I scrolled further, the emails started to change. The tone shifted. Jordan wrote about how much he missed her. How much he missed her pussy. How much he missed the way she sucked him off, the way she felt under him.

My stomach twisted as I scrolled down to see Lucy's replies. Her words stared back at me, raw and unapologetic. She told him she missed the sex too, that she missed his 'huge cock.' She wrote that she wished he hadn't taken the job so they could still fuck whenever they wanted. My heart raced as I read on—she told him about Steve, but added that it wasn't as good as it had been with him.

What the hell? I sat there, reeling, my mind trying to process everything. She had never told me that she was still thinking about Jordan like this. Why? I thought she'd moved on after he left, but clearly, that wasn't the case. She even asked him if he'd be visiting anytime soon, and if they could 'hook up' when he did.

Jordan's reply was just as blunt. He wasn't sure when he'd be back, but if he did come to visit, it would be a 'sure thing.' The casual way they talked about it, like it was inevitable, made my head spin.

And then, something else caught my eye. A paperclip icon. Attachments. My heart pounded as I clicked on it. The first few images were innocent enough—pictures of Jordan's new apartment, a few shots of the beach, and one or two photos of him standing by the water, smiling. I almost relaxed, thinking I was overreacting.

But then the explicit photos started. Jordan's erect cock filled the screen, unmistakable and brazen. In one, he was stroking it, his hand wrapped tightly around the shaft. Another showed him cumming on some flat surface, thick streams of white dripping down. My stomach dropped. There were more—pictures of him holding his cock in one hand, cum pooling in the other.

As I continued scrolling through the emails, something else caught my attention—pictures in her replies. My heart raced as I opened the first one. It was Lucy, naked, posing provocatively.

Her body was on full display, her skin glowing in the soft light of our bedroom. There were more—some of her masturbating, using the dildos she kept hidden in her bedside drawer, her face twisted in pleasure as she photographed herself mid-act.

There were several photos taken around our house: some on the bed, others on the couch, and even one where she was sprawled across our kitchen table, legs spread wide as she stared into the camera with that familiar, sultry look in her eyes. But what really caught me off guard were the others—the ones not taken at home.

One set was from her cubicle at work. They were upskirt photos, taken from a low angle, her skirt hiked up just enough to reveal she wasn't wearing any underwear. God, she was doing this at work? Another set was from the car, parked somewhere I didn't recognize. She'd taken these pictures during the day, by the looks of it, in broad daylight.

My stomach twisted as I realized the extent of what she had been doing. She was sharing these with Jordan. The man she described as the best sex she ever had. The Greek god she still couldn't get out of her system. And she hadn't told me a word about it.

The more I thought about it, the more underwhelmed and frustrated I felt. Why hadn't she shared this with me? I would've gotten off to this, knowing she was sending him provocative photos, living out her slutty fantasies. But the secrecy? That pissed me off. She'd kept this hidden, and for what? Was she afraid I wouldn't want to know? Or did she just want to keep it to herself?

But I couldn't bring it up. I couldn't confront her, not like this. Not when I wasn't happy with how I'd found out in the first place. I couldn't wait for her to tell me either, though—the emails were from over a month ago, and it was clear she had no intention of bringing it up. What now?

Hours passed before Lucy returned from the mall. I watched her walk in with Beth, her face flushed from an afternoon of shopping. She kissed me on the cheek, her lips soft and casual, like nothing was out of the ordinary. "Can you help bring in the bags?" she asked.

I obliged, carrying in the weight of her shopping trip while my mind raced with everything I'd uncovered. When we sat down at the table for dinner, the secrets I had unearthed gnawed at me. I wanted to ask her. I wanted to know everything. But how could I? She had no idea what I'd seen.

Instead, I decided to take a different approach. Something more subtle. I wanted to test the waters, see if she'd give anything away.

"So," I started, trying to keep my tone casual as we ate, "have you heard anything from Jordan?"

She didn't even flinch. Her fork didn't pause mid-air. In fact, she didn't seem the least bit surprised by my question. It was as if I'd asked her about something as ordinary as the weather.

"Yea," she replied, nonchalantly, her eyes not even meeting mine. She didn't offer more, didn't seem concerned by the fact that we hadn't talked about Jordan in over a month.

My chest tightened. So, this was normal for her. Just chatting with Jordan, sending photos, maybe even more, all while acting like everything was perfectly fine between us.

I kept eating, trying to keep my cool, but my mind was swirling with a thousand questions, none of which I felt ready to ask her. Not yet.

I sat there, chewing my food slowly, trying to calm the storm in my head. Maybe I was reading far too much into this. Maybe Lucy wasn't trying to hide anything from me. Was I being distrustful? Just because my wife had embraced the idea of fucking other men didn't mean she was suddenly hiding things from me. She loved me. I knew that. I was the one who encouraged her to explore these new experiences. I turned her into this confident, sexual woman.

"Oh, yea?" I said, playing it cool, taking another bite of my food.

Lucy didn't miss a beat. "Yeah, I get emails from him sometimes," she replied, casually, as if she were talking about something as mundane as grocery shopping. "He says he's really enjoying his new job and loves the beach."

I blinked, momentarily taken aback by her openness. She's telling me about the emails. Maybe there was nothing to hide. Maybe I was just letting my paranoia get the better of me.

"Anything else?" I asked, trying to sound as casual as possible, though my heart was racing slightly.

"Yeah," she said, looking up from her plate with a small smile, "we started sending dirty pictures."

What? I felt a momentary rush of shock. She told me. She wasn't hiding anything. She was being completely upfront. What the fuck was I doing? Of course, she wouldn't hide this from me. Lucy loved me. I was her husband. If it weren't for me, she'd never have even considered fucking other men. I was the one who'd turned her into this adventurous, sexually liberated woman.

"That's cool," I replied, trying to suppress the wave of relief that was washing over me.

"You're not mad, are you?" she asked, her tone light but with a hint of concern in her eyes.

I shook my head, feeling all the anxiety that had been building up drain out of me. "Nope, I think it's hot too," I said with a smile, my voice steady now.

She smiled back at me, her face relaxing as we continued eating. She wasn't hiding anything. It had all been in my head. Lucy loved me, and I had nothing to worry about.

We finished our meal, and later, we found ourselves back on the couch, scrolling through Netflix, looking for something to watch. The evening was peaceful, comfortable. But despite the relief I felt, there was still a part of me that wanted to keep asking questions, to dive deeper into what had happened last night. Even though I'd already read her deepest thoughts, I still wanted to hear it from her.

"Do you want to go out tonight?" Lucy asked unexpectedly, her voice carrying a hint of mischief as she lay comfortably on my lap.

I looked down at her, puzzled. "Where to?" I asked, trying to decipher her sudden proposal.

She sat up, pressing her lips to mine before pulling back just enough to smile. "I was thinking," she began, her grin widening, "you could sit in a corner booth and watch me flirt with the first attractive man I saw. And if things go well… we could get a hotel room, and maybe you'd be able to watch me fuck him."

Her words hung in the air, sending a jolt of excitement straight through me. We'd never done anything like that before. My mind raced with the possibilities. The idea of watching her, seeing her flirt, seduce, and then potentially fuck a stranger, was overwhelming. Where was she getting these ideas? I wondered. But I didn't care. Her newfound acceptance of being a slut, of embracing her sexual power, was intoxicating.

"Sure!" I exclaimed, a little too quickly, excitement creeping into my voice.

Lucy laughed, a deeper, knowing laugh that told me she could sense my eagerness. "Alright, let's go get ready," she said as she stood up from the couch, her hips swaying as she moved toward the stairs. She turned to face me halfway up, her grin still firmly in place. "By the way, I'm not going to wear any panties tonight," she teased.

My erection stirred immediately at her words. No panties. The thought of her out in public, teasing men, showing just enough skin to drive them wild, while she wore nothing underneath, filled me with anticipation.

As I waited by the door, fixing my hair in the mirror to hide my excitement, her voice floated down the stairs. "Don't worry, you look nice." I turned, seeing her descending gracefully toward me, a knowing smile on her lips.

"Y-yeah... sure," I stammered, my breath catching as she wrapped her arms around my shoulders, her body pressing softly against mine. I turned, my hands instinctively finding their way to her hips as I pulled her close, kissing her deeply. "Wow," I muttered, pulling back slightly to take her in.

She giggled, a soft, playful sound, and stepped out into the open to twirl around. She looked stunning. Her blonde hair was down, cascading in soft curls that framed her face. Her lips were painted a striking red, and a delicate diamond-encrusted butterfly necklace rested on her collarbone, shimmering in the light. But it was her outfit that really took my breath away. She wore a deep-v black blouse, the mesh around her breasts offering just enough of a tease, revealing ample cleavage while leaving the rest to the imagination. Her black mini skirt hugged her hips, ending just above mid-thigh, leaving her long legs exposed.

I pulled her closer again, my hand sliding up her inner thigh, under the skirt. My fingers brushed against her bare pussy lips, feeling the soft, warm skin. My eyebrows shot up in surprise as I looked at her. No panties.

"No panties," I whispered, feigning shock, though I already knew. She peered back at me seductively, her eyes gleaming as if she knew exactly the effect she was having on me. Without a word, she grabbed her coat from the recliner nearby, slipping it over her shoulders.

"I was thinking we should head to The Bellamy," she said

casually as she walked out the door toward the car.

I hesitated for a moment, the name of the hotel triggering a flood of memories. The Bellamy. It was an upscale, high-class hotel downtown. The place we had stayed for our honeymoon. It had been perfect back then—elegant, luxurious, intimate. Now she wanted to take a lover there. The thought thrilled me.

I eagerly followed her, my mind spinning with anticipation. The Bellamy. The idea of watching her flirt with a stranger, of possibly seeing her take him there, to the very place we had stayed on our honeymoon, was too much to resist. I hurried to the car, my pulse quickening as I imagined what the night had in store for us.

As we drove toward the hotel, the closer we got to our destination, the more the uneasy feeling in my stomach began to churn. That familiar tightness in my chest started building, the anticipation of what might happen—what I might witness —pushing me to the edge. She wasn't even doing anything yet. Hell, we hadn't even arrived, and already my mind was racing. The very thought of her seducing another man, of me watching her flirt and tease, had my cock straining against my pants. I was already hard.

When we finally arrived, I pulled up to the valet, stepping out to walk around and open her door. As Lucy slid out of the car, I got a perfect view of her exposed pussy, a fleeting but deliberate flash that sent a jolt of electricity through me. She smiled wickedly as she took my hand, tucking her arm into mine with a playful squeeze.

Before we could make it further inside, she leaned close, her lips brushing against my ear as she whispered, "We should separate, so it doesn't look like we're together."

I nodded, agreeing, my excitement building as I let her walk ahead. Watching her walk away, her hips swaying in that tight skirt, her bare pussy just inches away from anyone noticing—

it was intoxicating. I trailed behind, admiring the view before slipping into the hotel, where I requested a booth in the back, one that faced the bar. The perfect vantage point.

With a glass of scotch in hand, I settled into the booth, my eyes glued to Lucy as she perched at the bar, alone. She sipped her wine slowly, making small talk with the bartender, her eyes scanning the room. Waiting. I could feel my heart pounding in my chest, every sip of scotch doing little to calm me. Then, a man approached her.

I couldn't make out what he said, but I saw the way he patted her shoulder, smiled, and walked away. He must have struck out. I smirked, wondering what it was about him that didn't interest her. Maybe he wasn't bold enough.

About fifteen minutes passed before another man caught her attention. This one was different. Tall, just the way she liked them, with short dark brown hair and a clean-cut look. He had the appearance of someone successful—a stockbroker, maybe, or some kind of corporate professional. He was exactly her type.

I watched closely as he made her laugh quickly, though I recognized that laugh—her flirty laugh. It wasn't genuine amusement; it was the laugh she used when she wanted to please, when she was toying with someone. He sat down next to her, ordered two more glasses of wine, and leaned in, talking confidently. She lifted her glass, sipping it as he continued speaking, their conversation fluid, relaxed.

Then something unexpected happened. Her head nodded in my direction. The man followed her gaze and looked right at me. He smiled. I froze, the weird mixture of excitement and embarrassment swirling in my chest. What did she tell him? Did she say I was her husband? Did she tell him that I was sitting here watching because I liked to see her flirt with other men? Or did she go even further—did she tell him that we were here to find someone she could fuck while I watched?

The possibilities sent my mind spinning.

I ordered another scotch as the waiter passed by, my eyes never leaving Lucy. She was getting closer to him, more relaxed. They were on their second round of wine now, both leaning in more intimately. She'd occasionally place her hand on his leg, a casual but deliberate gesture. He responded by grazing her arm with his hand, inching closer with each touch. It was working.

Thirty minutes passed, and the tension was at its peak. This was going to happen. They were getting comfortable, the wine loosening them both up. I imagined how it would go—she'd suggest they get a room, maybe even invite me to join or watch from the shadows. My cock twitched in anticipation.

But then, just like that, the man stood up. He smiled, said something to her, and walked away.

What? That was it? Forty-five minutes spent watching, waiting, building up to this moment—and he was leaving? Fuck. I felt a wave of frustration hit me as I watched him disappear from view. All that time, and nothing.

I took a deep breath, trying to calm myself. Maybe it was just bad luck. Maybe he wasn't interested in taking things further. But as I sat there, the frustration grew. How much longer would she try? Would we end up leaving without anything happening tonight?

I sipped my drink, glancing back at Lucy, who was still seated at the bar, looking as calm and composed as ever. She hadn't even seemed phased by his departure. Maybe she had her sights set on someone else. Or maybe we'd go home, and this whole night would just be a tease. Either way, I couldn't shake the restlessness building inside me.

Just as I was about to let the night fade into disappointment, the man returned to Lucy. She glanced over her shoulder, caught my eye, and subtly motioned for me to follow as they made their way out of the bar and toward the elevators. His hand rested on her lower back, guiding her confidently through the lobby, while I trailed a few feet behind, my heart pounding. She looked radiant, glowing even. The sight of another man guiding my wife so intimately stirred something deep inside me, a strange mixture of excitement, jealousy, and arousal.

As we reached the elevator, I watched them step inside, the door closing softly behind them. I hurried to catch up, slipping in just in time. The moment the doors shut, they were on each other —pressed against the wall, wrapped in a deep kiss. His hands found their way to her breasts, squeezing and exploring through the fabric of her blouse, while she grabbed his ass, her fingers curling into what little she could grab of his muscular frame. I tried not to stare. I wasn't sure what the arrangement was— how involved I was supposed to be, if I was even supposed to be watching them this closely.

They broke their kiss just long enough for him to glance my way and mutter, "Just push 57," before diving back into Lucy's mouth. She didn't even hesitate, kissing him harder, her hands roaming across his body. I pushed the button, and the elevator hummed to life.

The entire ride up was strenuous for me. They never stopped their heavy make-out session, Lucy occasionally breaking away from his lips to stroke his package through his pants. His hands roamed all over her body—up and down her thighs, across her ass, and along her sides—but never ventured beneath her skirt, where the real prize lay, waiting, panty-less and ready. God, it was hot, and I was trying so hard not to lose control.

When the elevator doors finally opened with a soft ding, I stepped aside as he led her down the hall, pulling her along like she belonged to him. I followed closely behind, my pulse racing as we made our way to the room. He slid the key card through the door, and it clicked open. Inside, the room was as luxurious as I expected—modern and spacious, with a sleek kitchenette and a divider that led into the bedroom. In the corner, I noticed a large Jacuzzi tub, the kind that screamed high-end stockbroker or some corporate big shot.

I quietly closed the door behind me and noticed a couch off to the side. I quickly made my way to it, taking a seat, my eyes glued to the two of them. They didn't waste a second. The moment they were inside, they were back at it—kissing, pulling at each other's clothes. I could feel the heat in the room rising.

Lucy wasted no time undoing his shirt, her hands deftly working the buttons until he helped shrug it off. Underneath, his chest was broad, muscular—more defined than I had expected. A large tribal tattoo ran across his pecs, bold and striking against his tanned skin. He was more muscular than Jordan. I swallowed hard, feeling that familiar twinge of embarrassment creep in. He was bigger, more defined. My wife certainly knew how to pick them.

Lucy leaned in, kissing his chest while her hands roamed across his abs, tracing the firm ridges of muscle. Her lips moved lower, leaving a trail of soft kisses as she admired his physique. I could feel my breath catching, the scene unfolding before me more intense than I had anticipated.

Then she stepped back slightly, her hands moving to his belt as she kicked off her shoes. I watched in shock as she got down on her knees, fumbling with his belt until she slid it free and tossed it aside. She was going to suck his dick—already.

I was taken aback. Wow... Lucy was really a slut. I couldn't believe how quickly she'd embraced this role. There was no hesitation, no second thought. My heart pounded in my chest as I watched her slowly slide down to her knees, her hands trembling with excitement. Her fingers lingered on his belt for a moment, teasing the leather through the loops before tugging it free with a smooth pull. The sound of the belt sliding out was almost deafening in the quiet room.

Her eyes flashed with a mix of eagerness and hunger as she looked up at him, her lips parted in anticipation. She unbuttoned his pants, her movements deliberate, savoring the moment. The zipper came next, the metallic sound loud in the stillness of the room, each click sending a shiver down my spine. It was like she was peeling away the last layer of his restraint.

With a soft tug, she pulled his pants down just enough to reveal the bulge in his boxers, the outline of his hard cock already pressing against the fabric. She paused for a brief moment, her eyes widening slightly as she took in the sheer size of him. Even through the fabric, he was massive.

Lucy's fingers trembled slightly as she hooked them into the waistband of his boxers, slowly pulling them down to reveal the thick, swollen length of his cock. It was huge. Far bigger than mine—at least eight inches, but it wasn't just the length that shocked me. It was the girth. He was thick—so thick that when Lucy wrapped her hand around it, her fingers couldn't even touch.

Her breath hitched as she stared at his cock, her eyes widening with a mix of awe and arousal. She gave him a teasing stroke, her fingers barely able to grip his shaft. It was almost too much for her to handle, yet she seemed excited by the challenge. She glanced up at him, biting her lip before she leaned in closer, her lips parting as she brought the head of his cock to her mouth.

Slowly, deliberately, she ran her tongue along the tip, tasting him before sliding her lips over the head. The contrast between her delicate mouth and the sheer size of him was staggering. She struggled at first, taking him inch by inch, but she was determined. Her lips stretched wide as she worked her way down his length, her hand stroking what she couldn't fit into her mouth. The sight was overwhelming—her mouth barely able to accommodate his thickness, her cheeks hollowing as she sucked harder.

I watched, my breath catching in my throat. She was doing it. My wife, on her knees, was sucking this massive cock like it was nothing. The way her lips wrapped around him, the sound of her soft, wet moans as she worked her mouth up and down his shaft —it was intoxicating. She was completely lost in the moment.

Her hand moved to the base of his cock, but even with both her hand and mouth working together, there was still so much left exposed. He was enormous. Lucy's fingers barely managed to grasp his shaft, her grip tightening as she pumped the base while her mouth focused on the head. Her tongue swirled around him, tracing the thick veins that bulged along his length. It was like nothing I'd ever seen.

Her free hand reached up, cupping his balls as she continued to suck him, her rhythm steady, growing more confident with every motion. I could see her enthusiasm, her need to please. She wasn't just going through the motions—she was enjoying this. The wet sounds of her mouth, the slight gagging as she tried to take him deeper, and the soft moans that escaped her lips only heightened the intensity of the moment.

"She's so good at this," the man said, a wide grin spreading across his face as he looked down at Lucy, her lips stretched around his thick cock. His voice was casual, almost playful, as if he were complimenting her on something far more mundane. He looked over at me, his eyes glinting with amusement. "You really like seeing her suck cock, don't you?"

I nodded, swallowing the lump in my throat. This was happening. "I think it's hot," I replied, my voice barely steady, though my heart was racing.

He chuckled softly, enjoying the control he had over the situation. "Well, I'm from San Diego—here on business," he said, placing both hands on Lucy's head, guiding her rhythm as she let out soft, inviting moans around his cock. "But when I'm here... feel free to call me."

His hands tightened slightly, pushing her head down further, and Lucy responded eagerly, her moans growing more intense. He gave a few heavy pants, clearly enjoying the way she worked her mouth over him. His eyes flicked back to me, an almost taunting smile on his lips. "So, what do you do? Just jerk off while I fuck her?"

The question caught me off guard, and I stammered for a moment. "Not sure," I admitted, my voice shaky. "I've only been there one other time. Usually, she just tells me about what happened when she gets home."

He seemed to find that amusing, his focus shifting back to Lucy as he grinned wider. "Well, feel free to stroke it, bro," he said with a knowing look, his face contorting in pleasure as Lucy took him deeper into her mouth. His fingers tightened in her hair, his hips rocking gently as he guided her movements.

The invitation was clear. My cock, already hard and aching, pulsed painfully in my pants, practically begging to be freed. I glanced down, feeling a surge of arousal as I watched Lucy eagerly sucking this massive cock, completely lost in the moment. Fuck it.

I reached down, unzipping my slacks, my hands trembling slightly with anticipation. My cock sprang free, rock hard and throbbing. The relief was immediate, but the sight in front of me made it impossible to resist stroking myself. This was my wife, and she was sucking another man's cock with such enthusiasm.

As I began to stroke myself, Lucy turned her head just slightly, her eyes catching mine. Her lips curved into a wicked smile, her voice dripping with seductive pleasure. "Yea, babe, stroke that dick," she purred, her tone teasing. "Because I'm going to fuck the shit out of this cock." Her words sent a jolt of excitement through me, and I gripped myself tighter, stroking harder as she turned back to the man's massive cock, resuming her rhythmic sucking.

She was loving this. Her moans, the wet sounds of her mouth, the way her hands moved up to his hips as she took him deeper —it was all so overwhelming. I watched, completely absorbed, as Lucy pleasured him like it was the only thing that mattered. I stroked myself faster, my mind spinning with arousal, with the reality of what was happening in front of me.

For what felt like forever, Lucy continued sucking him, her head bobbing up and down, her hand stroking the base of his cock. He groaned, his body tensing as he pushed her further, his fingers gripping her hair tighter. Finally, he pulled her up, breaking free from her mouth with a wet gasp, and immediately kissed her, his hands roaming her body.

Lucy melted into his embrace, moaning into his mouth as his hands slid under her skirt, his fingers finding her soaking wet. She moaned louder, encouraging his touch as she reached down and pulled her top off, exposing her bare tits. She wasn't shy anymore. Her confidence was palpable, and I could see the effect she was having on him.

The kissing grew more heated, their hands everywhere, pulling at each other's clothes. He kicked his pants off completely, his cock still hard and glistening with Lucy's spit, as he guided her to the bed. Lucy shimmied out of her skirt, letting it drop to the floor. She was now completely naked, her body fully exposed to him, and to me.

"Should I strap up?" the man asked, glancing back at me, his voice casual but laced with expectation.

I shrugged, leaving the decision in Lucy's hands. "That's up to her," I said, my voice steady though my pulse was racing.

The man looked to Lucy, waiting for her response. She giggled, her eyes flicking between us before she murmured teasingly, "Well... baby, will you eat the cum out of me?"

Her words hung in the air, shocking both of us, but she

maintained that playful grin, clearly relishing the moment. The man raised his eyebrows, glancing back at me for confirmation. A wave of embarrassment washed over me at the boldness of her request. But then, the thrill of the situation took hold. What did it matter? This was all part of what we'd talked about, and I'd already crossed the line.

"Sure," I said, surprising myself with how confident I sounded.

A satisfied smirk spread across his face, and he turned back to Lucy, positioning himself between her legs as she opened up for him, her breath quickening in anticipation. He slid his hands along her thighs, lifting her legs slightly as his fingers grazed her slick entrance. She was ready for him, wetter than I had ever seen.

He didn't waste any time. Moving closer, he positioned himself at her entrance, the thick head of his cock pressing against her pussy. He paused for just a moment, savoring the tension, before pushing inside her in one smooth, deep thrust. Lucy let out a loud, guttural grunt, her body tensing as she adjusted to his size.

"Oh fuck..." she gasped, her voice shaky with both pain and pleasure. "He's so big, baby..." she moaned, her eyes fluttering shut as he began to move inside her. "Bigger than you... fuck, I can feel every inch." Her voice was thick with arousal, each word dripping with seduction as she teased me.

I couldn't help myself. I reached down, unzipping my pants and freeing my cock, which had been aching for release. The sight in front of me was too much—my wife, moaning about another man's size, while he stretched her open.

He began to thrust, slow at first, his hips moving with a deliberate, controlled rhythm. Lucy's moans grew louder, her body arching toward him as he filled her. She looked back at me, her eyes gleaming with lust. "Fuck, baby... you should see how deep he is. Can you see it? He's stretching me so good."

I stroked myself harder, my cock throbbing in my hand as

her words sent a fresh wave of arousal through me. She was enjoying every second of it, and she wanted me to know.

The man lifted her legs higher, gripping her thighs as he pushed deeper, his pace increasing. Lucy let out another moan, her fingers digging into the sheets beneath her as she threw her head back in pleasure. "Oh my God, baby, he's hitting all the right spots," she groaned, her voice filled with raw ecstasy. "He's fucking me so deep. You can't fuck me like this."

Her words were like gasoline on a fire, intensifying the scene. I stroked myself faster, my breath coming in ragged gasps as I watched him thrust into her, each movement driving her closer to the edge.

"Tell me how it feels," I managed to croak out, my voice strained with arousal.

Lucy looked back at me, her eyes half-lidded with pleasure. "It feels fucking amazing," she moaned, her voice thick with desire. "He's so much bigger than you, baby. I'm so full. I can't... I can't take it all." Her words sent another jolt of arousal through me, my hand tightening around my cock as I stroked myself in time with his thrusts.

He was relentless, pounding into her with increasing force, and Lucy's moans became more desperate, her body trembling beneath him. "Fuck, yes... don't stop," she begged, her voice a mix of pleasure and need. "I'm going to cum, baby... I'm going to cum on his big cock."

Her orgasm was like nothing I had ever witnessed before— intense, raw, and all-consuming. Lucy's body trembled with each wave of pleasure, her moans escalating into screams of ecstasy that echoed throughout the room. It wasn't just an orgasm; it was a release, a surrender to the moment. I could see it in her face, in the way her body arched and shook beneath him. Her orgasm went on and on, a prolonged crescendo that left both of us captivated.

Then he looked down at her, his voice rough with desire. "I want to hit it from the back, because that ass is amazing."

Without missing a beat, he flipped her over, guiding her effortlessly onto her knees. Lucy didn't resist—she wanted this. He positioned her so that her head was facing me, and as he moved behind her, he thrust into her with one deep, powerful stroke. She let out a gasp, her eyes locking with mine. The look she gave me—a mixture of surprise, pleasure, and something else—said everything. 'Wow,' her eyes seemed to say. This was more than she'd expected.

As he pounded into her, his thick cock stretching her from behind, his hands gripped her ass, squeezing tightly. "Damn, you're a lucky son of a bitch," he said, glancing over at me with a grin. "To be married to this ass and all this sexiness."

I forced a smile back, my heart racing, my hand still stroking my cock as I watched. He wasn't wrong. Lucy looked incredible, her body arching into each thrust, her ass bouncing as he took her from behind. His focus shifted back to her, his hands never leaving her as he pumped harder, his hips slamming against her.

Lucy began to grind back onto him, her head lowering as she pushed her ass into his thrusts. Her face told the story—her eyes glazed over, her lips parted in breathless moans, her brow furrowed with pleasure. She was lost in it, completely consumed by the sensation of him filling her.

I stroked myself harder, faster, unable to look away. Her yelps turned into sharp cries of pleasure. "Oh... oh... fuck, yea," she moaned, her voice trembling with the intensity of what she was feeling. Her hands gripped the sheets beneath her as she began to scream louder. "Fuck me faster! Fuck me harder!"

He obliged, bending her further over, one hand on her lower back, the other gripping her juicy ass, pulling her closer with every thrust. I could feel the tension in the air rising, the moment building to its inevitable climax.

"I'm cumming, baby," she screamed, her voice raw and desperate. "Fuck, I'm cumming! Oh my God, don't stop, Rick! Fuck me faster!"

Rick. That was his name. No one had bothered to tell me, and at this moment, it didn't seem to matter. The name seemed irrelevant to the overwhelming heat of the moment. All that mattered was what I was seeing.

Rick's thrusts became more frantic, and with a loud smack, he slapped Lucy's ass, his grip tightening as he leaned forward, his voice rough with arousal. "I'm going to cum all inside you, Lucy," he growled, his face contorting with pleasure as his hips jerked forward. His orgasm was written across his face—every nerve alive as he buried himself deep inside her, his cock pulsing with release.

Lucy moaned even louder, her body pushing back into him, grinding onto his cock as he came. She wasn't done yet. Her hips rolled, her ass pressing harder into him, as if she was savoring every last drop of his cum.

And all the while, she looked back at me, her lips curling into a teasing smile. "Baby... you're going to love this. He's filling me up so good. You should see how full I am. You want to taste it, don't you?"

Her words hit me like a shockwave. This was it. The moment of ultimate surrender. She knew exactly what she was doing. She had pushed me to the edge, teased me beyond what I thought possible, and now she was going to push me over.

Rick's thrusts slowed, his breath ragged as he rode out the last waves of his orgasm, but Lucy's movements only grew more deliberate, grinding back into him, milking him for every last ounce of pleasure. She was in complete control now. And I knew what was coming next. I was going to kneel. I was going to surrender everything.

As Rick's thrusts slowed and he slid out of Lucy, I knelt in front of her, feeling the weight of the moment descend upon me. This was it—the ultimate surrender. My heart pounded as I positioned myself beneath her, my face inches away from her dripping pussy, slick with their combined cum. The musky, salty scent hit me first, thick in the air, but strangely... it wasn't as revolting as I had always imagined it would be. There was something different about this moment—something powerful. I was kneeling here for her, for Lucy, and that made it all different.

"Baby, you know what to do," she said, her voice low and commanding, but with that playful lilt she always used when she was fully in control.

I leaned in, my breath catching as I tasted her, my tongue sweeping through the slick, slippery mess of her juices and his cum. The familiar saltiness of semen coated my tongue immediately, but it wasn't as jarring as I had expected. It should have been disgusting, but instead, it felt like a part of the moment—like I was meant to be doing this for her. For us. Each stroke of my tongue was deliberate, tracing the folds of her pussy as I cleaned her, my mouth filling with the evidence of their passion.

There was a strange intimacy in it, a connection. The taste of cum, something I thought would repulse me, was now just a part of this new reality. It was for her.

As I licked, I couldn't help but notice Rick standing behind her, watching us. My eyes briefly flicked up toward him, and the realization hit me with a sudden, uneasy jolt: he could see me—he could see my hard cock, standing out proudly as I knelt there, licking my wife clean. The vulnerability of the moment twisted in my chest, a mix of embarrassment and arousal flooding me all at once. I was exposed, naked, but it didn't stop me.

Lucy's hand tightened in my hair as I kept going, her hips moving slightly as she ground against my face. I could hear her breathing growing more ragged, her pleasure building again. Above me, Rick's hands roamed over her body, squeezing her breasts, teasing her nipples. I licked faster, driven by the need to push her over the edge again, to bring her to that place only I could take her.

"God, baby... lick me harder," she moaned, her voice thick with pleasure. Her dominance was undeniable now, and I wanted nothing more than to please her. I moved my tongue more urgently, the slick taste of their cum lingering in my mouth, each lick bringing her closer to the edge.

The room seemed to pulse with the weight of the moment, the air thick with tension and heat. Her legs trembled slightly, her body responding to every flick of my tongue. I could feel her tightening, her muscles clenching as she ground herself harder against my mouth. Her moans filled the air, louder and more desperate.

Then it hit. The moment I had been waiting for. Her legs began to shake—subtle at first, then more violently as the orgasm tore through her. Her entire body shuddered, and she let out a raw, breathless moan, her fingers digging painfully into my scalp. I stayed there, kneeling, my mouth still working against her pussy as I licked her through her climax.

It was overwhelming. The salty liquid of her release flooded my mouth, mixing with the last remnants of cum, making her pussy impossibly slippery. But I didn't stop. I couldn't. This was what I had been waiting for—the moment she lost control, the moment I was completely hers. Her legs shook so hard I thought she might collapse, but she steadied herself, her breath coming in sharp, uneven gasps.

I kept going, my tongue flicking over her sensitive clit, pushing her higher, deeper into the pleasure. She moaned again, the sound primal, desperate. Behind her, Rick watched, his hands still roaming her body, but in this moment, I knew she was mine, too. I had brought her to this—this leg-shaking, body-trembling, earth-shattering climax.

As her orgasm slowly ebbed, her hips began to still, but I could still feel the aftershocks rippling through her body. Her hand loosened its grip on my hair, but she didn't let go, her breath shaky as she leaned back slightly, savoring the moment. I knelt there, my face buried between her legs, still licking, still serving her, still surrendered.

As Lucy's orgasm finally subsided, her breathing began to steady, and she gently pulled away from me. I was still on my knees, watching as she walked with effortless grace toward Rick, who was now standing casually near the bed, completely naked. His cock, which had been so powerful moments ago, was now entirely soft, hanging between his legs with the same confidence he carried throughout the night.

Without hesitation, Lucy moved toward him, a look of satisfaction and affection in her eyes. She pressed her body against his, rising onto her toes as she kissed him deeply, passionately, as if thanking him with every breath. Her hands roamed his chest as their lips met, her fingers trailing across his skin, while Rick responded, kissing her back with the same relaxed confidence.

When the kiss finally broke, she looked up at him, her eyes gleaming with satisfaction. "Your cock was so good," she purred, her voice filled with genuine appreciation. "That was incredible. We're definitely going to have to repeat this."

Rick grinned, clearly pleased with himself, standing tall and unbothered by his softened state. He watched as Lucy slowly leaned down, taking her time, until her lips brushed against his cock once more. This time, the kiss was soft, almost tender—a slow, gentle kiss goodbye. It was a quiet moment, intimate in its own way, as if she were sealing a promise with that final kiss. She lingered there for a moment before straightening back up, the playful smile returning to her face as she turned to grab her clothes.

As Lucy began to get dressed, pulling on her top and stepping into her skirt, Rick's eyes drifted to me—still kneeling, still rock hard, my cock aching from the entire experience. He raised an eyebrow, his smirk returning as he casually asked, "So, is Lucy going to take care of that for you?"

I felt a sudden flush of embarrassment, but before I could answer, Lucy laughed, pulling her skirt up and adjusting the waistband. Her laugh was light, teasing, and completely in control. "Oh, no," she said, glancing back at me with a wicked grin. "He doesn't get that. Maybe... if he's good, he'll be allowed to sort himself out later."

Her words stung with both denial and excitement. This was her final reminder of who was in control. She didn't need to do anything more—just the suggestion that I might be able to take care of myself, but only if I earned it, was enough. I stayed kneeling, my hard cock still throbbing as I watched her finish getting dressed.

Lucy turned back to Rick, giving him one last smile before slipping on her shoes. She looked at me again, her expression softening slightly, but still with that playful dominance in her eyes. I was hers, completely, and she knew it.

"Come on, baby," she said, heading toward the door. "Let's go."

The drive home was quiet, the hum of the engine the only sound, but the tension between us was electric. Lucy's hand rested casually on my thigh at first, but I could feel the heat of her touch spreading through me. I gripped the steering wheel, trying to focus on the road, but I knew it was only a matter of time before she would take control again.

With a sly smile, her hand moved toward my lap, her fingers expertly finding the zipper of my pants. She slowly unzipped me, freeing my cock, which was already hard from the events of the night. I gasped softly as she wrapped her hand around me, her touch sending a shiver through my body.

"Baby, you've been so good tonight," she purred, her voice soft but dripping with playful dominance. Her hand moved slowly, deliberately, stroking my cock with just the right amount of pressure. "Watching me with Rick... and before that, Steve... and Jordan. You love it, don't you?"

Her words sent a surge of heat through me, and I couldn't help but nod. I did love it, even as the tension between pleasure and control consumed me.

She stroked me with steady precision, her hand sliding up and down my shaft, but just as I felt myself getting close to the edge, she slowed, her grip loosening. The frustration was immediate, and I groaned softly, but she just giggled.

"Remember how Steve fucked me in the woods?" she teased, her voice smooth and seductive. "Or how Jordan made me cum harder than I ever have before?" She squeezed my cock slightly, making my pulse race even faster. "You loved hearing about that, didn't you?"

I nodded again, my breath shaky. I was so close. The way her hand moved, the way her words dripped with seduction—it was almost too much. But every time I felt the familiar rush of an impending orgasm, she would slow down, teasing me further.

We turned onto our street, the house looming closer. My whole body ached with need, my cock throbbing in her hand, but she wouldn't let me finish. Not yet.

As we pulled into the driveway, Lucy's grip tightened again, her strokes becoming faster, more intense. I was right on the edge, about to lose control. But she wasn't done teasing me.

Her eyes sparkled with mischief as she turned to me, her hand never stopping. "So, baby," she said, her voice low and full of power, "how do you feel about having a hotwife?"

The words hit me like a punch. I knew what she wanted me to say. I knew I couldn't cum unless I admitted it. I swallowed hard, my breath coming in ragged gasps as I tried to hold on.

"I... I love it," I finally gasped, the truth spilling out of me in a desperate whisper. It was the truth. I loved it. I loved her control, her dominance, the way she teased me, the way she made me wait.

As soon as I said it, her hand moved faster, her grip tightening. "Good boy," she purred. "Now cum for me."

I couldn't hold back anymore. My body shook as I exploded, my orgasm tearing through me with an intensity I had never felt before. Lucy giggled, her voice light and teasing as she leaned in closer, watching me lose control completely.

"I'm so glad you like it," she whispered, her lips brushing against my ear. Her voice was soft, but there was an edge of playful cruelty in her words. "Because I'm not sure I could stop, even if you didn't."

BOOKS BY THIS AUTHOR

You Wanted This: A Husband's Cuckold Fantasies Are Brutally Exposed

As Ben sat in the living room, he could feel his heart rate rising second by second. He had just heard his wife Leah turn her key in the door, but tonight was different. Tonight was going to be very different. Leah wasn't the only person about to walk through the door. Leah had brought Carter with her. And this wasn't a social visit. Carter was there for one reason and one reason only. He was there to get his cock inside Leah.

He knew it, Leah knew it, and Ben definitely knew it. But as Carter walked into the living room, Ben's feelings of excitement and arousal suddenly vanished as his feelings of jealousy and insecurity overtook him. Did he really want to go through with it? Did he really want to watch his pretty little wife get on her knees in front of this stranger?

The thing is, Ben didn't really have a choice. A few weeks ago, Leah had discovered his fetish. She had discovered all of his fantasies about her with other men, and she had agreed to explore them.

"You wanted this, babe," was the last thing she said as her lips closed around Carter's big hard cock only a few feet in front of Ben.

But that was only the beginning, and all of Ben's deepest, darkest cuckold fantasies were about to be brutally exposed by Leah.

A Secret Between Friends: Discovering Their Married Friends' Swinging Secret

If you're expecting some sort of story about how we had always known we were swingers deep down, or how something was lacking from our sex life and how my husband couldn't satisfy me, then suddenly swinging filled that gap, then I'm sorry, but this will be a letdown.

This was all a lot simpler, really. We moved to a new area and made some new friends, all very normal friends, you know, the sort of friends that have BBQs and beers in the summer. The sort of new friends who might let you crash at theirs if you have too much to drink at the BBQ. Just normal, average friends.

Until things stopped being normal and average, which occurred about 0.01 seconds after a moment of madness following a drunken BBQ. Agreeing to skinny dip because we didn't have our swim gear. Well, that wasn't the crazy bit; our hosts getting naked was.

As soon as I saw his massive soft cock I couldn't help it. There was only one thought in my mind. It's so much bigger than my husband's. I felt terrible then, just for having the thought. But I'm a married woman, and I love my husband, so I didn't even let on how hot it got me.

But that's not the part that got weird. He just had a big cock, like some guys do. He got in the hot tub, and we chatted as a group and drank until me and my husband went to bed alone, just the two of us. And okay, I'll admit it, as my husband's face disappeared between my legs, I might have been thinking about that massive cock as he got in the hot tub.

But I was satisfied with my husband, in fact, more than that. I was happy. My husband can make me cum with that tongue like nothing else. And he did, again and again that night. But every time I shut my eyes, the image of that huge cock was there, hanging between his legs as he stepped into the pool.

So can you imagine how I felt when I finally opened my eyes, and he was standing there, in the slightly open doorway, watching my husband make me cum with his tongue, slowly stroking his even more imposing, now fully hard cock.

And here's the problem, ten minutes later, with my husband on top of me, all I can think of is his much larger cock. Suddenly 5 1/2 inches won't get the job done, and I'm left laying in bed next to my loving husband as he comes down from his climax, wondering why for the first time in years, I didn't cum.

That's how it started, I guess. That's how we discovered our friends' swinging secret. Now there's just one question. What do we do with that information?

Hedonism: A Couple's First Experience

When my wife told me she had booked a surprise vacation for my birthday, I honestly never would have expected this. Sure, we had talked about it, briefly, sometimes. But I think a lot of couples talk about it in the heat of the moment.

Hedonism - Just the name of the resort is all it takes to send vivid images flashing through your mind. Images of what you think the place will be like.

But really, no one has any idea until they get there.

You can go as far as you want, or you can just chill by the pool in the non nude area and see what happens.

But what surprised me the most was that although this had always been my fantasy, it was actually Sarah who seemed to be pushing it once we landed!

This is Hedonism; this is our first experience, and this is happening!